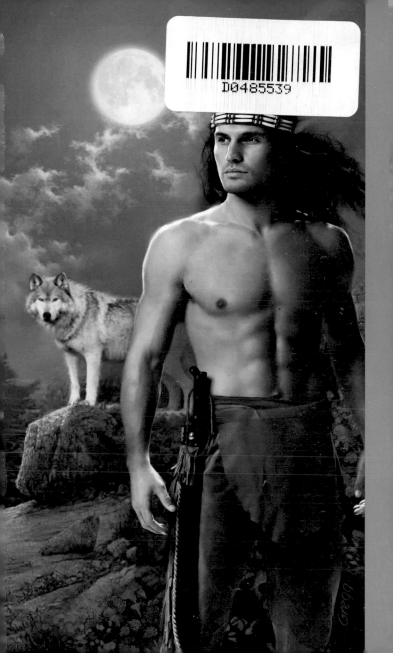

CASSIE EDWARDS,
AUTHOR OF THE *SAVAGE* SERIES

A WOMAN OF COURAGE

She had never considered any Indian handsome. But now? She knew how wrong she had been.

Yet how could she forget, for even one moment, that this man was responsible for the deaths of many people, among them her father and Malvina?

She gazed at him now with contempt, with hate, as he stopped beside her.

"Stand," he said in perfect English. "Or do you prefer to continue crawling like a lowly snake along the ground?"

Knowing that she had no choice, yet so afraid she was not certain her knees would support her when she did try to stand, Candy slowly pushed herself up from the ground.

She stood straight-backed, her chin held firmly high, as she tried to prove that she was a woman of spirit…of courage…despite the danger she was in.

CASSIE EDWARDS

SAVAGE BELOVED

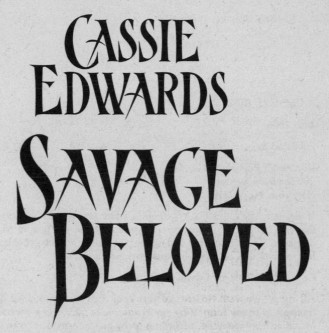

LEISURE BOOKS NEW YORK CITY

A LEISURE BOOK®

June 2006

Published by

Dorchester Publishing Co., Inc.
200 Madison Avenue
New York, NY 10016

ISBN 0-8439-5273-3

The name "Leisure Books" and the stylized "L" with design are
trademarks of Dorchester Publishing Co., Inc.

Printed in the United States of America.

Visit us on the web at www.dorchesterpub.com.

With the fondest of memories, I dedicate Savage Beloved *to my 1954 Mattoon High School (Illinois) graduating class, especially my special friends. Who could ever forget walking the halls of Mattoon High with friends between classes; the many sock hops and formal dances; the Tuesday nights with the Fifinellas (our sorority group); and Gill's Drive Inn, where everyone met after dances, ballgames, and dates, for a delicious hamburger and cherry Coke!*

Always,
Cassie Edwards

Kay Adams	Peggy Donley	Fred Hovis
Sue Armstrong	Louise Douglas	Jean Hunt
Madonna Arthur	Duane Duncan	Ralph Idleman
Walter Baker	Fred Duncan	Marilyn Janes
Linda Bales	Shirley Duncan	Harvey Janssen
Evelyn Banks	Geneva Edwards	Carl Jeffers
Tom Barber	Ina Rae Elder	Billie Johnson
James Beals	Pansy Elder	Katherine Jones
Donna Belt	Corinne Ellis	William Justice
Bernice Boruff	Ed Ethington	Pat Kelley
Susan Bowen	Joan Fickes	Mavis Kenny
Gerald Boyle	Robert Fickes	Marion Kirkendoll
Pat Bradley	Larry Fisher	Rose Knollenberg
Jack Branson	Fritz Furry	Patty Knowles
Tom Brewer	Ronald Geiger	Alice Landrus
Patty Bridges	Janice Gilbert	Leonard Lass
Joan Broers	Roxanne Gilbert	Joanna Lawhorn
Mac Bumpus	Sara Gover	Gene Lindsey
David Bunten	Yvonne Grafton	Jo Ann Lindsey
John Burns	Karlene Gust	Mary Lou Lundeen
Russell Camfield	Earl Haislip	Dean Marshall
Jahala Cannoy	Marilyn Hamby	Don Martin
Stephen Cannoy	Mary Hamilton	Carolyn Matthews
A.L. Carter	Joyce Hamma	Bob McCall
Phil Carter	Judy Harris	Bill McCleary
John Chamberlain	Norma Hash	Noah McFadden
Freda Chism	Phil Haskell	Gene McFarland
Doris Clark	Melvin Hebert	Charles McKibben
Raymond Crenshaw	Sara Helm	Jim McMillan
Bill Critchelow	Thelma Higgens	Ann Miller
Joann Cross	John Hill	Dixie Miller
Jim Daugherty	Shirley Hite	Wayne Mingus
Betty Davis	Evelyn Hogan	Barbara Montague
Howard Decker	Marcia Holloway	Kay Morse
Joe Delaney	Clara Hood	Larry Myers
Joyce Derrickson	Joyce Hood	Paula Neal

Nancy Neimeier
Craig Nelson
Nancy Newby
Richard Nighswander
Ronald Nighswander
Peggy O'Neal
Daisy Oakley
Eileen Overton
Mary Parker
Wendell Parkhurst
Delores Peterson
Edward Phipps
Mary Ann Pippin
Willie Podesta
Harlan Price
Carol Rardin
Shirley Rardin
Marjorie Rathe
Madonna Reinhart
Madonna Ritter
James Rominger
Jeannene Rose
Read Ross
Phillip Ryan
Marilyn Sampson
Joanne Schagemann
David Schwarz
Jack Scott
Duane Seaman
Lenora Seaman
Guy Seymour
William Shafer
Stan Sharp
Don Shepardson
Jim Showalter
Ruth Sloan
Lewis Smith
Sharon Smith
Mike Smyser
Bob Snapp
Kenneth Sparks
Patty Stevens
Harold Strater
Virginia Swango
Bernard Thompson
Pat Thompson

Shirley Thompson
Don Timmons
Susie Tomlin
Richard Tucker
Kenneth Wakefield
Bonnie Walker
Bill Wallace
Frances Ward
Dick Ward
Marilyn Waters
Shirley Weber
David Well
Barbara Welsh
Duane Wetzel
Don Whitford
Shirley Whitley
Steve Whitley
Ann Wilbur
Marilyn Wildman
Fred Winings
Paul Young

In Remembrance:

Claire Abell
Tom Clayton
Emil Czerwonka
Delores Hackett
Jim Hardin
David Hoop
Joe Eveland
Charles Ellis
Janice Fonner
Madonna Campbell
Jim Van Cleave
Mary Giberson
Jerry Pepperdine
John Keene
Dorothy Scott
Catherine Shoap
Roy Stewart
Le Titia Thomas
John Wheeler
John Kilman
Ernic Watkins
John Bone
Shirley Estelle
Shirley Maxey
Bill Biggs
Jim Trower
Ronnie Campbell
Charles Ryan
Tom Karpus
Mildred McGinnis
Janelle Russell
Jerry Zike
Joe Wade
Jim Whitley
Richard Rodgers
Ruth Howes
Suellan Mey
Shirley Logdson
Russell Sawyer
John Craig
Paul McAchran
Natresia Ballinger
Thea Rae Hovious
Carol O'Dell

My Warrior

His eyes so dark,
like the midnight sky,
would make any woman
want to die.
His hair is long and black,
and flows in waves
down his back,
his skin is copper
like the sky in autumn.
And his heart and mind...
so sweet and tender.
And he and his people
will never surrender.

—Crystal Marie Carpenter,
a fan and friend

Chapter One

Kansas, 1849

A slow fire burned in the fire pit of the large, cone-shaped council house, the smoke spiraling slowly upward through the smoke hole overhead. Two Eagles, a young chief of twenty-five winters, of the Eagle band of the Wichita tribe, sat in council with his warriors, making plans to go help his ailing uncle Short Robe escape from Fort Hope.

As his warriors obediently watched and listened, it was evident that their chief would tower in height over most of his band, as well as his enemies.

His bronzed, muscled body was clad today in only a breechclout. His face was sculpted, with a

1

CASSIE EDWARDS

small slash of a scar beneath his lower lip. He had flashing dark eyes, and his long, sleek, black hair hung down to his waist.

Today he wore a beaded headband that held his hair in place; a lone eagle feather was hanging from a coil of his hair, at one side.

He sat comfortably on a thick cougar pelt.

"My warriors, as you know, several days ago my uncle Short Robe was abducted while praying alone at his private place of prayer," he said tightly. His dark eyes glittered at his warriors, who were sitting cross-legged before him.

Two Eagles was attuned to all emotions around him. As a person of solitude may sense the feelings of others without their speaking, Two Eagles sensed his world, like the deer that lifts its head quickly from feeding on rich grass, sensing the invisible approach of danger from warnings that come clear and sharp as a clap of thunder.

"Only a short while ago did I discover who took my uncle, and why," Two Eagles continued. "Our scout, Gray Wing, came to me with the sad news that it was pony soldiers who wrongly took my uncle."

He paused as gasps of horror filled the council house, now that everyone finally knew the truth of Short Robe's disappearance.

"*Ho*, yes, it is with much sadness that I report this to you today," Two Eagles said solemnly. "The pony soldiers thought they were stealing away my father, our chief, for his brother looked so much like him. But in reality, my father, Chief Moon Thunder, was dying. Now that he has been buried, it is my plan to

2

attack the fort today and bring my elderly uncle back to his home."

The Wichita did not choose a chief through heredity alone. A chief's son must show not only marked ability to lead, but must also win the love and respect of all members of his band by acts of generosity and kindness. Two Eagles had done both during his father's time as chief.

It had not taken a second thought for the band to accept Two Eagles as their chief upon the death of his father.

A shout from outside the large tepee now caused Two Eagles to look quickly toward the closed entrance flap.

He stiffened when the person shouted that a small contingent of pony soldiers had been seen approaching in the distance. And someone was walking behind them, being led by a rope.

Two Eagles leapt to his feet and hurried outside to see his sentry, Running Wolf, dismounting from his steed a few feet away.

"My chief," Running Wolf said breathlessly. "Pony soldiers from Fort Hope are approaching. Short Robe is with them. He is shackled and being led by a rope behind the soldiers. But we cannot attack them in order to rescue your uncle, for there are many more soldiers visible along the horizon, watching and waiting to see if you and our warriors will start a fight."

Two Eagles's heart raced, for it was hard to imagine his uncle being treated so inhumanely. Yet for now, Two Eagles could not do anything about it. The pony soldiers were apparently just waiting for him to make the wrong move, so they would have an excuse to attack his village and kill everyone.

He kneaded his brow, puzzled as to why the soldiers were returning his uncle at all.

There could be only one reason: Surely they hoped to antagonize Two Eagles into a fight.

So he must keep control of his anger until his uncle was safely home. Afterward, those at Fort Hope would be sorry for having done his people wrong. Up until now, to protect his people from attack by the pony soldiers, Two Eagles had practiced restraint, as had his chieftain father.

But this was too much.

The white eyes had gone too far!

They must pay. And . . . they . . . would.

In the meantime, Two Eagles was relieved to know that his uncle was still alive, for he had been afraid that once the soldiers discovered their error, they would kill him. They had already dishonored another Wichita band by beheading their chief . . . Chief Night Horse, whose son Proud Wind was now chief. Proud Wind was also Two Eagles's best friend.

Two Eagles smiled when he recalled the day he had received the scar beneath his lower lip . . . on a youthful outing with Proud Wind.

It was Two Eagles's deep desire to help Proud Wind by attacking the fort, for there was something there he wanted to rescue for his friend: the head of Proud Wind's beloved father. He had been told this grisly trophy was kept in a jar in Colonel Creighton's study.

Ho, yes, it had been his plan to attack the fort, and soon. It would be easier to overwhelm the fort now that only a few soldiers remained. The others had left Fort Hope for their new post in Arizona.

But now things had changed, and Two Eagles wondered why the white eyes would return his uncle to the village.

Was it a trick?

Were they bringing his uncle back, only to kill him in front of his people? Would they then kill everyone else?

Thinking of this possibility, Two Eagles hurried back inside the council house. He quickly explained about his uncle being brought home, and how.

"I am glad my uncle is alive and is almost home, but there is much about this occurrence that does not seem right," he said tightly. "I believe it is being done for only one reason . . . to trick us. The pony soldiers might be planning a massacre of our people after releasing my uncle to us. *Looah*, go! My warriors, hurry to your lodges. Stay there. Arm yourselves well and be ready to fight if an attack is launched against our people."

"And what of you?" Gray Bear asked, rising quickly along with the others.

"I, alone, will stand openly as I await my uncle's return," Two Eagles said thickly. "I will leave my weapons in my lodge so that it will look as though I am no threat to the pony soldiers. I do not want to do anything that might antagonize those who are bringing my uncle back. It is still possible that no attack is planned against our Wichita people."

5

"But you will be vulnerable without a weapon," said another warrior, who loved his chief so much he did not wish to see him take such a chance.

"For my uncle I must do this," Two Eagles said. "For our *people* I must do this. The pony soldiers speak too often with forked tongues. Today, who is to say what their true purpose may be? *Ho*, I will feel naked without a weapon, but I have no other choice but to act so."

He nodded toward the entrance flap. "*Looah*, go, quickly," he said. "*Wissgutts*, go home. You must be in your own personal lodges before the pony soldiers get close enough to see you go there. They must be the ones who are surprised if they try anything against us."

His warriors nodded almost in unison, then left the council house at a run.

Two Eagles removed the knife that was sheathed at his waist, the only weapon he had with him during council. His lethal arrows and his great, strong bow were in his personal lodge, as were his rifle and ammunition.

With pride in his steps, his chin held high, Two Eagles left the council house and walked to the edge of the village. He would be the first person the soldiers saw when they got close enough to identify people.

He stood straight and tall beneath the burning rays of the sun. The day was unusually hot for this time of year. Normally the temperature was mild enough so that fires were left burning day and night.

Two Eagles wondered if the pony soldiers had deliberately chosen this stifling day to bring his uncle home, perhaps thinking he would not survive the journey.

But they did not know the constitution of such a man as his uncle. Short Robe was brave and strong, a warrior who would bear much to prove that he could withstand anything the white men chose to do to him.

Two Eagles kept his eyes directed straight ahead, aware now of the muffled sound of horses' hooves striking thick prairie grass as they came closer and closer to the village.

Ah, but Two Eagles did feel naked without a weapon to defend himself. Still, he knew that what he was doing was right. He would do nothing to antagonize the soldiers who were bringing his uncle back.

As he stood there gazing out at the land, he felt so proud of his people . . . of his village, which was surrounded by fields of corn, beans, squash, and other plants the women had lovingly planted.

Two Eagles loved the high, rolling prairie and the sandy river bottoms and banks that were a part of his people's land. Clusters of scrub oak with heavier timber of elm, cottonwood, and willow stood along the water courses.

The Great Spirit, *Tirawahut*, had been good to the Eagle band of Wichita. Their crops had grown well, and there was plenty to feed their people.

As Two Eagles continued to wait and watch, his heart pounded with worry over whether his uncle was alright.

Short Robe was Two Eagles's only remaining

blood kin. All the others had been killed by whites, or by their enemy the Sioux, or had died of natural causes.

His mother and sister had been killed together while working in the cornfields. They had been alone that day, instead of with the usual larger group that kept the women safe.

Two Eagles knew not who was responsible.

And then there was his cousin Spotted Bear, whom he missed terribly. He had died one day a summer ago in a skirmish with the Sioux.

When Two Eagles had heard about the fateful ambush of Spotted Bear and his warriors, and that Spotted Bear had died, he had gone to retrieve Spotted Bear's body for burial, but to no avail. No body had been found, yet the bloody ground attested to his death.

Two Eagles could only conclude that his killers had taken his body, perhaps to mutilate it.

It saddened him to think of such a thing happening to such a proud warrior . . . his cousin!

He had searched far and wide for that Sioux camp, but they had disappeared into the wind, and had never been heard of again.

Two Eagles had prayed often for his cousin's spirit, hoping that it returned often to be among his people, even though his body was far away.

The hatred Two Eagles felt for the white eyes ran deep. The white eyes were killing hordes of buffalo as a way to discourage the Wichita from staying on the plains, where the buffalo had once been so plentiful.

Of course the Wichita hated to see such waste, but they no longer depended solely on the buffalo hunt as they had in the past. They ate other meats hunted by their warriors, and enjoyed the good fruits of their labor in their gardens.

Ho, the United States government had thought that once the buffalo went, so would the Wichita, saying that with the buffalo disappearing, in time there would also be no more red men.

But it was Two Eagles's father who had boldly told the uniformed spokesman for the United States government that the Wichita did not always give the Great Spirit meat and he still favored the Wichita!

Two Eagles's spine stiffened as he caught his first sight of a dozen bluecoats on horses. The animals snorted and blew their nostrils as they were made to ride onward in the blistering heat. Their riders must surely see Two Eagles alone and waiting for them at the edge of the village.

And then Two Eagles's heart cried out within his chest as he caught his first sight of his uncle. He was being led by a rope looped about his neck as though he were an animal.

Two Eagles clenched his hands into tight fists at his sides when he saw how his uncle was being forced to jog, not walk. The leg irons that shackled him hit his ankle bones with each of his movements, and his hands were bound with chains.

Straight as an arrow, Two Eagles still stood there, even though he longed to run and help his uncle, who seemed unable to go much farther.

But Two Eagles knew that if he went beyond

where he stood now, he might goad the soldiers into killing his uncle or Two Eagles, himself. They might then swarm into the village like mad hornets and kill everyone else.

So Two Eagles continued to stand there, watching and waiting, as the group came closer and closer. When his uncle was close enough for Two Eagles to see him fully, the numbness of the shock he was feeling became a hot rage. His uncle's bare feet were bloody, with flies and gnats buzzing around them.

Two Eagles fought off the nausea that came with seeing his beloved uncle being so mistreated, as though he were less than human.

Two Eagles's body became even more rigid as the pony soldiers stopped only a few feet away. Short Robe's gaze locked with his nephew's.

Two Eagles could tell that his uncle's will to survive until he was reunited with his people might be all that had kept him alive. One of the soldiers dismounted and lifted the rope from around Short Robe's neck, then slapped him with it across the buttocks before remounting his horse. His uncle stumbled and fell to the ground at Two Eagles's feet.

That was when Two Eagles saw his uncle's back and the deep, bloody scars that must have been made by the lash of a blacksnake whip.

Holding back an even stronger urge to leap past his uncle and yank the soldier from his horse, then choke the life from the heartless man, Two Eagles gazed coldly into the soldier's eyes.

"Why did you treat a helpless old man so inhumanely?" he asked, fighting hard to keep his voice steady, while everything in him cried out to lunge at that soldier and pull him from his horse, but not kill him with his bare hands. Instead, he would wrap his neck with the bloody rope that had held his uncle prisoner.

"Why?" the soldier said tauntingly. "Why did we bring this old geezer home in chains?" He laughed and held his face down closer to Two Eagles's. "Because we could, that's why."

That response made the heat of hatred rush through Two Eagles's heart so intensely, he had to reach deep within himself for the willpower to refrain from acting out his anger.

Instead, he could only watch as the mocking soldier wheeled his horse around and cantered away with the other bluecoats. In the next moments all the Wichita came from their lodges, stunned silent by how Short Robe had been treated.

Short Robe gazed up at Two Eagles. "Two Eagles . . ." he said in a voice that was hardly discernible. He continued his communication in the silent Indian way, signaling the Indian sign for "Everything will be alright." He held his right palm down, fingers extended straight out, with his arm in a horizontal position near his heart, then made a swift motion forward about six inches.

Fighting back tears, Two Eagles knelt down and picked up a handful of sand. He tossed it at his uncle's feet, causing clouds of flies and gnats to rise in the air from them.

He gazed into his uncle's faded, old eyes, and nodded in affirmation of what Short Robe had said in sign language. Yet he knew that everything was not alright, for his uncle was too old to have been treated in such a way.

He knew that soon his uncle would die because of it!

A hunger for vengeance such as he had never felt before swept through Two Eagles!

Chapter Two

Portraits are to daily faces
As an evening west
To a fine, pedantic sunshine
In a satin vest.
—Emily Dickinson

The sun streamed softly through the bedroom window as Candy Creighton sat on the floor in front of her travel trunk, neatly placing her folded clothes in it.

But she was only halfheartedly preparing herself for departure from Fort Hope with her colonel father. She just couldn't get what she had witnessed these past few days off her mind.

It was the old Indian whose name she now knew was Short Robe whom she saw in her mind's eye. She flinched even now as she remembered the snapping sound when the soldiers had taken turns lashing the old man's bare back with a blacksnake whip, over and over again.

She cringed as she thought of the soldiers' mocking laughter, proving how much they had enjoyed torturing the old Indian warrior. She couldn't understand how anyone could enjoy raising the whip and bringing it down across another human being's back.

And she knew the men *had* enjoyed it. They had tossed coins, gambling amongst themselves over who would be the next one to whip the old man held in bondage with chains.

It had taken all the willpower that Candy could muster up to keep herself from going out to the parade ground and grabbing the whip to give those who were beating the old Indian a lash or two. She longed to let them know just how it felt.

Instead, she had gone and asked her father why the elderly Indian was being treated so cruelly. Her father had given her an explanation that made her heart turn cold with horror.

She shivered as she again heard her father's nonchalant reply: "To set an example."

That seemed the worst reason of all, for it most certainly would be the beginning of trouble with the Wichita, and perhaps even before she and her father left the fort for Arizona. Her father was to be the colonel at a new fort built purposely for fighting the "redskin savages," as most soldiers referred to the Indians.

Her father's reason for whipping the old Indian made her skin crawl. Although her father would no longer be in charge of this area, he wanted to leave something behind for the Wichita to remember him by. He was angry that the Wichita had ignored all he had urged them to do. What irked him most was their refusal to agree to reservation life.

Her father had so badly wanted to achieve that goal as a way to win recognition in Washington, and another medal on his uniform.

So, since the Wichita had showed her father no respect, he had decided to make this old man suffer.

Actually, Candy knew that Short Robe was lucky to be alive. In a sense, he had unknowingly tricked her father. Her father had thought he had abducted the Wichita chief, Moon Thunder, that day the soldiers found the old Indian praying on a butte, away from his village. Only later did he discover that his men had captured the chief's brother, a man who had no power, or voice, when it came to decision making among his people.

And when he learned that the true chief had died, her father felt even more foolish.

He had told Candy that the old man was lucky he didn't kill him with his bare hands, and the only reason he hadn't done so was because he wanted to use Short Robe as an example. For that, he needed him to be alive.

Candy trembled again at how horribly the old man had been treated. Would those at the village retaliate once Short Robe was returned there and they saw the condition he was in?

More than once, her father had enjoyed lifting the whip against Short Robe himself.

When Candy had begged him to stop and expressed her concerns about retaliation, he had said, "Nonsense. The Wichita are too busy mourning their chief to come and take revenge for what was done to one old man."

Candy could hardly wait to leave this horrid place of bad memories. Surely when they arrived at the new, larger fort in Arizona, she could relax without fearing that an arrow might suddenly slice into her back at any moment.

Candy's insecurity was not helped by the knowledge that her mother, Agnes, was gone now. She had finally had enough of the sort of life her husband offered and had fled to God only knew where.

Tears shone in Candy's eyes at the memories of her mother. Oh, how she missed her, but she was glad that her mother had found the courage to follow her heart and go where she might find true happiness.

Candy pushed herself up from the floor and went to her dresser to stare into the mirror.

She gazed at her face as she slowly ran her fingers over it. She felt much older than eighteen after all she had seen at Fort Hope.

She was glad to be leaving.

Perhaps after she left Fort Hope and went to live at the new fort, she would find her white knight in shining armor, a man who would take her away from this military life that had been forced upon her from the day she was born.

But she knew how improbable that was.

The only men she would meet would be more soldiers, and she certainly didn't want to marry her "father."

No, she would never allow that to happen. Like her mother, Candy hated military life.

She had never understood why the U.S. government sent soldiers to fight the people who had owned this land long before the white man. The Wichita, one of the tribes that lived in this area, had always sought peaceful solutions with white people.

If it were up to Candy, these peace-loving Indians would still have all of the land that whites were now occupying.

When *she* saw Indians, she didn't see savages. She saw a people who were standing up for their rights . . . their land . . . their freedom.

She wondered if the Indians in Arizona would be out for blood like the Sioux, who also lived in this area. Or would the Indians in Arizona be more like the Wichita, who always worked things out with white people in a peaceful manner?

Yet how would the Wichita behave when they knew how cruelly Short Robe had been treated during his incarceration in Fort Hope? When he was returned to them, one look at him would tell the tale of how his time at Fort Hope had been spent.

Oh, Lord, what would their reaction be?

Thinking of the possibility of their attacking the fort before Candy and her father left made her hope that their few remaining days in Kansas would go by quickly.

She gazed at herself again in the mirror and ran her fingers through her long, golden hair. She was tiny in build, so petite her father often referred to her as his "fragile porcelain doll."

Her oval face *was* of a porcelain color, with a touch of pink at her cheeks, and with a nose slightly tilted at the end.

Her eyes were azure blue, shadowed by long lashes.

Today she wore a high-necked, beautiful delicate pale blue silk dress that fell in deep ruffles around her tiny ankles. Her waist was so small her father could fit his hands around it, his fingertips touching.

"And, Lord, my name," she whispered to herself, hating the name Candy.

But her mother had insisted on it. She had said that the first moment she looked at her tiny newborn daughter she thought her as sweet as candy. Besides, her mother's best friend, a woman she'd known before she had met Candy's father and married him, was called Candy.

Candy had discovered only a few years ago that her mother had been a "dance hall queen," and her friend Candy had been the same.

"But my father, as he put it, 'saved' my mother from sin by taking her away from such an ungodly place," she whispered to herself.

But he could never change everything about her as he had hoped to do. From the moment her mother had married the esteemed Colonel Earl Creighton, she began to long for her former life as a dancer, and for her friend Candy—who, the young Candy had heard not long ago, had been run down by a team of horses on the streets of Laredo.

Candy prayed that her mother wouldn't meet the

same sort of end, now that she had fled the life of a military wife.

Sighing, Candy went to a window and gazed out. She saw her pet wolf asleep not far away on the parade grounds.

She would never forget the day her father had brought the tiny abandoned animal home for her to raise. Candy had named the wolf Shadow, and now felt as close to her grown wolf as she would have any brother or sister.

She looked into the distance, beyond the fort where there were no protective walls. She gazed at the rolling hills, where she heard wolves howling even now in broad daylight.

The sound emerged from the forest, eerily low at first, and then grew.

It sounded as if the forest were teeming with wolves, but Candy knew that these howls were coming from a small pack that she had become familiar with.

She looked at Shadow to see if she had been awakened by the wolves. Candy sighed with relief when she saw that her pet was still sound asleep.

She looked again into the distance, glad that the wolves were no longer howling and had surely gone on their way.

She was sorely afraid of those wolves, even though she had one as a pet herself. But her main fear was not so much for herself as it was for Shadow.

Candy had seen this pack of wolves more than once, led by an animal with snow-white fur. It had looked like a ghost with its white fur and mystical pearly blue eyes.

Those wolves had coaxed Shadow to join them more than once.

Candy had always been afraid that her wolf wouldn't return, for surely the call of the wild was imbedded so deep inside her heart, she was destined to one day live among those of her own kind.

Candy returned to her half-finished chore of packing her trunk. Sighing heavily, she went and sat down on the floor before it, again carefully placing her folded clothes inside.

She then picked up a doll that her mother had given her when she was a small girl.

Tears glistening in her eyes at the thought that she might never see her mother again, she held the doll to her bosom and hugged it.

"Mama, I hope you are alright," she whispered. "I . . . I . . . hope you are happy." She swallowed back a sob. "I hope to one day find my own true happiness."

Chapter Three

The smitten rock that gushes,
The trampled steel that springs;
A cheek is always redder
Just where the hectic stings.
—Emily Dickinson

It took a while, but finally the bloody irons and chains were off Short Robe's ankles and wrists. Short Robe was in his lodge now, where he lay unconscious, emaciated and weak, on a thick pallet of furs and blankets.

Two Eagles solemnly, gently washed his uncle's wounds free of blood as Crying Wolf, his people's shaman, prepared medicine for the cuts.

Two Eagles's heart skipped a beat when he saw his uncle's eyelashes flutter as he began to awaken from his deep sleep.

Two Eagles laid aside the soft buckskin cloth that he had been using to bathe his uncle's wounds and leaned down over him to hear what Short Robe was whispering.

Short Robe reached out a shaking hand and placed it on his nephew's arm. "Two Eagles, my . . . life . . . was spared for a purpose," he managed to say in his pain-filled voice. "After the pony soldiers realized they had captured the wrong man, they . . . they . . . took their mistake out on me and . . . and . . . beat and whipped me almost to unconsciousness. They . . . they only returned me home for one reason."

When his uncle's eyes closed and his voice faded, when his hand fell away from Two Eagles's arm, Two Eagles felt panic rush through him.

He breathed a heavy sigh of relief when his uncle's eyes opened again, his quivering hand again on his muscled, bronzed arm.

"I was brought back to my people to . . . to . . . set an example," Short Robe said, his voice cracking with pain.

"An . . . example?" Two Eagles said, rage entering his heart. "They did this to you for such . . . a reason as that?"

"Listen while I can speak," Short Robe said, his faded brown eyes pleading with Two Eagles. "There are not many pony soldiers left at the fort. Only . . . a . . . few remain, but even they are going soon, to another fort."

Two Eagles saw a sudden panic in his uncle's eyes, and felt his grip tighten on his arm as he again forced words from deep within himself.

"Two Eagles, it would be easy to attack the fort, but I encourage you not to, for vengeance is a low law that weakens the soul," Short Robe said. "Two Eagles, you must resist the temptation of vengeance. It is something that will bring more *wakan*, bad, to our people, than good. Think past what happened to me and concentrate only on the future of our people. Forget . . . what . . . happened to this one old man."

Two Eagles looked at his uncle's scarred, bloody feet and ankles.

He then looked at his uncle's bloody wrists, where the irons had cut mercilessly into his flesh.

And he knew that as long as Two Eagles lived, he would never be able to put the sight of his uncle's scarred back from his mind.

"Uncle, how can I not hunger for vengeance against those who did this to my father's brother?" he said thickly.

"You . . . will . . . only play into their hands if you pursue the vengeance that is eating away at your gut," Short Robe breathed out, each word now becoming harder to say.

He was so weak, so tired, but he forced himself not to drift off into unconsciousness again. He must not, not until he had said everything to his nephew that he knew must be said.

"They must be made to pay," Two Eagles hissed out between clenched teeth. "Do not ask me to forget this thing that must be done. I must avenge you, or our Eagle band of Wichita will lose honor as a people."

"Worse has happened to others than what happened to me, yet they remain unavenged," Short Robe said softly.

He patted his nephew's arm. "At least my head was not removed and put on display in a jar as a trophy as is our friend Chief Night Horse's head. It is being shown to any white who wants to see it," he said, his voice breaking with emotion. "The . . . the . . . colonel boasted of his triumph over Chief Night Horse and showed me his . . . his . . . head."

He closed his eyes as tears spilled from them, down over his leathery cheeks.

Then he gazed into Two Eagles's eyes. "You see, nephew," he said, wiping tears from his cheeks. "I was nothing to the colonel since I was no chief or shaman. The colonel said that he would not even waste a bullet on someone as useless as me."

Again, hot rage flooded Two Eagles. He was not certain he could hear any more of what had been done to his uncle or others of their skin color.

He stroked Short Robe's brow. "Uncle, have you had anything to eat since you were taken from your people?" he asked softly, trying to change the subject that pained him so. "You are terribly thin."

"A few times I was given a handful of raw meal alive with weevils," Short Robe said. "And I was fed stringy and half-rotted meat."

Hearing this was the last straw for Two Eagles. Despite Short Robe's words to the contrary, Two Eagles could not let this go. He and his chieftain father had practiced patience and restraint for too long now. He must show the white pony soldiers that they could not treat an old man like Short Robe as though he were less than human.

Ho, yes, Two Eagles must . . . *would* . . . make the

24

pony soldiers pay, especially Colonel Creighton, who had given the orders to do these humiliating things to his beloved uncle!

"I will get you food," he said as he rose. The shaman was still treating Short Robe's worst wounds, while saying prayers beneath his breath.

Short Robe nodded, then again floated away into a restful sleep.

After Two Eagles got outside his uncle's lodge, he had to stop and inhale deeply, over and over again, in order to get control of his fury.

He was already planning his vengeance.

This time he would not just stand aside and let such things happen to his people. He had nothing to lose by attacking the fort. He was probably already on the list of "savages" to be taken and punished, or killed, by the white pony soldiers. Now that the evil colonel knew Two Eagles was chief, surely he would try to capture him.

As shadows lengthened all around him and the air grew cooler, Two Eagles went to a maiden and requested she bring broth to his uncle; then he returned to his uncle's tepee and sat down cross-legged beside Short Robe's bed.

He was alarmed when he found his uncle asleep again, for Short Robe looked as though he had fallen into a deep unconscious state, possibly never to awaken.

It seemed that Short Robe had stayed alert only long enough to tell Two Eagles what he knew, and to ask his chieftain nephew not to seek revenge for what had been done to him.

25

To ward off the chill of the night, Crying Wolf lit a fire in the fire pit, then sat down on the opposite side of the fire from Two Eagles.

The shaman saw how the flickering of the fire sent light and shadows playing over the young chief's face, and how his eyes held great sadness.

He did not like what he must say to his chief, but it had to be done. His chief had to be prepared for the worst.

When Crying Wolf spoke, he drew Two Eagles's eyes quickly to him.

"My chief, your uncle's heart is very weak," Crying Wolf said softly.

He paused, when from somewhere afar, wolves howled at the rising moon.

He continued to speak after the wolves went suddenly silent.

"My chief, your uncle's old body has suffered terribly at the hands of the pony soldiers," he said solemnly. "Short Robe . . . is . . . dying."

Those words renewed the rage that had earlier filled Two Eagles's being. Recently he had lost not only his father, but also his only cousin, his mother, and sister.

And now his father's brother?

Before his family had begun leaving him, one by one, he could not have imagined life without one, much less all of them.

Two Eagles knew he would have had his uncle with him for at least a few more moons had the white eyes not come and taken him away to torture him.

26

Ho, Two Eagles thought to himself, he *must* avenge this injustice. He could not bear the thought that soon he would not have his uncle to sit with him beside the night fires; never again would they speak of things long past that no one else would know to tell Two Eagles.

His eyes glittered when he recalled what his uncle had said about there being only a few white pony soldiers left at the fort. Surely among them was Colonel Creighton, who had given the orders that brought such harm to Two Eagles's uncle.

This colonel, and those who remained at the fort with him, would pay.

They would pay for their sins against humanity with their lives!

To the Wichita, war was sacred, Two Eagles reminded himself, trying to find justification for what he planned to do, when for so long he had used only peaceful means to achieve his goals.

Long ago, before his father and grandfather reigned as peace chiefs, war was what had gained the Wichita all that they had.

It was time for warring again.

Ho, yes, it was time.

It was time for Two Eagles to take his place in that long line of warring chiefs.

"My chief, I read much in your eyes that frightens me," Crying Wolf said. "Is it the need for vengeance that I see?"

"Do you not also feel the same cry inside your own heart?" Two Eagles demanded. Then he turned and sat facing his uncle once again.

Outside he could hear his people congregating before Short Robe's tepee. Prayers were being offered to the God of the Wind, which was breath, hence life.

Two Eagles heard the prayers, then spoke one aloud, himself, as he gazed lovingly down at his uncle. "Now, good wind, I ask you to come and breathe on my uncle, so that he may be healed and feel comfortable," he cried. "I pray you, good wind, enter my uncle, so that he may breathe and be healed."

When he was finished with his prayer, he nodded a silent farewell to the shaman, who continued his vigil at Short Robe's side.

Just as Two Eagles stepped outside, he saw a red-tailed hawk flying from a tree, screaming as it rose upward into the star-speckled sky. The moonlight cast a white sheen on its outstretched wings.

A shiver raced across Two Eagles's flesh, for he could not help believing that what he had just seen and heard was an omen.

But was it a good omen?

Or . . . *wakan*, bad?

Only in time would he receive his answer.

Chapter Four

The little leaves hold you
as soft as a child,
The little path loves you,
the path that runs wild.
—*Max Eastman*

A full day and night had passed since Candy had watched the old Indian walk listlessly from the fort as chains rubbed against his raw flesh.

Dressed today in a fully gathered cotton skirt of a soft green color, and a white drawstring blouse, Candy shivered again at the memory as she stood at that same window in the dining room. Out on the parade grounds, the haunting notes of a bugle sounding taps floated in the air.

Candy watched the familiar ritual, one that had always touched her from the time she'd understood what an American flag was, and what it stood for. A soldier was lowering the flag; then several carefully

CASSIE EDWARDS

folded it. Soon one soldier would carry the flag, marching stiffly, slowly, and formally across the parade grounds toward her father's study in their cabin. It was this fort's main headquarters even though it was also where she and her father lived.

Candy turned and gazed at the grand oak dining table where a white linen tablecloth was spread out neatly.

Tall tapers burned at each end of the table, and a turkey, all browned and smelling delicious, sat on a large platter in the center. It was surrounded by dishes of mashed potatoes, gravy, and even green beans that her mother had grown and canned.

Tears came to Candy's eyes as she recalled her mother outside planting the beans, her skirt dirty with the black Kansas soil, and even some smudges of dirt on her cheeks.

Never in a million years would Candy have believed that her mother would soil even one finger to plant a garden.

But that had been a warning to Candy that things were not right with her mother, that she was bored to tears with military life. Filled with restless energy, she had found as many ways as possible to fill up the lonesome hours of her day.

"Even going as far as canning beans," Candy whispered to herself, recalling, too, how patient their family's black servant, Malvina, had been while teaching her mother how to do it.

Just as she was thinking about Malvina, the tiny black woman came into the room.

Malvina gazed at her in a troubled fashion, glanced at the table, where the food was cooling much too quickly for Malvina's liking.

"Where is your father?" Malvina asked, going to the table and smoothing out a wrinkle in the table-cloth. "The food won't stay warm forever, you know."

"Yes, I know," Candy murmured, loving Malvina almost as much as she did her own mother, for Malvina had been there for Candy since she was a small girl longing for someone to rock and sing to her.

Malvina had done those special things.

Not Candy's mother.

Candy hurried to Malvina and hugged her, feeling the familiar stiffness of the starched black dress against her arms, for Malvina was as exact in her washing and ironing as she was in her cooking and keeping house for the Creighton family.

"I'll go see what is delaying Father," Candy said, hurrying from the dining room.

She walked down a narrow corridor that opened up to various rooms in this large log cabin, which had been the family's quarters since her father had been transferred to this fort from one not far away in Missouri.

Candy would never forget that particular fort, which sat atop a huge bluff overlooking the Mississippi River. Jefferson Barracks Fort had been lovely and was never threatened by Indians.

Candy's family's home had been on the parade grounds of that fort, too, but it was much more elaborate than this cabin at Fort Hope. It had been a tall, two-storied plantation-type house, with beautiful furniture, draperies, and many servants besides Malvina.

When they had departed, Malvina was the only one who joined them, for they knew the sort of house they were moving into, and it was barely enough for the family, much less a dozen servants.

Candy missed Missouri, for she had loved exploring along the Mississippi River, even paddling out into it with friends in canoes. Her mother had been horrified once she heard about such escapades.

Candy believed it was those escapades that had caused her father to leave Jefferson Barracks and take his position at Fort Hope.

"Oh, well, just another piece of my life that is gone," Candy whispered to herself as she stepped up to the closed door of her father's private study.

Before knocking and disturbing her father, Candy gazed at the closed door. As long as she could remember, there had always been two rooms forbidden to her, from base to base, home to home: her parents' bedroom and her father's private study.

Her father had said there were things negotiated in both rooms that had nothing to do with Candy.

Of course she understood why the bedroom was off limits when her mother still lived with them. But never would she understand why she couldn't at least enter her father's private study.

What . . . could . . . he be hiding?

What rankled her nerves was the fact that the military staff entered her father's study freely through the door that led outside to the parade grounds. All official business was transacted there in his study. Perhaps her father just hadn't wanted Candy to get involved.

That had to be the reason she was not allowed there. She was a part of her father's other world, which had nothing to do with the orders being handed out in his study.

Surely it had been in that very room that he had made the decision to abduct the Wichita chief . . . a decision that had gone badly awry.

Realizing how more impatient Malvina must be getting as she watched the steam spiral from the food she had labored so hard over in the day's heat, Candy knocked gingerly on the door.

"Father, Malvina has made your favorite meal," she said. "It's getting cold."

When there was no response, even though she knew her father was there, probably packing his important papers in his briefcases, Candy softly spoke his name again.

"Father—"

"Candy, for heaven's sake, go on," he finally said through the door. "Go and tell Malvina I'll be there soon."

Having heard the same response countless times before, knowing that "soon" meant perhaps another thirty minutes, which would be the ruination of Malvina's delicious meal, Candy started to say something else, but decided not to.

It wouldn't matter.

Her father was set in his ways.

If he wanted more time before eating, he would have that time, no matter that it would also make Candy eat the same cold food as he!

Disgruntled, she went back to the dining room and settled in a chair just as Malvina came and poured her a cup of tea.

Candy admired Malvina's patience so much. Even though her many hours of slaving over the stove might be for naught, Malvina said no more about the absence of Candy's father.

"Father will be here soon," Candy offered, then looked up in surprise as he came into the room and took his place at the table, opposite Candy.

She always admired how neat he looked in his blue uniform. He even kept the brass buttons on his jacket polished. And his thick, golden hair, worn to his shoulders, framed a handsome face that sported a small sliver of a mustache.

Although he had proven to be calculating and cold at times, even cruel, as evidenced by the way he had treated the elderly Indian, he had kindness in his blue eyes. She would never forget how they'd softened with love and pride when she was a small child and loved sitting on his lap.

Even now he could give her a look that melted her heart.

Candy smiled softly at Malvina as she began ladling food onto her father's plate, then served Candy.

To try to make Malvina feel better about the

rapidly cooling food, Candy ate several bites, then smiled at her. "Delicious," she murmured.

"It's too cold," Malvina fussed, as she poured Candy's father a cup of hot tea.

"Malvina, I believe you've made your point," Candy's father grumbled. "I'll try not to be so late next time. It's just that I have a lot on my mind with the upcoming move."

"Do you have your trunk packed and ready, Malvina?" Candy asked as she stabbed beans onto her fork.

"Yes'm, I do," Malvina said, frowning. "But I must say, I do hate this movin' 'round from place to place. I just get used to a kitchen and then I'm gone from it."

"I'll make sure you have the best kitchen in Arizona," Candy's father said, giving Malvina a grin.

"That'd be nice," Malvina said, then left the dining room.

Candy and her father ate in silence for a while, but after a few minutes Candy just couldn't help speaking her mind. What the old Indian had endured ate away at her heart, and she was scared to death to think of the Indians retaliating.

"Father, I just can't forget that old Indian and the condition he was in as he was taken from the fort," Candy blurted out. "Just think of how he must have looked to his people when he arrived home. They surely will be out for blood. We should all leave here as soon as possible."

Her father paused before taking another bite of turkey. He glared over the table at Candy. "Yes, there could be repercussions over what happened to that old man," he said thickly. "And I was a fool to have abducted the wrong man. How was I to know that the chief had a brother who looked exactly like him? It was an honest mistake, Candy, but intolerable."

"Don't you think you should tell everyone to hurry their packing so that we can leave soon?" Candy said. "I just have a feeling that something terrible is about to happen."

"Am I to guide my actions by your feelings?" her father spat out. He slammed his fork on the table. "Just leave it be, Candy. Do you hear? Leave it be."

"Well, I have one more thing to say about the matter," Candy said, shoving her plate away. She had suddenly lost her appetite. "I'm just so glad you aren't planning another abduction. I was afraid that you would decide to go and abduct the new chief."

"I've lost interest," her father said, sipping his tea.

"Father, do you know anything about this new young chief?" Candy asked. "I've heard that Indian chiefs are like our president, and that the Indian people can't do anything without them."

"Yes, that's how they are looked upon and treated," he said. "That's why I abducted the man I thought was the chief. I wanted to gain control by showing that I could abduct him from right beneath his people's noses."

He shrugged. "But that's water under the bridge," he said. "I couldn't care less now what that band of Wichita do. I made a mistake and must learn to live with it."

"Father, when I talked with the old Indian, he spoke so highly of his nephew, and how he would make a great chief one day," Candy said solemnly. "And now it seems that day has come."

"You actually spent time with the old man?" her father said, his eyes filled with sudden rage. "When? Why?"

"You were away from the fort and everyone else's attention was on other things," Candy said. "I just couldn't pass up the opportunity to talk with him. I . . . I . . . felt so sorry for him."

"Sorry?" he shouted. "Don't you know how many innocent white people have been slaughtered by Indians?"

"I have heard the Wichita are not among those who slaughter white people," Candy said. "The old man said that his nephew, who is now chief, is a highly moral man who seeks peace, not war, with whites."

She swallowed hard. "Father, you know what you did to that old man was wrong," she said guardedly. "He told me that it would be hard to find any people of a finer nature than is possessed by his people, the Wichita."

"And will you still say that about them if they decide to get back at us for what we did to that old coot?" her father snapped.

"Surely they won't retaliate," Candy murmured, trying to convince herself, while in truth it turned her heart cold to think of what might happen because of her father's actions.

"Not if what the old man said about the young chief is true," she added.

"And since when would you believe a savage . . ." her father began, but stopped, alarmed when a spattering of gunfire and barbaric war cries outside interrupted him.

Candy flinched with alarm at the sound.

Her face drained of color as a cold, stabbing fear entered her heart.

And then she screamed wildly when an arrow shattered the dining-room window and pierced her father's chest. With a look of shock on his face, he clutched his chest and fell to the floor.

Panic and grief filled Candy's very being as she went and knelt over her father to feel for a pulse. She could hardly believe that only moments ago they'd been eating and talking.

And now?

What her father had most feared, but would not admit to, had come to pass.

There was no heartbeat, no pulse. He was dead!

"Oh, Father, what am I to do?" Candy cried, staring blankly at the arrow and the blood that oozed from the wound, spreading along his jacket as if the fabric were a sponge soaking up water.

She knew that she couldn't stay there any longer.

Her father was dead.

She could do nothing for him now.

She had to think of herself and Malvina, for the war cries, the whooping and hollering and shooting, continued outside the cabin.

"Malvina!" she cried as she looked down the corridor toward the kitchen, just in time to see Malvina stumble from the room, clutching an arrow that had pierced her back and was protruding through her chest.

"Go—" Malvina managed to say before she fell to one side, dead.

Candy gasped in horror. In a matter of moments she had lost the only two people left to her to love.

She was now alone.

Or would she die, too, in the next few minutes?

She knew where she must go, if she could only get there quickly enough. At any moment another arrow could slice through a window and claim her own life. Or an Indian could burst into the cabin and drag her away and . . . violate . . . her, then kill her!

All of her positive feelings about the Wichita had just been swept away in a heartbeat, for she had no doubt it was the Wichita who had come to retaliate for what had been done to one of their own.

She lifted the hem of her dress and ran hard down the corridor to the library at the far back of the cabin.

Breathing hard, she shoved a portion of a braided rug aside and saw the handle to the trapdoor that had been placed there to make escape possible if something like this happened.

She lifted the trapdoor, went a few steps down, then closed it behind her. She knew that when it was closed, the rug that was nailed to it would fall into place, hiding the trapdoor beneath it.

Trembling, she reached around for a lantern and

match, and soon had light to guide her onward to the passage ahead.

She held the lantern out before her and fled through a long underground tunnel that had been dug long ago for such an escape.

When she was almost at the end, she stopped to catch her breath.

She winced as she heard the thud of horses' hooves overhead and continued gunfire and screams.

She knew that she must wait a while longer, and then, when all became quiet and she was sure that the Indians were gone, she would go on to the end of the tunnel and, hopefully, make a successful escape.

She breathed hard and sobbed as she recalled the sight of her father on the floor, dead, and then Malvina.

In all reality, she doubted that she would come out of this alive either.

It didn't matter which tribe had come today to slaughter those left at the fort. It might be the Sioux, who had been on the warpath for some time now, and who were the most warlike of the tribes in the area, or it might be the young chief who had decided to seek revenge despite his usually peaceful nature. In either case, she doubted they would allow anyone to come out of the attack alive.

She thought back to the old Indian and how he'd spoken so favorably and lovingly of his nephew. A part of Candy wished that the attack was being led by Chief Two Eagles, for if she did somehow survive this ambush, might not he take pity on her, a mere woman?

Then another thought came to her.

She sobbed out the name Shadow.

Her pet wolf!

Was . . . she . . . also among the slaughtered?

Chapter Five

It, past escape,
Herself, now; the dream is done,
And the shadow and she are one.
—Robert Browning

As the sun lowered further toward the horizon and the air quickly cooled, Two Eagles sat on his black stallion, stunned silent by what he had just witnessed.

Just before he and his warriors had reached the fort, they had spotted many Sioux on horseback, looking fearsome in war paint. Screeching the war cry, the Sioux had sprung out of hiding and attacked the fort as Two Eagles and his men stayed back, in hiding, amid a thick stand of cottonwoods.

They had witnessed a full massacre. It appeared that no Sioux had died as the warriors rode away now, singing their victory songs. For no empty-

43

saddled Sioux horses were among the many rider-
less horses that followed the warriors—horses they
had stolen from the fort.

Ho, the Sioux had come and killed, and departed
victorious, before Two Eagles had been given the
chance to claim the same victory for himself and his
warriors.

Wearing his breechclout and moccasins, he had
his powerful bow slung across his left shoulder and
a quiver of many arrows on his back. His thick, black
hair hung loosely down his back to his waist as Two
Eagles gazed from one of his warriors to another.

He saw the same shock on their faces that he felt
within his own heart, knowing it was mixed with
disappointment that they had been outdone again
by the Sioux.

Two Eagles watched the Sioux ride away from
the massacre until they were totally out of sight.

A strange sort of quiet had descended over the
fort. The breeze rustling the leaves of the cottonwoods overhead was the only sound now, except for
a horse that suddenly whinnied, and another responding in kind.

"My chief, what are we to do?" Running Wolf
asked as he sidled his horse closer to Two Eagles's.

Two Eagles did not respond right away.

He gazed hard at the fort and listened to the silence. Only moments ago the air had been split by
war cries, screams of pain, and the sound of hun-
dreds of arrows being loosed from their bowstrings.

"My chief, should we retreat now and return

wissgutts, home?" Running Wolf asked, again trying to draw his chief's attention. "It is done. All are dead. That should be enough, do you not think?"

Two Eagles turned his head quickly and gazed angrily into his sentry's eyes. "Do you think it is enough?" he asked thickly. "Do you not recall any reason besides besting the pony soldiers that brought us here this evening?"

Running Wolf's face twisted in puzzlement, and then Two Eagles saw that his warrior finally remembered the chore that still lay ahead of them.

He spoke no more of it now, for he knew it was no longer necessary to say it aloud. The knowledge of what he was thinking was visible in the eyes of his warrior.

He looked past Running Wolf at the others.

He raised a fist in the air. "Come with me," he said in a low voice that would carry to his men but would not travel on the wind to the crafty ears of the murdering Sioux.

It would be a double victory for the Sioux if they realized that the Wichita were so near. They would surely defeat their traditional enemies, for the number of warriors that rode with the Sioux chief were double those who were with Chief Two Eagles.

Two Eagles kneed his *arrus*, his horse, snapped his reins, and rode onto the parade grounds, which were easily accessible because Fort Hope had no protective walls around it.

Urging his steed to a slow lope, as did those who rode beside and behind him, Two Eagles gazed from one dead white man to another. They were sprawled on the ground in their own spilled blood, making a gruesome spectacle. When he had covered the full length of the parade grounds, Two Eagles stopped.

He wheeled his horse around and again studied what the Sioux had left behind.

Except for the slight whispering of the breeze, nothing could be heard. There were no sounds; just the strange silence that came after a massacre.

His gaze then went to the buildings that lined one side of the fort, homing in on the main cabin that stood in the center of the parade grounds. Two Eagles knew it was the home of the colonel, as well as the main headquarters of the fort.

He looked slowly and carefully from one building to the other for any signs of life.

All he saw was how the red sunset reflected from the glass of those windows that had not been broken by Sioux arrows. The light seemed to spread like bloody stains.

"All are dead, do you not think?" Running Wolf asked as he again came and rested on his steed beside Two Eagles.

"We must be certain," Two Eagles said flatly. He nodded toward several of his warriors, one at a time. "You go and check all the buildings but the one that stands alone. I will go there myself."

"And what then, my chief?" Running Wolf asked. "Do we leave the buildings as they are, or do we burn them?"

Two Eagles looked in the direction of the fleeing

Sioux, then gazed into the eyes of his questioning warrior. "We will burn everything. It would be best to do it before full night comes. Otherwise, the reflection of the fire in the dark heavens might bring the Sioux back to see what causes it," he said tightly.

His gaze moved around him, studying each building more carefully, then he frowned as he again focused on the one in particular that set his heart afire with anger. He would never forget how these white pony soldiers had treated his beloved uncle, or forgive the man who had been in charge at this fort.

Colonel Creighton.

"Running Wolf, you come with me to the main headquarters building," he said thickly. "It is there that we will find our reason for remaining here tonight."

Everyone knew what he was referring to.

They nodded, then went their separate ways as Two Eagles and Running Wolf approached Colonel Creighton's cabin.

When they arrived at the main headquarters of the fort, Two Eagles drew rein and dismounted, nodding to Running Wolf, who did the same. They walked up the two steps that led to a closed door.

Being prepared for anything, even the possibility that somehow someone in this building might have come through the attack alive, Two Eagles yanked his large, sharp knife from the sheath at his right side, then with his free hand opened the door. The resulting creak sounded ominous in the stillness of the evening.

Two Eagles stepped inside with Running Wolf close behind him, his own knife ready in case it was needed.

But silence again ruled, with only a whistling sound coming through the broken glass of the windows.

Seeing many arrows lodged in the walls on the left side of the corridor, Two Eagles realized just how angrily the Sioux had fired them from their bowstrings.

He wondered what these pony soldiers had done to this band of Sioux to create such hatred.

He did not think about that for long, for he had spotted someone on the floor in a room to his left, where candles had burned down to their wicks on a sprawling table covered with a white cloth. He could see food on platters and cups turned over, from which a brownish liquid had spilled onto the white cloth.

But most of his attention was on the man who lay lifeless there on his back. An arrow had pierced the strange-looking medals on the man's blue jacket, and blood had stained them.

Two Eagles looked cautiously from side to side.

When he felt sure that no one else was left alive there, he stepped into the dining room and knelt beside the dead man.

An instant revulsion flowed through his veins, for he was looking onto the face of the very colonel he had despised. This man had the blood of his uncle on his hands, for Short Robe had told him that Colonel Creighton, himself, had made some of the scars on Two Eagles's uncle's back when he had heartlessly beaten him with the whip.

"And so the Sioux took the satisfaction of killing you from me," Two Eagles said between clenched teeth as he glared at the dead colonel. "But the important thing is that you are dead and can cause no other man humiliation or pain."

Hardly able to look on the face of the white man any longer, Two Eagles hurried to his feet and went out into the corridor where Running Wolf was kneeling beside a woman and studying her as though he had never seen a woman before.

Two Eagles went and knelt beside him, now understanding why his warrior was so curious about the woman. None of his people had seen many black-skinned people, and here one lay in a pool of blood, an arrow protruding from her chest.

He watched Running Wolf reach a hand to the woman's face, then draw it quickly away.

"Her skin is soft to the touch, but . . . but . . . so cold," he said, visibly shuddering.

"Her skin is cold not because of its color, but because she is dead," Two Eagles said solemnly. He placed a hand on Running Wolf's shoulder. "*Hiyuwo*, come. Let us find what we came here for and then return to our village. I have had enough of this place. Never before have I seen as many dead as I have here today. It is good that our people are not a warring people, for I would not have the stomach for such as this."

"Nor would I," Running Wolf said, swallowing

hard. "It is good that we have solved our problems in a peaceful way. But today . . . ?"

"*Ho*, we had planned to leave that peace behind us today in order to avenge my uncle and those of our friends who were terribly wronged by Colonel Creighton and his men," Two Eagles said, rising. He looked at the doors that lined the corridor. "Let us find what we are here for, quickly. *Hiyu-wo*, come. Follow me."

They hurried from room to room until they finally found the one they sought—the colonel's study.

"It has to be here," Two Eagles said stiffly. "Our scout, Fire Eyes, who the colonel did not know was a friend to us, saw it here."

Together they began searching, throwing books from shelves, opening and emptying the drawers of a massive oak desk, until they came to a closed, windowed piece of furniture.

Slowly Two Eagles opened the glass doors, again finding books that stood stiffly, side by side.

Angry that he still had not found the jar with the chief's head in it, Two Eagles began tossing books from the shelves.

He stopped short, his eyes wide, when the lowering sun's rays came through a broken window and settled on a jar that had been hidden behind the books. It was covered by a maroon scarf.

"This . . . must . . . be it," Two Eagles said as he slowly pulled the scarf away.

His stomach churned when he found eyes, locked in a death's stare, looking back at him, from sockets that had sunk into the bone. Only a few remains of flesh clung to the skull.

Two Eagles swallowed hard, turned his eyes away and closed them. Then he looked at Running Wolf, whose stomach had betrayed him after only one look at the face of an old friend.

Running Wolf was bent over and vomiting.

Then, breathing hard, Running Wolf wiped his mouth clean with the back of a hand and gazed in apology at his chief.

"Do not feel *wakan*, bad, about what you did," Two Eagles said, reaching a comforting hand to Running Wolf's bare shoulder. "My stomach rebelled, too, but just did not go as far as yours did."

"How could the white leader do this terrible thing to such a wonderful, admired, and powerful chief?" Running Wolf asked, gulping hard. "Please cover it. I do not want to look into those eyes ever again. There . . . there . . . is such pain there. Think of the misery he endured before . . . before—"

"Do not say any more," Two Eagles said thickly, quickly covering the jar with the scarf. Slowly, almost meditatingly, he wrapped the fabric securely around it.

When he turned to leave, his eyes settled on something else that the sun's rays seemed to purposely illuminate. He gasped when he saw several scalps hanging along the far wall.

Among them were two that he readily recognized. There was no doubt whom they belonged to.

His mother and sister!

Theirs had a unique trait that no other scalp hanging there had.

His mother's black hair had had one wide streak of gray that went straight down the back of the scalp, as had his sister's. She had inherited this trait from her mother.

Anger seethed inside Two Eagles as he placed the jar on the desk, then went and took those two scalps from the others and attached them to the belt of his breechclout. Now he could take them where they belonged . . . to the graves of his mother and sister. Finally their bodies would be complete in their final resting place.

He grabbed the jar up and held it securely, for he was glad to have found it. Now he would be able to return it to his close allies and friends. The head of their chief could finally be placed with the body!

Instead of returning to the part of the house where the colonel's body lay, Two Eagles and Running Wolf went through a back door and hurried to their steeds. Two Eagles never wanted to see that man again, especially now that he knew it was the colonel who had stolen his mother and sister away and murdered them.

Anger still flashing in his eyes, Two Eagles placed the jar inside the huge buckskin bag that he carried with him at all times at the side of his horse.

He placed the scalps there, too, then went and stood before his warriors.

"Do not leave anything of these people standing!" Two Eagles shouted, knowing that enough time had elapsed so that the Sioux could not hear him. "Burn it all! Burn everything!"

He mounted his steed and sat stiff-backed in his saddle as he watched torches being thrown on first the main building, and then the others. When they were all aflame, he wheeled his horse around and rode away, his warriors close behind him.

He had gone only a short distance before he was stopped by an unusual movement in the brush. There was just enough light left for him to see a woman crawling along the ground.

From this vantage point, he didn't see any blood on her person, nor did she seem injured, so he assumed that she was crawling in an effort to keep him and his warriors from seeing her.

Suddenly he saw her stop and look over her shoulder. She had spotted Two Eagles, who was now riding toward her.

Candy's heart was thudding with fear as the handsome young Indian, who was scarcely clothed, now slowly circled her.

She noticed a scar on his face, beneath his lower lip; it slightly marred his perfect, noble features, as did the tattoos on his hands. She bit her lip when she realized where her mind had taken her. There she was in mortal danger, her father and Malvina behind her now in the burning building, and she was thinking about how handsome this Indian was.

But she had never considered any Indian handsome. She had always thought they all looked alike.

But now?

Up this close?

She knew how wrong she had been.

Yet how could she forget, for even one moment, that this man was responsible for the death of many people, among them her father and Malvina?

She gazed at him now with contempt, with hate, as he stopped beside her.

"Stand," he said in perfect English. "Or do you prefer to continue crawling like a lowly snake along the ground?"

Knowing that she had no choice, yet so afraid she was not certain her knees would support her when she did try to stand, Candy slowly pushed herself up from the ground.

She stood straight-backed, her chin held firmly high, as she tried to prove that she was a woman of spirit . . . of courage . . . despite the danger she was in. She knew that one arrow could snuff her life out, as so many lives had been ended this evening at the fort.

Two Eagles knew this woman must be related to one of the men who lay dead now at the fort. Yet he couldn't help noticing her tininess, and the attire she wore, which was so different from what his Wichita women wore. And her eyes. They were beautiful and the same color as the sky. And he could hardly take his eyes off the golden color of her hair.

But it was her show of courage, of spirit, as she stood so boldly before him, her hands now moving slowly to her hips in an act of defiance, that truly awed him.

He had always thought that white women were

weak, especially in the presence of their enemy, the red man.

But this woman was different, much different from the one who lived among his people now. That woman, who was called by the name Hawk Woman, had come crying and screaming and begging for her life when she had been found wandering alone on the prairie.

It had not taken her long to realize, though, that those who had come to her rescue were not there to kill her or take her scalp. She lived now among his people, a part of them.

He had ignored Hawk Woman's many invitations to join her among her blankets, for there was nothing about her that appealed to him.

But this woman standing before him now?

Everything about her seemed to draw him near. She could change his mind about white women and bedding with them.

He saw her as someone he would enjoy sleeping with, and . . . more.

"What name are you called by?" he asked, his voice tight.

Candy tried to keep her voice from quivering, for thus far she had proven to be strong in the eye of danger, although inside herself she felt like a mass of quivering jelly.

"Candy," she managed to say in a murmur. "My . . . my . . . name is Candy."

She did not dare speak her last name to this red man, for surely he had come to the fort to kill her colonel father.

If this warrior knew her true identity, he might snuff out her life in one blink!

She saw how his eyebrows lifted when she said the name Candy.

She had received similar responses many times before when she told someone her name; she understood this Indian's reaction to it.

Suddenly Two Eagles reached down and whisked Candy up from the ground and onto his horse.

Holding her around the waist before him, he rode away.

Breathless at how quickly he had done this, and stunned to know that her fate surely lay in the hand of this one Indian, Candy felt her fear mount as they rode from the ruined remains of the fort.

Oh, Lord, surely she would die, for why would this Indian spare her life after having taken so many others? She was swept by a stark fear that he would use her sexually, then scalp and kill her.

She closed her eyes and said a silent prayer, then sobbed as she recalled the instant of her father's death, and then dear Malvina's.

She was oh, so alone in the world.

She had even lost her beloved pet wolf!

Perhaps dying would not be all that bad if it would save her from the disgrace of being savagely taken by this Indian, and those who rode with him.

She gulped as she looked from side to side, and noticed that some of the warriors were giving her hard stares. The day had turned to night, yet the moon was high and bright enough for her to see everything and everyone around her, and . . . for them to see her.

She closed her eyes, hoping to blank out as much as she could until the moment of decision came . . . whether she lived or died!

Chapter Six

Thy voice, slow rising,
like a spirit, lingers,
O'ershadowing me with soft
and lulling wings.
—Percy Bysshe Shelley

Trembling, her stomach churning with fear, Candy hugged herself as she sat beside a low-burning fire in the fire pit of a tepee she had just been taken to. The tepee was devoid of furnishings or utensils of any sort. All that was there, on the bulrush mats covering the earthen floor, were blankets rolled up and tied, a few feet from her.

When voices spoke from outside the lodge, she looked quickly at the closed entrance flap. She recognized one of the voices.

It belonged to the man who seemed to be the leader, who had brought her on his horse to the village.

She was in awe that the conversation was being conducted in perfect English.

She leapt to her feet and went to stand beside the entrance flap, listening to what was being said, for she knew it was about her.

The one Indian, whom she thought so handsome, had remembered her name and used it now as he gave the other man instructions.

She cringed when she heard that she was to be guarded at all times. Even if she got brave enough to try, she wouldn't be able to escape whatever fate awaited her.

When the voices stopped, she again heard only the same sounds that she had been listening to before the conversation began.

She heard women's voices and children at play who seemed happy as they laughed among themselves. She also heard what sounded like the voices of older men.

Before being taken inside this lodge, she had gotten enough of a glimpse of the village to see a huge outdoor fire burning in the center of many tepees. Older men were sitting around it smoking pipes; they had been conversing among themselves until they spotted her being brought into the village. As she was led to this tepee she could not take her eyes away from the big, roaring fire with its flames leaping skyward, lighting up the dark heavens.

Seeing that fire made a lump rise in her throat, for the burning inferno of the fort was the last thing she had seen as she had been taken from the scene of the massacre.

Not only had the Indians come and killed everyone there except herself, they had also set all the buildings aflame.

What had happened to the many horses that belonged to the soldiers? What had happened to those that belonged to her father, to her own strawberry roan, which she had adored riding on the days her father allowed her to leave the fort?

She jumped with alarm when the entrance flap was suddenly shoved aside and the handsome Indian came into the tepee. He caught her standing there, and surely guessed that she had been listening to his instructions.

But his discovery of her eavesdropping was not what frightened her. She grew pale, and the sick feeling that had overcome her since the beginning of the horrible massacre worsened when she saw what the warrior was bringing into the lodge.

As he turned to her, his eyes gleaming, she trembled at the sight of the irons and chains he was dragging behind him. The dried blood on them made her gulp hard in order to keep from losing everything that was rolling around in her stomach.

"What . . . are . . . you going to do with those?" she finally had the courage to ask.

She flinched when she suddenly recalled the last time she had seen such irons and chains.

The old Indian had been forced to wear them, and then made to walk from the fort with them on; the soldiers had been riding in front of him, leading him by a rope around his neck.

She gagged as another thought came to her. Was the blood on these iron and chains the old Indian's?

It made her feel ill to think of the kind old man being forced to wear those horrible things, and for such a length of time.

Two Eagles lifted and began swinging one of the chains before Candy's fearful eyes.

She watched it as though it were a pendulum, slowly moving back and forth, each swing counting off another moment of time.

She was afraid that each swing of the chain was counting off the moments before she would be killed for the sins of her father.

"You do recognize these, do you not?" Two Eagles asked tightly. He had seen a look of recognition and horror in her eyes as she watched the chain moving back and forth.

When Candy didn't respond, Two Eagles stepped closer to her and leaned into her face. The chain now hung quietly at his left side.

"You know that these chains are the very ones that were placed on my uncle by the white pony soldiers at the fort," he said, his teeth clenched. "You will now wear them. My uncle's blood will mingle with yours when they cut into your tender white flesh. Flies and gnats will buzz around your bleeding flesh and eat the blood as they did while my uncle wore them."

Candy was mortified to know that the old man was this Indian's uncle.

That made the situation even worse for her than she had imagined. Surely he was going to make her wear these nasty chains for a few days, and then kill her.

As she looked onto his face, the scar that ran in a jagged line beneath his lower lip was clearer; she noticed that the tattoos on the backs of his hands were in the design of a bird's foot, and on his right arm there were tattoos in the shape of a small cross. She found it hard to speak. Her words seemed frozen inside her. Her fear was so acute that she now felt cold all over.

"You have nothing to say?" Two Eagles demanded, finding it hard to be cruel to her, since everything about her spoke of innocence and loveliness.

But he could not allow himself to forget what had happened to his uncle and that Short Robe was even now surely dying because of his horrible treatment at the hands of the white soldiers.

For a moment, Candy seemed to see a softening in the handsome Indian's midnight-dark eyes, as though he realized that what he was doing was wrong.

But then, in the very next blink of an eye, there was that fierceness and anger again as he glared at her.

Still, she did have a glimmer of hope because of that one brief moment when his conviction had wavered.

He had a good reason to hate her.

She, too, would hate anyone who had treated her beloved uncle in that manner. God rest his soul, he had died while she was living in Saint Louis with her parents at the lovely fort that overlooked the Mississippi River.

He had loved taking walks with her as they gazed down at the paddlewheelers passing down below in the muddy Mississippi. It was on one of those outings that he had suffered a heart attack. He had died in her arms after he had fallen to the ground, unconscious.

Yes, she did understand how one could hate so much, but . . .

"I am not responsible for any of this," she blurted out. "Especially not for what happened to . . . your . . . uncle. I was horrified by all that was done to him. But I had no voice in the matter. Please believe me. I could do nothing to stop his mistreatment."

Two Eagles leaned closer to her until their breath mingled as they gazed into each other's eyes. Again he found it hard not to weaken beneath the pleading in her lovely blue eyes.

Even her voice had momentarily entranced him. Never had he heard such a soft, sweet voice.

But he forced himself to remember his uncle and what had happened to him. And he would never forget the two scalps he had found in the colonel's office . . . scalps of his mother and sister.

He had already taken them to where they should have been all along . . . to their graves.

"Did you plead for my uncle when you saw him being beaten?" he hissed out. "Did you ask that he not be treated in such a way? Did you ask for his release?"

"I did, but nothing I said helped, for I had no say

in anything that happened at the fort," she said, her voice breaking. "My father . . . was . . . the colonel. He . . . listened . . . to no one, especially not his daughter."

Candy suddenly realized what she had said when she saw a fire leap into the warrior's eyes at the news that her father had been the commanding officer of Fort Hope. It was the worst thing she could have told him.

She was doomed now!

Two Eagles took a step away from Candy, only now realizing that he had achieved more than he could have hoped for. The very man who had ordered the inhumane treatment of his beloved uncle, who had abducted and scalped his mother and sister, was this woman's father!

Ho, Two Eagles would get much pleasure in having her at his mercy, yet . . . yet . . . he saw much about her that said she was not like the man her father was, even though they shared the same blood. She was strong and courageous in the face of danger, and she had spoken in behalf of his uncle. She seemed helpless, sweet, and oh, so beautiful.

But he would not be sidetracked by his emotional response to her.

She would be used as an example to the white eyes, just as his uncle had been used.

Tears spilled from Candy's eyes as she tried one last time to make this Indian see reason. "After I saw how the old man . . . your uncle . . . was being treated, I gave him food and water when none saw me do it," she murmured. "I . . . even . . . washed his bloody feet."

Two Eagle was filled with rage at her words, for when he had asked his uncle if he had been fed while he was incarcerated at the fort, he had spoken of weevils in his food, and stringy, spoiled meat. He had most certainly not said one word about a woman being kind enough to bring him food, much less bend low and wash his feet!

"You lie!" he spat. "You lie in order to be treated better by the Wichita than my uncle was treated by whites!"

Candy's eyes widened. "I . . . I . . . have never lied about anything in my life," she said, her voice breaking again. She gazed into his eyes. "How . . . how . . . is your uncle?"

"You want to know how my uncle is faring?" Two Eagles asked, dropping the chains to the mat-covered floor of the tepee. "Come with me. You will see firsthand the damage done to the man I have admired and loved all my life."

Candy's heart sank, afraid now that the elderly man was dying. If he was, what then would be her own fate?

Chapter Seven

*I love your hair when the
strands enmesh your kisses
against my face.*
—Ella Wheeler Wilcox

Two Eagles grabbed Candy by an arm and shoved
her outside.

She was very aware of the quiet that suddenly descended on the village. The people nearby stopped
their activities and stared at her until she was taken
inside another tepee.

The light of the flames in the fire pit was enough
for Candy to see Short Robe lying on the far side of
the fire in a pile of blankets.

He was so lifeless, she thought he was dead.

She saw her own life flashing before her eyes, because she knew that she would be made to pay for
the crimes of her father.

She was very aware of a medicinal smell that permeated the lodge, and another aroma she was not familiar with that stung her nostrils. The smells gave her hope that perhaps the elderly man had been doctored; perhaps he would survive his terrible treatment.

Yet . . . he was lying so still. She could not see him taking breaths.

"Is . . . he . . . dead?" she blurted out, her knees trembling so terribly, she felt they might not hold her up much longer.

Her eyes widened, and she gasped when Short Robe opened his eyes and saw her there with his nephew.

He reached a shaky hand out toward her, but it fell limply at his side and he again drifted off into a deep sleep.

Candy was immensely relieved that he was alive. As long as he lived, she herself had a chance, especially if he eventually told his nephew how she had tried to help him.

Two Eagles interpreted his uncle's gesture very different from the way Candy wanted him to. He glared at her and strengthened his hold on her arm. "My uncle looked at you and pointed at you because he saw that you are rightfully the captive of his people," he said tightly.

"No!" she cried. "You misinterpreted what he was trying to do . . . to say . . ."

She yanked herself free of Two Eagles's grip and went to her knees beside Short Robe. "Short Robe, oh, please, Short Robe, awaken again," she cried. "Please tell your nephew what I did for you. Please, Short Robe. I'm afraid . . . my . . . life depends on you."

Two Eagles's eyebrows rose when he heard Candy calling his uncle's name and pleading with him, as though she might really have spoken to him before.

Could it be true that she had helped him?

Then he recalled his uncle's description of what he had been fed. He had said nothing about a white woman bringing him food, or doing anything else for him, for that matter.

Two Eagles could not allow himself to be misguided by this woman's soft voice and lovely eyes. She was as guilty as her father; did she not have his evil blood running through her veins?

He went to her and yanked her to her feet, then took her from the tepee and back to the one where she would be held captive.

Terrified now, truly believing that nothing she said or did would save her life, Candy sobbed as she watched Two Eagles place the bloody irons around her wrists and ankles. The chains attached to them were bloody and heavy.

She already felt the discomfort and feared moving; surely the metal would cut into her flesh.

She recalled the gnats and flies that had buzzed around the old man's sore, bloody flesh.

Soon they would be on hers!

Rage replaced her fear and nausea. "You are heartless!" she cried out as she glared into Two Eagles's dark eyes. "How can you do this? I . . . I . . . am not guilty of any crime." She lowered her eyes. "You are wrong to do this to me," she sobbed out.

Two Eagles placed a hand beneath her chin and raised it so that she had no choice but to look directly into his eyes. "All you knew at the fort, especially your colonel father, were the heartless ones. They not only treated an innocent old man inhumanely, but also removed heads from red men they saw as their enemies!"

The horror of his accusation made Candy shiver with disgust. "No!" she cried. "Never! My father was a strict colonel, and he did despise Indians, but he could never do such a heartless thing as that."

He gave her a long, last look, then stormed out of the tepee.

Candy sat there numbly, the chains weighing down her wrists and ankles.

Tears pooled in her eyes at the thought of her father's death, as well as dear Malvina's, and the deaths of all the men who had followed her father's lead.

And then there was her beloved wolf, Shadow. Surely she had been killed by an arrow, too!

Candy hung her head, torn apart by grief and fear of where this would end for her.

What Two Eagles had already done to her was awful. Yet she knew it could get much, much worse.

Suddenly she was no longer alone. Candy was shocked to see a white woman who was dressed in Indian attire, and who had hair the same golden color as hers. The woman was calmly adding wood to the fire.

The woman ignored Candy when she asked who she was. "Why are you here?" Candy inquired. "Are you also a captive?

Hawk Woman, who was anything but a captive, frowned at Two Eagles's prisoner. She had been in love with the handsome young chief ever since she'd joined the band, but he rebuffed all of her advances toward him.

Hawk Woman saw this woman as possibly a threat to her own standing among the Wichita.

Hawk Woman, whose real name was Sara Thaxton, had been rescued by these people and taken in. They welcomed her as a part of their lives and guarded her against the white man she had fled from.

Candy could not understand why this other white woman refused to speak with her. Bemused, she watched the woman place yet another log on the fire.

Before Candy could say anything else to this unfriendly woman, she was gone.

But to Candy's surprise, she returned very soon with a platter of food.

"Ma'am, thank you for adding wood to the fire, and . . . and for bringing me food," Candy said softly, trying once again to get the woman to speak with her. When the woman met her gaze, she saw instantly that this woman was going to be anything but a friend.

Candy knew resentment when she saw it, and she saw much of that emotion in this woman's flashing green eyes. It was hard to understand why the woman should resent her so much. Candy had done nothing to earn it.

"Will you please stay awhile?" Candy said, trying one last time to reach the woman's heart as she gazed up at her, watching and waiting for her response.

"Would you want to eat with me?" Candy blurted out.

"Just shut up," Hawk Woman said, her eyes narrowing angrily. "You will cooperate if you know what's good for you. Chief Two Eagles, the warrior who brought you into this tepee, will kill you if you don't behave."

Hawk Woman's eyes glittered even more when she reached down and ran her fingers through Candy's long, golden tresses. "You hair would make a good decoration for Two Eagles's scalp pole," she said, laughing mockingly.

Horrified by what this woman had just said, Candy stiffened and leaned away from her. She was truly afraid now. It seemed that this woman hated her with a strange sort of passion.

Candy gazed at the woman's beautiful golden hair, which was braided in a single long plait down her back. She wore a white doeskin dress with a flashing necklace of beads around her thick neck.

Candy could not help wondering how the woman had come to this village, and why she was free to come and go among the Wichita people.

Now Candy felt even more afraid than before, not

because of the threats that came from this spiteful woman's mouth, but because Candy now knew that her captor was the chief of this village of Wichita. If *he* had such hate for her, all his people would feel the same.

Now she didn't believe that she could possibly come out of this alive. Would her hair sway from Two Eagles's scalp pole someday? Or would she be cast out of the village, to become food for wolves and birds?

She suddenly heard the baying of wolves from somewhere in the distance, reminding her of her dear Shadow.

Even though she realized how much the white woman obviously resented her being there, Candy tried one more time to gain her sympathy.

"You are white, I am white; how can you not want to help me?" Candy murmured. "Why do you resent me so much?"

Hawk Woman gave Candy a cold glare, stuck her nose in the air, then flounced from the tepee.

A moment later Two Eagles returned.

Candy noticed that he carried something covered by a piece of maroon cloth.

She was afraid to ask what it was, and didn't have to. Two Eagles seemed eager to show her what he had brought into the lodge.

"Do you see what I am holding?" Two Eagles asked tightly. "I took this from your father's dwelling."

The color drained from Candy's face when he

yanked the cloth away from the jar, revealing a head inside it. The eyes of the skull stared blankly back at her. . . .

She felt dizzy, then floated away into a dark, deep void as she fainted to the floor.

Chapter Eight

No sister flower would be forgiven
If it disdained its brother.
—Percy Bysshe Shelley

Candy awakened with a start when she heard someone step up to her bed of blankets. She had no recollection of having unrolled the blankets. She had no
recollection of having gone to sleep.

Then she remembered.

She had fainted!

And she shuddered as she now recalled why. The
jar with the head in it.

Tears filled her eyes at the realization of who was
responsible for such a ghastly act.

Her father.

She hated to think of the other horrendous acts her
father might have committed while in command as a
powerful colonel.

She had to put such thoughts from her mind or she just might go crazy.

She thought again of where she had spent the night; she knew it was morning now, for the sun was slanting its golden rays down the overhead smoke hole.

She looked up at the white woman who was standing over her, holding a bowl of food. Had this woman put her to bed the night before?

Or had it been Two Eagles?

If it had been Two Eagles, she was glad that he had not removed her clothes. She was still wearing the same skirt and blouse she had been wearing at the horrendous moment of the attack on Fort Hope.

Candy's stomach growled at the thought of eating, for she had not eaten the food that had been brought to her the night before. Her stomach was too unsettled from the terrors of the day to even try to put food in it.

She had been afraid her dinner might come back up as soon as she ate it.

But realizing that she must eat to keep up her strength, she sat up and was crudely reminded once again of her bondage. The irons had already rubbed her wrists and ankles raw.

"Ma'am, I can't eat with these irons on my wrists," she said. "It is too difficult to move, and the dried blood on them sickens me."

"First off, quit calling me 'ma'am,' " Hawk Woman spat out. "My name is Hawk Woman. Do you understand? Hawk Woman!"

"Alright, Hawk Woman, I'll remember to call you

that from now on," Candy said, her voice breaking. She was still stunned by this woman's attitude toward her and the fact that she seemed so Indian, not only in the way she dressed, but also in the name she was called.

"Hawk Woman, will . . . you please remove the irons?" Candy asked, hating the timidness of her tone.

Hawk Woman's eyes glittered, and her lips twisted into an amused smile. Then she set the bowl down next to Candy.

She gave Candy one more mocking look, then spun around and left Candy alone again.

Candy wasn't used to being treated so callously. But she now knew that she could not expect anything else from Hawk Woman. For some reason, the woman disliked her.

Sighing heavily and trying to put Hawk Woman from her mind, Candy gazed at the tempting food. Her stomach growled again as she spotted a piece of corn on the cob. It was one of her favorite foods. There was a small portion of cut-up meat, which she assumed was venison, and a ripe cantaloupe, which had been cut into slices.

The various aromas smelled delicious.

She couldn't *not* eat.

She must at least try.

She grimaced as she tried to reach for the corn, then stopped and rested her hand on her lap. The irons rubbing against her raw wrists caused her too much pain to continue.

Tears filled her eyes as she stared into the fire.

Her tears sprang from many mixed emotions—

her feeling of total helplessness, her aching hunger, and the loneliness she felt as she missed her father, and also sweet Malvina and her beloved Shadow.

For the first time in her life, she was totally alone with no one to help, or love her.

She then remembered the head in the jar and the horrible sight of her father whipping the old man's bare back for no good reason. He had done it just because he could, since he was in charge of Fort Hope.

She would never forget Short Robe's silence as he had been whipped, too proud to let her father realize the pain that he was inflicting.

No.

He had never cried out, not even one time.

It was at that moment when Candy accepted the sort of man her father was. She had known for a long time, but just hadn't been able to face up to it. He was her father, the person she had adored as a child, before she knew what he was capable of. He had loved her and held her close to his heart until she was too old to hold.

Then he had taught her the wonders of riding horses and everything else that he would have taught a son.

She had not allowed herself to be insulted, or hurt, to know that in his heart he resented the fact that she was not a son and could never enter the military with him.

But no father could have been prouder of a daughter than he had been of her. He had always thought her fragile because of her petiteness, but although she was not all that strong, she had been strong enough to fend for herself when the need arose.

Several times she had been caught away from the fort in a rain storm. She knew that her father had been frightened for her on those occasions. He knew, much better than she, the dangers that lurked away from the safety of the fort.

Of course she knew all about Indians and what some were guilty of doing to whites.

But she hadn't allowed that knowledge to make her a prisoner of her own home, for if she had, she would have felt only half alive.

"And now I am a true prisoner," she whispered to herself, again looking at the food.

She had never been so hungry in her life, yet . . . yet . . . each movement of her wrists brought renewed pain and fresh blood as the irons scraped against her already raw flesh.

Again she thought of her father. She knew that if he were alive, he would be sending the military out everywhere to look for her.

She could even now envision him sitting in his study, staring into the fire, as he waited for her to return.

The thought of the study brought more than her father to her mind. She shivered as she again recalled the head in the jar, and where Two Eagles had found it.

In her father's study!

Now she understood why he had never allowed her to enter it. He was hiding something ugly beyond belief. How could any man do such a thing to another human being?

Her thoughts were interrupted when she heard footsteps outside drawing near the tepee. They were not the footsteps of a woman, so she knew not to expect Hawk Woman.

Her heart pounded at the thought of who had come for a morning visit. A moment later, Two Eagles nudged the entrance flap aside and came to stand over her.

As before, he wore only a breechclout, moccasins, and a headband holding his long, thick, black hair back from his magnificently sculpted face. The scar beneath his lip was certainly no hindrance to his handsomeness.

But today there was something about his attire that was different. He wore a huge knife sheathed at the right side of his waist.

It looked deadly.

He also carried a lovely white, fringed dress across one arm, and held a pair of moccasins in his left hand. A thin, long piece of hardened leather was in his right.

She knew immediately what that strip of leather was: the hardened remains of a leather strop.

She grimaced at the memory of a time long ago when one of her friends, Sam, a twelve-year-old boy, had been punished by his father for bloodying the nose of a playmate. His punishment had been a whipping with his father's leather strop.

She would never forget Sam's yelps of pain as his father brought the strop down across his back at least a dozen times. Nor would she forget that afterward, his father had taken Sam by an ear and forced him to apologize to the other boy, even though as far as she was concerned, that boy had earned the bloody nose because he had yanked so hard on Candy's pigtails. The pain in her head had lasted for a full day.

So . . . why had Two Eagles brought a razor strop into this tepee? Was it a way to frighten her even more?

Did he use the strop to punish anyone who disobeyed him?

She closed her mind to the possibility that he would use the horrid thing on her; surely he could not do such a thing to someone as innocent as she.

Her insides tight, and scarcely breathing, Candy watched as Two Eagles laid everything down.

She saw how his eyes went to the uneaten food, and then gazed questioningly at Candy.

As though he could read her mind, he bent to his haunches and removed the irons at her wrists.

"Eat," he said, nodding toward the bowl of food.

Stunned that he had been thoughtful and understanding, Candy just stared into his midnight-dark eyes for a moment. Then when her stomach growled and she was reminded how hungry she was, she gave him a soft smile.

"Yes, I am terribly hungry. Thank you," she murmured. She knew that after she was through eating, he would more than likely place the irons on her again, but for the moment she was free of them. Forgetting that he was there watching her, she ate ravenously.

While she was eating she was only scarcely aware that he had removed his knife from its sheath. But when he began slowly sharpening it on the dried-up leather of the razor strop, slowly slapping and sliding the blade up and down the strop, a sick feeling rushed through her. Why was he gazing at her golden hair?

Was he sharpening his knife so that he could scalp her?

Had he fed her her last meal before killing her?

Suddenly her appetite was gone. Gagging, she shoved the bowl away from her.

She felt icy cold when Two Eagles paused in his work, then carefully plucked a hair from his head and held it dangling in the air before him.

Candy gasped and felt faint when he suddenly swept the knife blade in a vicious swing, cutting the hair in half. Nodding, he went back to sharpening the knife on the razor strop.

Candy reached inside herself for all the courage she could muster and asked, "Why . . . are . . . you doing . . . that?"

Two Eagles ignored the question. Instead, he gazed at her as he left off sharpening his knife. He could not help noticing how slender and supple she was, her hips curving into a slim waist.

Her face was oval and delicate, with blue eyes that mesmerized him.

Her lips. Ah yes, her lips. They were perfectly

shaped and tempting; he found himself longing to taste the wonders of her lips.

And then there was the golden hair tumbling down her back.

Although Hawk Woman had the same color hair, it seemed more beautiful and lustrous on this tiny, fragile white woman.

But he reminded himself that no matter how much he admired her hair, soon it would be gone from her.

Candy sat rigidly still as she was scrutinized by this man who held her fate in his hands. She felt as though she were on display as his eyes lingered here and there on her, resting longest on her hair!

Oh, surely he did plan to scalp her!

Would she die immediately, or slowly bleed to death?

She wanted to shout at him that it was wrong to kill her. She was innocent of any wrongdoing against him or his people.

But she couldn't.

She would not beg, not even for her life, for she would never forget the courage of the old man as he stood in the parade grounds being whipped, too dignified and proud to ask the soldiers to stop.

She would be just as dignified and proud!

She would show this young chief that she would never beg for mercy, not even at that moment when he touched her scalp with that horrid, sharp knife!

Her eyes widened in wonder when he began talking about his people, surely in an effort to distract her from what he was doing.

Candy tried hard to look attentive, while all along her heart was crying out to him to set her free!

She could ride to the next fort and seek refuge there. If Two Eagles agreed to let her go, she would promise not to tell anyone that it was he who had massacred everyone except herself at Fort Hope.

But she knew that her words would be wasted. She had to patiently wait to see what her final fate would be.

"The Wichita women are tilling the fields today around the plants that will soon be harvested," Two Eagles said nonchalantly.

How could he be so casual about what was happening in this tepee, as though Candy were there just to be talked with, instead of his enemy and captive.

"After the final harvest of our corn, there is a great feast," Two Eagles said as he went back to sharpening his knife. The blade occasionally caught the light of the fire, sending its glow into Candy's eyes. "Corn is my people's main food. It is sacred and called *aitra*, which means 'mother.' There is an ancient legend telling that when the plants fail to come up, the Wichita people will cease to exist."

That made Candy's eyes widen even more. She was surprised that these people's lives seemed to be dictated by superstition. She listened, her curiosity making her momentarily forget her fear.

"When the first shoot of corn comes up, an old woman goes there to perform a rite of thanksgiving over the plant," he said. "She rubs the plant with her hands in blessing, saying, 'Oh, big bow,' which

84

means corn stalk. Then she rubs a baby with her hands in a similar fashion, passing on the blessing from the plant to the child."

He paused, smiled at Candy, then said, "Everyone is happy at the sight of the first plant."

Candy was unable to sit still any longer. What he was telling her was interesting enough, but the constant sharpening of the knife finally unnerved and unraveled her.

"Go ahead!" she cried. "Scalp me! Get it over with! I can't stand it any longer. Oh, please, just . . . do it . . ."

Two Eagles stopped and stared in disbelief at Candy. He was stunned that she actually thought he was going to scalp her.

But as he thought about it, he understood her fear.

There he was, sharpening his blade and occasionally looking at her beautiful hair. He could not help admiring the golden tresses. Surely it would feel like corn silk to the touch. He wanted so badly to run his fingers through it.

And he would.

Soon.

He would lay the locks he cut from her head in his hands. . . .

Suddenly Candy's attention was drawn to a commotion outside.

When someone shouted that a wolf had entered the village, Candy and Two Eagles exchanged quick glances.

Laying the knife and razor strop aside, far enough away that Candy could not get to them, Two Eagles held the entrance flap aside. Outside, everyone was moving aside as a wolf with singed fur and burned paws came limping toward the tepee. The creature did not act wild at all, but meek; it ducked its head and kept its tail tucked between its hind legs, only occasionally glancing up at Two Eagles.

Two Eagles knelt and reached his hand out to the injured wolf. It seemed to be coming to him, but then suddenly leapt past him and rushed into the lodge.

Candy gasped. "Shadow! Oh, Shadow, you are alive!" she cried. "Oh, Shadow, you found me."

Two Eagles stepped back inside the lodge and watched the reunion of the wolf and the woman, stunned at the sight.

He went and knelt beside them.

"This is my wolf," Candy murmured as she gently inspected Shadow's singed fur and sore paws. "Oh, Two Eagles, she escaped both the arrows and the fire! She is alive!"

"You call the wolf by the name Shadow?" Two Eagles said softly, touched by the love between the woman and the animal.

He saw that the animal was of the red wolf family. They were generally brown and buff-colored, whereas most wolves in this area, except for the lone white wolf he occasionally saw, were gray.

"Yes, Shadow," Candy said, feeling happy that one part of her former life had survived the terrible massacre. "A few years ago my father found a pup abandoned and afraid. He brought her home to me."

She paused, then said, "I thought she was so beautiful with the reddish tint of her fur behind the ears, on her muzzle, and on the back of her legs. She was like no wolf I had ever seen."

She gave Shadow a hug, then continued, "I nursed the sweet thing to health, fed her, and named her. I called her Shadow because the wolf became my shadow, following me everywhere I went. Only recently have we been separated when she occasionally started heeding the call of the wild, going to join her own kind for several days at a time. But she always came back to me."

Candy wiped tears from her eyes. "Just . . . as . . . she found me today," she murmured.

Suddenly she recalled what Two Eagles had been doing just prior to Shadow's arrival. She looked at the knife, and then glanced into the young chief's midnight-black eyes.

Chapter Nine

Which masters Time indeed, and is
Eternal, separate from fears.
—Alfred, Lord Tennyson

Witnessing Candy's love for the wolf, and the wolf's love for her, Two Eagles was almost convinced of her goodness. He had always seen wolves as mystical, wise animals.

Yet he could not allow anything to get in the way of the vengeance he could achieve by holding her captive.

For now, however, he would not interrupt the reunion of animal and woman.

He slid his *nezik*, his knife, back inside its sheath and knelt down beside Candy.

Candy clung to Shadow, then looked up at Two Eagles. She glanced at the knife he had sheathed.

"My wolf's paws need medicine," she said softly. "Can . . . will . . . you do something for her?"

She hoped that Two Eagles could be distracted from what he had been about to do. She hoped that the longer she lived, the more he would doubt his decision to take her life in such a terrible way.

Never wanting to see an animal in pain, Two Eagles nodded, then left the lodge.

"I think he's going to help you," Candy murmured, gently hugging Shadow. "I'm so sorry, Shadow, for what happened to you. But . . . but . . . there was nothing I could do for you. I wasn't even sure where you were."

Shadow placed a paw on Candy's arm as though she knew what Candy had said, whined softly, then turned her head and let out a low growl when an elderly Indian man came into the tepee with a large buckskin bag at his side. Two Eagles was right behind him.

"I have brought my people's shaman," Two Eagles said. "His name is Crying Wolf. He will treat your wolf's paws."

Hearing the shaman's name, Candy wondered if he had some sort of affinity for wolves. If so, Candy hoped that this old man with the long, flowing, gray hair would treat her wolf gently and give her the best care he could.

"Thank you," Candy murmured to Two Eagles. She didn't take her eyes off the shaman as he took a vial from his bag.

She quietly watched Crying Wolf as he placed a

creamy substance on Shadow's paws, then wrapped soft doeskin around them.

Crying Wolf gazed into Candy's eyes. "Your wolf will be well soon," he said in the same perfect English that the other Wichita people had used.

Shadow crawled onto Candy's lap, snuggled against her, and was soon fast asleep.

"Thank you," Candy murmured. "I so appreciate your kindness."

Crying Wolf gave her a smile and a nod, then lifted his bag in his arms and left without another word.

Candy's heart now thumped wildly inside her chest. She was alone again with Two Eagles. Anxiously, she waited to see what his next move would be.

When he pulled his knife from its sheath again and knelt in front of her, her hopes plummeted.

"I am going to cut your hair," Two Eagles said, lifting the knife toward it.

"Do you mean that . . . you . . . are going to scalp me?" Candy gulped out, her hopes of living past the next few moments waning.

She could not help recalling how Hawk Woman's eyes had gleamed when she had said Candy's hair would look good on Two Eagles's scalp pole.

A look of surprise entered Two Eagles's eyes. "I am not going to scalp you," he said. "I just want to cut your hair so that when you work in the fields with the Wichita women, you won't be so noticeable."

"You . . . aren't . . . going to scalp me?" Candy said, sighing heavily. "When I saw you sharpening your knife, I thought it was because . . ."

"Do not say it again, for you were wrong," Two Eagles commanded. He gazed at her hair, then reached out and touched it. "I do not like having to remove any of it. It is so soft, like a butterfly's wings. But to ensure that you are not noticed by those who might come near my village, I must cut it."

Relieved, Candy sighed heavily, then smiled. She would gladly part with a portion of her hair if it meant that she wouldn't be scalped, even though she had always been proud of her long hair.

Knowing now that he wasn't going to scalp her made Candy begin to hope that Two Eagles did not intend to harm her. Perhaps in time he would even release her.

"I understand," she murmured. Then, with Shadow still sleeping on her lap, Candy closed her eyes as Two Eagles used his knife to cut her hair, one lock at a time.

When he was done, she opened her eyes and saw her hair laid out smoothly on the mat beside her.

She questioned Two Eagles with her eyes.

"It is yours to do with as you please," he said. He then lifted the dress that he had brought into the tepee and handed it to her, along with the moccasins. "These are yours to wear. Change into them. You will join the women in the fields soon."

She glanced down at the irons and chains, then up into his eyes. "Will I be forced to wear these while I help the women?" she asked guardedly, afraid to hear the answer.

"Yes," he said flatly. "You are no less my enemy now than moments ago. I will step outside so that you can change your clothes; then I'll return and place the chains and irons back on you."

Knowing that no matter what she said, she would still be chained, Candy watched Two Eagles step outside.

She gently laid Shadow aside.

Then she changed into the wonderfully soft dress and moccasins.

She reached up and touched the blunt ends of her hair.

"I wonder what I look like," she whispered to herself, then flinched when Two Eagles came back into the lodge and placed the irons and chains back on her.

"I must leave now," he said, standing over her. "I must go into council with my warriors. It is the time of the waxing of the moon, when people feel and think less narrowly. They are more giving." He gazed at Shadow, then into Candy's eyes. "This is also the time the wolf and coyote are more successful in hunting."

It was at that moment that Candy heard the baying of wolves in the distance. She shivered at the wild sound, fearful of what they might eventually do with Shadow. She was afraid they might lure her wolf away from her.

As it was, Shadow was the only part of her old life left to Candy . . . the only one that loved her.

She saw a look she did not understand in Two Eagles's eyes as he gazed at her in silence for a moment. Then he turned and left the tepee.

Having never felt so alone in her entire life, Candy

gazed into the flames of the fire, and then looked at Shadow sleeping so snugly beside her.

If not for Shadow, she wasn't certain she could remain sane.

Tears filled her eyes when she thought of her father. She brushed them away when she recalled the severed head in the jar, and the look of pleasure on her father's face as he whipped the old Indian's back.

She still loved her father and would always miss him horribly, but she had lost all respect for him.

She had herself to think about now . . . and how she could escape.

But it seemed impossible. Shackled in such a way, she wouldn't be able to get far.

Eventually Two Eagles would remove the bonds and leave them off, though, for if he wanted her to work in the fields like a slave, he would get more out of her if she wasn't shackled. That thought gave her some hope.

Again the wolves howled in the distance.

She looked quickly at Shadow when she moved in her sleep, one ear lifting as though hearing the call of the wild again.

"Please don't ever leave me," Candy whispered.

Chapter Ten

I fear thy kisses, gentle maiden,
Thou needest not fear mine;
My spirit is too deeply
Ever laden to burthen thine.
—Percy Bysshe Shelley

Two Eagles went to his private lodge and sat down before his fire.

He drew his knees up to his chest and circled them with his arms, his eyes watching the slowly lapping flames as they curled around the logs.

But he wasn't truly seeing the fire.

He was full of conflicting feelings about the white woman.

His thoughts were too often filled with how sweet she was; she was so soft-spoken, and looked so very helpless wearing the irons and chains against her tender, white flesh.

He felt that he was wrong to make her wear them, yet none of her people had shown mercy when his uncle was wearing them while imprisoned at Fort Hope, or later, while he was forced to walk from the fort to his home.

Of course Candy had told Two Eagles that she had felt deep sympathy for Short Robe. She had even said that she had fed him and bathed his raw ankles when no one was around to see her do it.

"But would not anyone tell the same lie in order to win over a man who was holding them hostage?" he argued aloud.

He ran his long, lean fingers through his hair, pulling it farther back from his sculpted face.

No! He refused to let himself think about Candy any longer.

He had his duties as chief to occupy his mind. His warriors were waiting for his arrival even now at the council house, where important business was to be discussed.

And then tonight was storytelling time for his people's children around the large outdoor fire. He just might allow Candy to sit outside and listen to the stories in order to show her how wrong it was for her people to mistreat the red man.

Knowing that he had made his warriors wait too long already while he got his mind in order, he rose to join them in the council house. But first he wanted to see how his uncle was faring.

He hoped that by now his uncle was awake, for there were questions he would like Short Robe to answer . . . questions about the woman whose lovely hair he had just cut, and whose beautiful eyes haunted him every time he thought of them.

He did not see how she could be guilty of anything *wakan*, bad, and he felt guilty for making her pay for something she had had no control over.

He stepped softly into his uncle's tepee and found Hawk Woman sitting devotedly there on the far side of the fire, beside Short Robe.

There were many things about this woman that Two Eagles loathed, but her kindness toward Short Robe was something that he could not help being thankful for, and admiring.

Sometimes that kindness helped erase the other spiteful things she did from his mind.

"How is my uncle faring?" Two Eagles asked as he knelt beside Hawk Woman. He had eyes only for his uncle. He did not so much as glance at the woman who always tried to attract his attention with her eyes, which were as lovely as Candy's, yet did not hold such kindness in them.

Too often Two Eagles saw something sinister in the depths of Hawk Woman's eyes, something untrustworthy.

She had proclaimed her love for him more than once, but he did not trust her words. He saw her as someone looking for an opportunity to better her life. If she was married to the chief of this band of Wichita, she would have many privileges the other women did not have.

He knew that she would abuse the trust placed in her as the wife of a powerful chief, and he would never give her this opportunity.

"Short Robe has awakened only in short spells," Hawk Woman murmured, placing a gentle hand on

Short Robe's brow. "He wakens, then drifts off again quickly into another deep sleep. He hasn't said anything to me yet, only stares at me as though he is seeing someone else."

That made Two Eagles's eyebrows lift, for he could not help thinking of the other white woman and how similar her appearance was to Hawk Woman's. They had the same golden hair and blue eyes.

But their personalities seemed very different. Although Hawk Woman was kind when it came to his uncle, she had a strange temperament that Two Eagles would never be able to understand. The woman named Candy seemed as sweet as her name suggested.

He could not forget how she had shown her loving side with her pet wolf. And always while in his presence she showed herself to be anything but calculating and conniving, as Hawk Woman too often showed herself.

Ho, there was also a caring side to Hawk Woman, but he just could not feel anything warm or special for her.

"Thank you, Hawk Woman, for sitting with my uncle," Two Eagles said softly. "I will leave now and be in council with my warriors. If there is any change in Short Robe, do not hesitate to interrupt the council."

"But you have always told me it is forbidden to interrupt your council," Hawk Woman said, her eyes widening.

"Nothing is ordinary now, so do not hesitate to let

me know if my uncle worsens, or improves," Two Eagles said, rising. "If he wakens and is aware of things around him, come for me immediately."

"*Ho*, I will do that, my chief," Hawk Woman said.

She started to reach out and touch his arm, but jerked her hand quickly back when she saw him flinch and lean far enough away to avoid her touch.

She watched Two Eagles until he was gone from the tepee, then leaned low over Short Robe. "Please wake up," she whispered. "You are the only one who can convince Two Eagles that I am worthy of his love. I have treated you kindly only to have you as my ally. Have all of my efforts been for naught?"

She doubled her hands into tight fists on her lap. "You'd better not die," she said fiercely. "Do you hear me? You'd better not die."

Chapter Eleven

I love to rise in a summer morn,
When the birds sing on every tree;
O' what sweet company!
—William Blake

Two Eagles had sat in council the whole afternoon, discussing things of importance to his Wichita people, yet not mentioning their prisoner once, for he did not feel it was anyone's affair except his own that he had brought the white woman among them as a captive.

Of course they all understood the reason for her capture, but no one spoke of being in favor of his action, or against it.

It was up to him whether he would eventually release Candy back to her world, or make her stay among the Wichita forever.

Perhaps in time she might even be happy there,

for her world had been torn asunder because of the Sioux's attack on the fort.

He glanced at the smoke hole and saw that the sky was growing dark. He could hear the excited chatter of children outside; they were ready for a full evening of storytelling. Two Eagles quickly drew the council to a close.

In hurried steps, he went to the tepee where Candy was held hostage.

He saw that she had been fed; the empty bowl was sitting beside her.

He even saw a bone that had been stripped of meat beside Shadow, the wolf was peacefully sleeping now with a full stomach.

Candy watched wide-eyed as Two Eagles knelt beside her and first removed the painful irons from her wrists, and then from her ankles.

"Why are you doing that?" she finally asked, rubbing her raw wrists as he laid the chains and irons aside.

"There will be many stories told tonight beside the outdoor fire, and I think it would be good if you were there to hear them," Two Eagles said, wincing when he saw some blood ooze from an abrasion on one wrist. He looked away from it and instead into her eyes. "Come. I will take you there."

Candy was stunned that he had removed the horrible, painful irons, yet so glad. She was also surprised that he would allow her to sit amid his people to hear their stories.

But no matter why he was doing any of this, she welcomed the reprieve from being a hostage, if only for a little while. She knew that when the stories were over, Two Eagles would make her wear the dreadful things again.

Candy rose to her feet and trembled inside when Two Eagles very gently took her by an elbow and helped her outside. The touch of his hand on her flesh seemed something born of magic, for although he was her captor, and she should hate him with every fiber of her being, there was nothing inside her that could hate him.

Although he had attacked the fort, she could not really blame him. He had been pushed to the end of his patience after seeing what had been done to his uncle.

She would never forget the kind words that Short Robe had had for his nephew, about how he had always been a man of peace.

Outside, the large fire painted its glow across the dark heavens. The children sat in a large cluster at one side of the fire, where an elderly man of about Short Robe's age sat before them. The parents of the children sat back a little from them. All were attentive as the storyteller began his first tale.

The scene brought Candy a strange feeling of peace. For a moment, she could forget the ugliness of the world and her own plight.

She sat down beside Two Eagles on a blanket spread out on the ground. She felt many eyes on her and realized some of the people were not pleased to see her sitting beside their chief as though she belonged there.

And then she felt another pair of eyes on her.

103

She looked slowly over to where Hawk Woman was standing back from the others, at the entrance of a tepee. The other woman was gazing contemptuously at Candy, sending icy shivers of warning up and down her spine.

Candy sensed that Hawk Woman saw Candy as nothing but an interference. She realized that she must be aware of Hawk Woman's every movement, for she did not trust her one iota. Candy would only feel safe at night because Shadow would be protectively at her side.

Nothing would get past her wolf.

Just as she thought of Shadow, she saw her wolf leave the tepee and come limping toward her. When she reached Candy, the wolf lay down beside her opposite Two Eagles.

When Shadow scooted closer and rested her head on Candy's lap, Candy stroked her fur.

When Candy gave Two Eagles a glance, she found him gazing kindly at the wolf, and . . . then . . . he looked into Candy's eyes, revealing feelings far different from what a captor should feel for his captive.

Candy's pulse raced, for she now knew that he did not hate her, or want to harm her. He was being drawn into caring for her as she was for him, yet it was an impossible attraction . . . one that could lead nowhere.

Candy looked quickly away from him and forced herself to think of something else.

She listened to the Indian lore being told by an old man who called himself Blazing Sun. She found it hard to concentrate, yet the more she listened, the more intriguing she found the stories.

She was fascinated by these people who were so different from her. She found it hard to understand how whites could hate them so much . . . and call all Indians savages.

Living among soldiers, she had seen many white men who could truly be labeled savage; they needlessly killed innocent people just because their skin was red.

She had heard tales about the cavalry riding into an Indian village and slaughtering not only the warriors, but also the women and children.

Her father had tried to keep these stories from reaching Candy's ears, but being so inquisitive about life in general, she had heard more than she sometimes wanted to hear.

She had had nightmares those nights.

Tonight, after hearing such wondrous tales of the Wichita, she did not expect to have nightmares.

Yet there was one person who might cause them: Hawk Woman.

Candy looked toward the tepee where she had seen Hawk Woman and was relieved to see that she was no longer there.

"It is time to return to your lodge," Two Eagles said, interrupting Candy's thoughts and making her realize that the tales were over and the people were returning to their homes.

She watched some children lagging behind, their heads together, probably going over the tales told tonight. She could tell they had enjoyed them.

CASSIE EDWARDS

Dreading being chained up again, she rose slowly to her feet.

When Two Eagles placed his hand at Candy's elbow, walking her away from the central fire, she hoped that his kindness would outweigh his need for revenge.

She gazed heavenward and silently prayed for Short Robe's recovery. He was the only person who could tell Two Eagles just how wrong he was in mistreating her so.

Shadow came limping up to her and then went on ahead into the tepee as though she knew it was now her home, if only temporarily.

When Candy heard wolves in the distance howling at the moon, she hoped that Shadow would not choose tonight to join her kin, leaving Candy to fend for herself against the likes of Hawk Woman.

Strange how she did not feel as though she needed protection from Two Eagles. She was almost certain now that he would not harm her, except for forcing her to wear the painful irons at her wrists and ankles.

Something told her that he would soon end that bondage, for he seemed to show more feeling for her every time he looked at her.

She believed that deep down inside himself he knew how wrong he was to hold her hostage.

Chapter Twelve

Sudden, thy shadow fell on me;
I shrieked and clasped my hands
  in ecstasy.
—*Percy Bysshe Shelley*

Despite Candy's hopeful belief that Two Eagles would not keep her bound much longer, the following day found her still in chains at her ankles and wrists. And worse, she was made to go with the women to work in the large communal garden.

Every step she took was grueling, and none of the women took pity on her. No doubt they knew she was there on the orders of their chief.

In her mind's eye she saw the old Indian carrying heavy armloads of wood while in chains. Each step he had taken had caused pain inside Candy's heart.

But he had endured it all without so much as a grimace on his proud face.

So would she!

She was on her knees, clearing the garden of weeds, while other women tilled around the corn plants. Still others followed behind them, piling the loosened earth up around the corn hills, then smoothing it out with their hands.

Before sunrise, Candy had been awakened by Two Eagles and told what she must do that day.

She had left moments later along with several other women, some women carrying hoes on their shoulders, while others carried pots of hot porridge and bowls.

The porridge had been eaten after they reached the garden; immediately afterward they had started their long day of labor.

Upon first arriving there, Candy had noticed a huge pumpkin patch off to one side of the cornfield. She had also seen a patch of green squash with curved necks, as well as much larger pumpkins with deep grooves. There were also green squash with tapering ends, and big, fat cantaloupes.

Candy observed that the women seemed content at their labor, some smiling, some talking, but never halting in their chores.

Her eyes widened when some women broke into song, singing, "You are hoeing around in the great ground, in the blessed ground . . ."

As they repeated the song over and over, Candy got lost in thought again about Hawk Woman. She hadn't seen Hawk Woman anywhere near the huge communal garden. She wondered how the other white woman had gotten out of helping.

And she also wondered why Hawk Woman's golden hair had not been cut as Candy's had been.

She paused and looked at the women who labored so hard in the garden, thinking about how she had been ignored every time she had tried to strike up a conversation with any of them.

She again tried to talk to the one kneeling in the next row, smoothing dirt around a tall stalk of corn.

If only she could get even one woman on her side who might give her some answers.

But again she saw that she had no ally in any of the women. The only response she got was an icy stare.

Sighing, Candy gave up trying.

She grimaced when she stood, the chains pulling on her ankles and wrists with each of her movements.

She then went slowly onward until she found more weeds and eased to her knees once again. She proceeded to pluck the plants from the earth.

Candy found herself looking over her shoulder now in the direction of the village. She kept hoping that Two Eagles would take mercy on her and realize that she had had enough hard work for one day. It was more difficult for her to work than for the other women because she had the encumbrance of her chains to deal with.

Oh, surely Two Eagles realized how tiring this was—how painful.

Even now she felt trickles of blood around the bonds at her wrists and ankles, but refused to look at them and complain.

She would prove to these women that she was strong, even perhaps stronger than they.

Surely they could not withstand such pain for as long as she had been forced to endure it today!

Besides the pain, she was also worried about her wolf. When she had awakened this morning, Shadow was gone.

Candy cringed when she recalled the howling of the wolves last night.

She hoped that Shadow did not stay away for long, for her wolf made her feel safe. She was such a comfort to Candy at a time when she had lost everything, even her dignity!

Chapter Thirteen

Two Eagles sat with his uncle, who was finally awake.

Short Robe's condition was not encouraging. He was finding it hard to breathe, and he had refused food, even the thin gruel that Two Eagles had just tried to spoon-feed him.

Two Eagles feared that his uncle's time on this earth was now short.

It had been too long since Short Robe had taken nourishment into his body; he was even refusing water.

It was as though he were wishing death on himself, his tired old body having taken all that it could withstand.

Two Eagles set the bowl aside and took one of his uncle's hands in his.

Short Robe gazed into Two Eagles's eyes. "I have not long to live, but it is long enough to tell you my feelings about the white woman," he said softly. "Two Eagles, the white woman that you have taken captive is a woman of pure kindness. While . . . I . . . was captive at the fort, she came and . . . and . . . gave me water . . . and nourishing food. She . . . she even washed my bloody feet."

Those words struck at Two Eagles's heart, for had not the woman said that she had done such favors for his uncle? Yet Two Eagles had ignored her, thinking she would say anything to spare herself the torture of having to wear the irons and chains.

One thing did puzzle him, though. Why had his uncle said earlier that he had only been fed weevil-infested food and stringy, rotten meat?

But he was reminded that of late his uncle's mind came and went, sometimes remembering things distinctly, and sometimes not remembering things at all.

Two Eagles had to believe now, after hearing his uncle's words, that Candy *had* tried to help his uncle!

And that she had truly washed his bloody feet was remarkable. A white woman stooping to the ground and actually soiling her hands by washing an old red man's bloody feet?

The burgeoning feelings he had for Candy grew stronger. He no longer felt guilty for being attracted to a woman of a different people.

She had become a woman with the heart of an Indian the moment she had chosen to be so kind to an ailing elder of the Wichita tribe!

"Two Eagles, do you hear me?" Short Robe asked, squeezing his nephew's hand to draw his attention back to him.

Two Eagles looked quickly into his uncle's watchful eyes and realized that his own thoughts had strayed too far from him.

"*Ho*, I heard you," Two Eagles said thickly. "You said favorable things about my captive. You told me of kindness that one would not expect from a white person."

"What . . . I . . . said is true," Short Robe gasped, his voice weaker now. He blinked his eyes nervously as Two Eagles seemed to be fading away.

Short Robe pulled his shaky hand from Two Eagles and patted his nephew on the arm. "Nephew, the woman . . . deserves . . . to be treasured as one treasures a newly carved bow," he said. "Go now. Do not delay any longer about making things right for her. Before you perform duties for anyone else today, first tend to your duties toward a woman you have sorely wronged."

His uncle was using what might be his last breaths of life to defend Candy. Two Eagles realized that she was like no woman he had ever known before.

Ho, Two Eagles was touched deeply by what had just transpired between himself and his dying uncle. Because he knew the goodness of his uncle's heart, he was convinced of Candy's goodness, too.

"I will go for her now," Two Eagles said.

He leaned low over Short Robe and embraced

him, then stiffened when he heard his uncle take one last gulp of air. Short Robe then lay perfectly still, his old eyes staring into space, lifeless.

His uncle had practically died with Candy's name on his lips. Two Eagles would never forget that.

Tears filled Two Eagles's eyes as he again embraced his uncle, knowing that his life would be terribly empty without him. His uncle had filled many voids in Two Eagles's life. Short Robe had taught him to take his first step, showed him how to make his first bow.

Two Eagles's chieftain father had been too occupied by his duties to his people to do these things. His mother had been too immersed in her obligations as a proud chief's wife to take the time for her son.

Ho, Two Eagles's uncle had become his second father, especially since Short Robe never married or had a family of his own. To Short Robe, Two Eagles was his family.

"I will miss you so," Two Eagles whispered against his uncle's ashen cheek. "And I will listen to your last words and obey them."

He gently closed Short Robe's eyes, then fought the urge to cry as he stood over him and gazed lovingly down, knowing that soon he would be preparing him for burial. His uncle had told him oh, so long ago that brave little boys did not cry when they were hurt. When he had become a strong warrior, his uncle had said warriors did not cry.

It was hard not to now, when his heart hurt so much at the loss of his beloved uncle. But as he had listened to everything else his uncle had taught him, this, too, he obeyed.

There would be no tears, only a lingering love inside his heart for this old man who was everything to his nephew.

Two Eagles glanced over his shoulder at the closed entrance flap.

He knew that he had something else to do before readying his uncle for his long journey to the hereafter.

It was his uncle's last wish, so it would be done, and immediately!

He went outside and looked all around him. In a matter of moments he must tell his people the sad news of his uncle's passing. He would tell them that it had been a peaceful transition from life to death for Short Robe.

But now, before he got further immersed in his duties as nephew, he must take care of one important matter that his uncle had requested of him.

He turned and gazed at the communal garden and at the many women working there.

With his eyes, he found Candy and saw how she dutifully worked with the other women.

She was on her knees, pulling weeds, even though he knew what a struggle it had to be with the irons at her wrists, the chains pulling at them.

He would put a stop to that.

Now!

With determination in his steps and a tight jaw, he went into the garden and directly to Candy.

As the women stopped to stare in disbelief, Two

Eagles removed the shackles from Candy's wrists and ankles, then stood before the freed woman as she pushed herself up from the ground. Their eyes met.

"Why . . . did . . . you do that?" Candy asked, rubbing one raw wrist and then the other as her gaze held his.

Something inside her melted at the way he was gazing into her eyes.

It was with a mixture of emotions—apology, kindness, and she even felt that she saw something akin to love!

She wondered what could have happened to make everything change between them. Whatever it was, she was thankful.

"Moments ago my uncle revealed the truth to me about how you treated him so kindly at Fort Hope," Two Eagles said. He felt a strange pain in his heart for not having believed her, and for having put her through such misery.

She did not deserve what had happened to her!

"My uncle said that your kindness should not be repaid with cruelty," Two Eagles said thickly, his eyes searching hers.

"He . . . did?" Candy gulped out, feeling many things now. She was mesmerized by how Two Eagles was looking into her eyes so deeply, so searchingly.

And she was thankful that Short Robe had finally told Two Eagles the truth about her kindness toward him. It seemed that his uncle's words had freed this young and handsome chief to show his feelings for her . . . feelings that up until now he had been carefully guarding.

"That has to mean that he has awakened," Candy said. "Oh, Two Eagles, I'm so glad. Please tell me that he is going to be alright. Surely he is, if he took the time to tell you about his feelings toward me."

She saw something else enter Two Eagles's eyes, but could not interpret it.

She hoped that he would take her quickly to his uncle so that she could tell Short Robe how glad she was that he had regained consciousness. She wanted to thank him for speaking on her behalf.

"*Hiyu-wo*, come with me," Two Eagles said, kicking the chains and irons aside.

Chapter Fourteen

Bright eyes, accomplish'd shape,
And lang'rous waist.
—John Keats

Candy walked proudly beside Two Eagles from the garden, aware that all the women were watching her. They surely resented her being singled out in such a way.

"Thank you so much for taking me to your uncle," Candy said softly, touched by what was happening to her now. Just minutes ago she had felt that if she did not escape soon, she might not live long enough to try again.

When Two Eagles said nothing in reply but instead kept walking beside her toward Short Robe's tepee, she glanced over at him.

Suddenly things seemed to have changed. The look on Two Eagles's face was anything but pleasant.

Yes, she could tell that something was troubling him very deeply, especially as they approached Short Robe's tepee.

She knew that the change in Two Eagles's attitude must have to do with his uncle.

And if Two Eagles was so solemn, surely Short Robe was not all that well after all, even though he had defended Candy in such a wonderful way.

"We are here," Two Eagles said thickly. He stopped and turned to Candy. "I have brought you for this last visit with my uncle because of your feelings for him and because of his for you. It is only right that you have a chance to say a final good-bye before his burial rites begin."

"Burial rites?" Candy gasped, paling, her heart turning cold with dread. "Oh, no. Please don't tell me . . ."

"Come," Two Eagles said, gently taking her hand. "It is right that you are here. He would want it this way."

Tears fell from Candy's eyes as she stepped into the tepee. It smelled of medicinal herbs and of cottonwood burning slowly in the fire pit.

The sun's glow shone through the smoke hole overhead, casting its soft light on the wall behind where Short Robe lay. It illuminated the stillness of the elderly man's body.

Candy could hardly bear to look at this wonderful old man who would never speak again, or laugh.

And it was all because of her father!

Oh, Lord, she felt such guilt in her heart because

she was the daughter of someone who had heartlessly tortured an innocent, elderly man.

She fell suddenly to her knees beside Short Robe. She bowed her head as she sobbed out her grief beside him.

Two Eagles was stunned by the way she was reacting to his uncle's death. Her grief was deeply heartfelt.

Ho, he had brought her there for a purpose, to see her reaction when she learned his uncle was dead.

What he was witnessing proved the sort of person she was. Just as his uncle had said, she was goodhearted, kind, and oh, so much more.

She truly did have feelings for Short Robe.

Two Eagles was feeling his own guilt heavy in his heart now. He wished he had not made Candy wear the irons. He gazed down and saw the dried blood on her ankles and wrists.

He hoped he could find a way to make all of this up to her.

He knew that if he did, his uncle would look down at him from the heavens and smile upon him.

He bent low next to Candy and twined an arm around her waist. "*Hiyu-wo*, come," he said.

Candy looked up at him through her tears, nodded, then left with him.

She was surprised when he did not return her to the lodge where she had been held captive, but to a much larger one which she guessed was his.

It was not far from his uncle's, so they'd been able to easily come and go when one or the other had needed to talk.

She noticed how neat and clean his lodge was even though he never had a wife. The women of the village surely took turns caring for him.

The tepee was large, the floor slightly more egg-shaped than circular. It was supported by slender poles arranged and lashed together in a cone-shaped framework. At the top was a smoke hole with directional flaps, and at the bottom edge the only door, facing east.

Inside the tepee were many skins and furs of mountain lions, bears, and deer. At one side she saw a bed with a mattress made of slender willow rods and coverings of buffalo hide.

Hanging down in front of the bed was a long curtain of buffalo hide, which she could tell could be raised or lowered at will. The half-lowered hide seemed to be painted with war scenes.

Farther back were Two Eagles's weapons.

She was drawn from her thoughts when Two Eagles suddenly spoke.

"Sit beside my fire," he said, gesturing toward a thick, plush pelt that was spread over the rush mats on the floor. "The sun is lowering. Soon the air will be cool again and the heat of the fire will feel good against your skin."

"Thank you," Candy murmured.

She smiled at him as she sat down, welcoming the softness after being in the garden the entire day. She was not used to such manual labor, and every bone in her body seemed to be aching.

For a moment, nothing was said between Candy and Two Eagles. She didn't turn to watch what he was doing, but when he came with a wooden basin of water, in which was a soft cloth, she questioned him with her eyes.

She was then taken, heart and soul, by his gesture of kindness when he began washing the dried blood from around her ankles and wrists, as she had from his uncle's.

The feeling was magical as he softly bathed her.

Then suddenly he stopped and left the tepee.

She was full of wonder over his change of heart toward her, yet understood it since his uncle had spoken the truth. She wondered where Two Eagles had gone.

But she was no longer afraid of what might happen next. She thrilled at the very thought of how gentle he had been as he washed the blood from her flesh.

And the way he had looked into her eyes made a sensual thrill ride her spine.

There were many things that she hoped she had interpreted correctly. Only in time would she know.

She looked quickly at the entrance flap as it was shoved aside and the shaman came into the tepee with his bag of cures. Two Eagles entered behind him.

Candy scarcely breathed as Crying Wolf medicated the wounds caused by the irons. All the while Two Eagles stood back, only watching.

Soon Candy and Two Eagles were alone again.

She started to thank him for his change of heart toward her, but stopped when he reached for her hands and drew her to her feet before him. He gently took her into his arms, their gazes meeting and holding.

"I have wanted to hold you in my arms since the first time I saw you," he said thickly.

When she stiffened, he wondered if she was misinterpreting his behavior toward her.

Did she feel threatened?

"Are you afraid?" he asked. "Should I not have done that?"

Candy gazed into his eyes. "No, you . . . should . . . not have done that," she replied, for she was suddenly thrown back in time. She recalled the screams overhead when she was hiding in the tunnel beneath the ground at the fort, and then the unbearable silence which meant that the slaughter was complete. Not only were her father and Malvina dead, but also everyone else who was stationed at Fort Hope!

How could she forget for one moment that this man who held her in his arms was the one who had done these horrible things?

How could she have ever wondered what it would be like to be loved by him?

How could she have ever allowed herself to feel something besides loathing for him?

She yanked herself away from him and lowered her eyes. "I am your enemy," she said, her voice breaking.

She then gazed into his eyes. "And you . . . are . . . mine," she murmured. "You might as well place me in captivity again, for I will never want anything from you except . . . except my freedom."

Torn between her need to hate him and her want of him, Candy quickly turned her back to him.

Two Eagles was momentarily stunned silent by Candy's sudden change in behavior. He hated the fact that she believed he and his warriors had killed those she knew. Two Eagles placed his hands on her shoulders and turned her slowly to face him.

"You are wrong," he said, causing Candy's eyes to waver. "It was not me nor my warriors who attacked the fort. It was the Sioux. They killed, rode away, and then we came and saw the slaughter. So you see, you are wrong to condemn me. I only want to be the one to protect you, now and forevermore, since your father is no longer alive to do it."

He drew her closer in his arms. "Will you allow me to protect you?" he asked thickly, his eyes searching hers. "Will you allow me to love you, for I do. My heart beats only for you."

She was so glad to know that he had not done the horrible deed. And she was so glad that he had just confessed to her how much he loved her, for she loved him just as much.

It was hard to believe that she was now free to love him, but she was, and she did!

"Just . . . please . . . kiss me," she murmured, finding it, oh, so natural to twine her arms around his neck.

He did not have to be asked twice. He drew Candy tightly against him, her lips sweet against his as he kissed her.

Candy couldn't understand how she could be doing this. All of her life she had heard horrible tales about what savages did to white women.

Yet even then she'd known that the true savages were the soldiers, among them her father, who so openly mistreated the Indians.

Oh, yes, she did care for Two Eagles. She knew that she had, almost from the moment she was alone with him and knew the gentleness of his touch and voice.

She just hadn't allowed herself to show anything but loathing for him because she thought he had killed everyone at Fort Hope.

Even now that she knew the truth, she was afraid of loving him. He was an Indian, someone taboo to a white woman.

And she had never been with a man, sexually, before.

She had never loved before.

She was afraid to love . . . and to . . . make love.

She slipped away from him. "Things are moving too quickly between us," she said, searching his eyes. "Please understand that this is all so new to me . . . living among your people, learning to trust them, and especially finding myself caring in this way for their young chief."

His eyes brightened at those words. "I have loved you from the moment I saw you, although I needed to take you captive to avenge what had been done to my uncle," he said. "In time you can tell me that you love me. Your body will let you know when you are ready to share the ultimate pleasure with me."

He stepped away from her. "I have the duties of a chief and of a nephew to tend to now," he said, his voice breaking. "I must tell my people of my uncle's passing and arrange the funeral rites. I alone will be the one to prepare my uncle's body for burial."

"Is there anything I can do?" Candy asked. She had grown to care for the elderly man so much, yet she knew before Two Eagles answered her that it was not her place to mingle with the Wichita people at such a sad time.

"Just rest. Stay in my lodge. I will return when I am free to do so," Two Eagles said, stepping close to her again and sweeping his arms around her.

They gazed into each other's eyes for a moment, then kissed passionately.

And then he was gone, leaving Candy in awe of the wonders of this man, his kiss, his gentleness!

Sighing, she sat down beside the fire and gazed into the flames. Life was complicated, but perhaps it would finally be good again!

But could she . . . should she . . . trust this easily?

Hawk Woman stood at the side of Two Eagles's lodge, stunned by what she had witnessed only moments ago. She had watched, mortified, as Two Eagles went into the garden and removed the white woman's bonds. Then he had taken her to Short Robe's lodge. Hawk Woman knew now the old man was dead. But she would not announce it to anyone, for she knew it was Two Eagles's place to do so.

Hawk Woman saw the gentle way Two Eagles was now treating Candy. As Hawk Woman had walked past Two Eagles's lodge a moment ago, she had seen through a tiny space at the side of his entrance flap how he had been holding Candy in a tender embrace.

She had even seen them kissing.

She realized now that she had no hope of getting Two Eagles to love her, not while this Candy person was still alive.

Hate seething inside her, she went to her own lodge and began plotting ways to rid Two Eagles of the other woman!

Chapter Fifteen

O, cunning Love! With tears
thou keep'st me blind.
Lest eyes well-seeing thy foul
faults should find.
—William Shakespeare

The next day the air was filled with the steady throb of the *esadadnes*, the drums that were being played for Short Robe. Everyone in the village had stopped their normal activities to mourn the passing of one of their most beloved men.

Candy was alone in Two Eagles's tepee. It was still hard to believe how things had turned around for her, and it was all because of that blessed old man who had found the breath and strength to speak in her behalf before he died.

Little had he known how much those few words he spoke would change her life. Not only had she gained her freedom, but now she also had a man in her life to love.

Two Eagles's tenderness toward her, his gentleness, and ah, the love in his eyes when he looked at her, had made all the wrongs in her life right.

He had given her his love. And she had given him hers. But she had not actually told him that she loved him.

Her fear of loving him, or any man for that matter, made her hesitant to declare her feelings. She had seen the cruelty of men . . . such as her father and his soldiers.

But she ached to feel Two Eagles's arms around her again, to be kissed by him. Those longings were all the proof she needed to know that she did love him with all her heart and soul. He was not like any of those men of her past who killed and mocked innocent people.

Two Eagles had a deep caring for humanity.

Even if he had been the one who attacked Fort Hope, she would have seen him as a caring man, for his need to fight the men at Fort Hope was understandable.

But she was so glad it hadn't been Two Eagles who had claimed so many lives at the fort. Even though she loved him, she was afraid she might have relived the horrors of that day every time she gazed into Two Eagles's eyes.

Now all she saw was an adoration of her that made her melt inside.

Yes, she would tell Two Eagles that she loved him when his duties to his uncle were over.

But for now, she was restless for another reason.

She could not get Shadow off her mind. Her wolf had been gone for far too long this time.

Candy had accepted Shadow's need to rejoin the wild wolves every once in a while, but this time it was different. Her wolf was not all that strong. If she needed to, she probably could not defend herself.

"I can't wait any longer," Candy whispered to herself as she scrambled to her feet.

Yes, she must go and search for Shadow. And she must do it alone. She could not ask for help from Two Eagles, or anyone else.

No one would want to think about a mere wolf while mourning the loss of a great, wronged man.

Now that there was an understanding between herself and Two Eagles, he had left her alone without sentries posted outside the entrance flap. She could leave and search for Shadow. No one would even notice her departure because all were preoccupied by their sadness, crying and wailing mournfully while the drums continued thumping.

Candy knew that Two Eagles was preoccupied, too, especially today, for he was preparing his uncle's body for burial.

Wearing the soft doeskin dress and moccasins, Candy crept from the lodge. She stopped and looked toward the huge council house where everyone had gathered.

There was no one in sight. They were all inside, sharing the mourning.

Even the sentries had been pulled from their posts so that they could join the gathering.

Eager to begin her search for Shadow, Candy left

the village. She did not go on a horse because she was afraid that if she took one from Two Eagles's corral, he might think she'd left to return to the white community.

If she went by foot, Two Eagles would know she hadn't planned to go far.

She knew that most white people would find it odd that she didn't want to leave the Wichita and find someone who would help her get her life back in order among her own people.

They would be shocked to know that she wanted to be a part of Two Eagles's life, for he was Indian . . . taboo.

They would be utterly stunned to know that without him she would be nothing. Without him, she felt she would be alone in the world.

Smiling as she slipped away without being seen, she walked farther and farther from the village. She stopped suddenly in alarm when a red racer snake slithered across the ground in front of her. Fortunately, it went on its way without even noticing her.

Sighing heavily with relief, Candy walked onward, hoping that Shadow would somehow sense that she was there, searching for her, and come out of hiding.

She halted abruptly again when she saw something else that was a danger to her. A little ways off, three stray buffalo were facing down a pair of grizzly bears.

She was stunned when the three buffalo attacked the bears, striking them over and over with their hooves and eventually killing the grizzlies.

She stared at the bears, still finding it unbelievable that the buffalo had actually overpowered the massive animals, then hurried onward herself.

When she was a good distance from the village, she began shouting Shadow's name, cringing in fear when she heard the howling of wolves not far from where she was walking.

She only now realized the mistake she'd made in coming this far from the village weaponless, into wolves' territory.

To them she was a threat, because she was too close to their home.

If they chose to, they could come and . . .

No. There was no point in terrifying herself. She was thankful when the wolves went quiet.

Now realizing just how foolish it was to be so far from the village alone, Candy started to turn around, but realized that there was no clear path back to the village.

She had lost her way!

With fear like a cold poker in her belly, she stared up at the lowering sun.

Soon it would be dark.

Surely Two Eagles would return to his tepee and discover her missing. Yet he was so busy with duties to his dead uncle, he might not return to his lodge until long after dark.

A chill rode her spine at the thought of spending time alone in the dark. At any moment she could become food for some wild animal.

Frantically she looked around her. She had to find something she recognized, some landmark that could help lead her back the way she'd come. Yet nothing looked familiar to her.

Nothing!

Near tears, Candy fell to her knees beside a stream.

She splashed water on her face, then flinched when she heard the snapping of a twig behind her.

Frozen with fear, she turned her head slowly. She almost fainted when she saw an Indian that she knew wasn't one of Two Eagles's warriors.

He was like something from a nightmare, grotesque in appearance. His bare head was badly scarred, and she could see that a part of his scalp was gone.

His only weapon was a sheathed knife and he wasn't threatening her with it, only resting his hand on it as he silently studied her.

Candy slowly stood up. She tried to hide her fear as she held her chin bravely high.

She jumped with alarm when he finally spoke to her, but felt slightly reassured when he used English as good as Two Eagles and his people spoke.

"My name is Spotted Bear," he said slowly, as if it had been a long time since he had spoken. "I am Wichita, a warrior banished by my tribe."

Hearing that he was Wichita, not Sioux, who were the fiercest Indians in the area, gave Candy some hope.

Surely if this man was Wichita, he knew Two Eagles.

Yet could it have been Two Eagles who had banished him from the tribe?

If so, why?

Had he done something deplorable which caused his banishment?

But no matter why he was no longer able to be with his people, she knew that she must try to get on his good side.

"My name is Candy," she murmured, purposely not telling him her last name. The name Creighton was anathema to those who knew her father and of his evil doings against redskins.

She saw the same puzzled reaction that always came from those who heard her name for the first time.

"Are you one of the Eagle band?" she blurted out. "Do you by chance know Two Eagles?"

The look in his eyes told Candy that he did recognize the name, and he soon confirmed it.

"Two Eagles was from my band, but we have not seen one another for some time," he said. "I am not welcome among my people any longer, for I am known now to all red men as a Ghost, one who is no longer seen as a living man."

"What?" Candy gasped, surprised that he would tell her something so personal. She was relieved that he was being kind, not threatening, to her.

"Why are you called a Ghost?" she quickly added. "Did you do something wrong that caused your people to banish you? Is that why you are called a Ghost?"

She was beginning to fear that this man might be dangerous, especially if his own people had just cause to turn their backs on him.

"I did the same as all the warriors who rode with

135

me on that fateful day of the Sioux ambush," Spotted Bear said, his voice tense. "But I was the only Wichita warrior who was downed by a Sioux, scalped, and left for dead."

She gazed at his head again and now understood why he was so disfigured.

She was stunned that he had survived such a thing as a scalping!

The more she knew about him, and the longer she was with him, the less afraid she felt.

She listened intently as he told her his story.

"I was scalped and left to die," he said, looking humbly at the ground. Then he raised his head quickly and gazed into her eyes. "But I managed to live and treat my wounds with herbs. Since I was too weak to hunt, I survived by eating berries. Now I am healed, and strong enough to hunt again. But even now I cannot return home. I am now a man without a people, without a friend. I am to walk this earth alone, forever."

"But why?" Candy asked, pitying this man whose heart seemed broken because he'd been abandoned by those he loved.

She could not imagine Two Eagles being so heartless.

There had to be a misunderstanding here.

"All Indian warriors who survive a scalping such as I did are feared," he said. "We are called the Living Dead. I have always been a man of peace and have never been an energetic fighter. That is why the Sioux got the best of me and scalped me. I have lived alone ever since."

His gaze moved slowly over her. When he noticed that she was dressed in the clothes of his people, he looked more closely into her eyes. "Tell me about yourself," he said softly. "Tell me why you are not with your own people and why you are dressed in the clothes of the Wichita."

She told him about her father's death and the massacre at Fort Hope, and how she had thought it was the Wichita who had done this horrible thing. She told him that she and her pet wolf were the sole survivors of the massacre, and that Two Eagles took her in, first as his captive, and now . . .

She paused and then blushed as she confessed that she was something more now than a captive to Two Eagles.

"I am free to come and go as I please," she said. "When my pet wolf went off, as she is wont to do now that she is grown, I set out on my own to find her. I am afraid that the wolves might see how weak she is now and possibly kill her."

She looked over her shoulder, still disoriented and unsure as to which way to go to get back to the village.

Then she looked again at Spotted Bear. "I had to search for my wolf alone because Two Eagles could not go with me," she said. "He is mourning his uncle's death."

"Short Robe is dead?" Spotted Bear said, his eyes revealing his sadness. "It is wrong that I am not there to mourn him, too, along with my people."

"I am sad for you," Candy said, truly feeling sorrow for this man whose world had been torn asunder by the Sioux, just as her own had been. She was more fortunate than Spotted Bear, though. The Sioux had unknowingly fulfilled two destinies when they attacked Fort Hope: hers and Two Eagles's.

Thinking of Two Eagles brought her back to her current predicament. She slowly shook her head back and forth. "I am lost," she said, her voice breaking. She looked again into Spotted Bear's dark eyes. "I can't find my way back to the village. If you aren't allowed there, you can't take me back, but can you at least point me in the right direction?"

Spotted Bear looked at the sky and then at Candy. "You should not leave now to find the village," he said. "Soon it will be dark. It is not safe to travel during the night hours. Come to my camp with me. Eat. Rest. Sleep. Tomorrow I will lead you back to the village, or if you prefer, I can take you near a white person's home."

Candy didn't have to think twice about where she would rather be taken. "I prefer going back to Two Eagles's village to be a part of his life," she said, seeing the shocked look on his face.

Candy blushed when she realized what she had just said about being a part of Two Eagles's life. That was vastly different from saying that she wanted to be a part of the Wichita's lives.

By singling out Two Eagles she had practically admitted her feelings for Two Eagles to this banished warrior.

She felt suddenly uneasy over her openness with this man, who might disapprove of any relationship between a white woman and a red man.

She watched closely for his reaction, relieved when he didn't seem perturbed by what he had just learned.

For his part, Spotted Bear was surprised to learn that this woman was in love with Two Eagles, which was taboo. But that did not concern him. Her safety did, for if she was so open about her feelings for Two Eagles, surely he cared as much for her.

"Will you come with me?" he asked, searching her eyes. "Will you trust me as much as you do Two Eagles, or is that asking too much? You have not been with me long enough to know if you can trust me." He lowered his eyes. "Knowing that I am a Ghost, banished by my people, you may see me in the same light as they."

Truly not feeling threatened by this man, in fact feeling sorry for what had happened to him, Candy nodded. "I will go with you," she murmured, feeling that was the best way to answer his question. "I truly appreciate your kindness."

She saw how her trust in him brought a smile to his face. Surely she was the first person to be kind to him since the day of his scalping.

He nodded toward his left. "Come, and I will show you my home," he said. "You will be the first to sit with me by my fire."

She smiled at him, then walked beside him for a short distance to a tepee in the shelter of some trees.

She stepped inside with him where a fire burned within a circle of rocks. Meat was browning on a spit over the flames.

They both sat down, and soon Candy was eating

with him; she had not realized just how ravenous she had been until now.

"It is good to have someone with me who does not see me as a Living Dead," Spotted Bear said, his voice breaking. "Thank you."

"Thank you for your kindness toward me," Candy said. The food was soon eaten and her stomach was comfortably full, but she grew a little anxious inside when he handed her a blanket. Had she been wrong to trust this man, especially since he had obviously been without a woman since his banishment?

Had his kindness toward her been only to make her relax so he could rape her?

"I will sleep outside beneath the stars so you can have privacy," he said, lifting another blanket into his arms and quickly dispelling any doubts about him that she had.

"Again, thank you," she murmured and watched him leave.

Candy stretched out beside the fire, and, worn out by her long day's travel on foot, she was soon fast asleep.

She was not aware of a hand shoving the entrance flap quietly aside, or eyes that watched her as she slept so soundly . . . so trustingly. . . .

Chapter Sixteen

Awed by a thousand tender fears,
I would approach, but dare not move;
Tell me, my heart, if this be love?
—George Lytleton

His heart aching, his sadness deeply felt, Two Eagles stood over his uncle, who was now wrapped in what had been his favorite robe.

Two Eagles had sat vigil at his dead uncle's side for some time after preparing him for burial. He had chanted and prayed the entire day, the only one there for these final hours before Short Robe's burial tomorrow.

Needing to return home, not only to rest but to see how Candy had managed all by herself for the whole, long day, Two Eagles stepped outside into the darkness of evening. He found Hawk Woman standing there, a strange look on her face.

"Why are you here?" he asked, his voice a little

harsh. "Everyone else has returned to their homes to prepare themselves for the burial tomorrow."

"Candy is gone," Hawk Woman said, trying to keep from smiling.

She was hoping that Candy had taken this opportunity to escape and return to the white world. If she had, it would prove that she had toyed with Two Eagles's affection in order to gain his trust and the opportunity to escape.

"She . . . is . . . gone?" Two Eagles asked, looking quickly at his lodge. His insides tightened when he saw in the moon's light no smoke spiraling from his smoke hole. No one was there.

He looked quickly into Hawk Woman's eyes and placed his hands on her shoulders. "How long has she been gone, and why did you not alert me to her disappearance before now?" he demanded, trying to control his anger with the woman.

"I have no idea how long she has been gone, and I did not disturb you because you were spending many hours with your uncle," Hawk Woman said, stunned that Two Eagles would be so upset over Candy's disappearance.

Panic filled Two Eagles as he ran to his tepee, where he had last seen Candy. When he did not find her there, he went to the tepee where she had been confined upon first arriving in the village.

She was not there either!

He hurried outside to his corral and checked his horses to see if any were missing.

None were.

That meant she had left the village on foot, and if so, surely had not planned to be gone for long.

He turned and found Hawk Woman standing behind him. "Do you have more to say about this?" he asked, searching her eyes.

"I believe Candy was worried about her wolf," Hawk Woman said.

"And why would you think that?" Two Eagles asked.

"When I left the council house earlier today to see to personal business, I saw her step outside your lodge more than once. The wolf was not with her," Hawk Woman said. "I saw how Candy gazed into the distance, especially when the wolves there howled."

Having heard enough, Two Eagles mounted his steed and headed out to search for Candy, even though the sky was already dark and he could not see her tracks.

He rode onward until he realized how far he was from the village, and alone, which was dangerous at night.

The murdering Sioux were always waiting for an opportunity to catch him alone.

He could not make it easy for them!

He wheeled his horse around and headed back for home. As soon as dawn broke, he would take many warriors with him to search for his woman, even if his uncle's burial must be delayed.

He knew that his uncle had cared deeply for Candy and would want it no other way. Short Robe would want her found and brought home safe.

143

And Two Eagles would not be able to speak freely over his uncle's grave while his heart was heavy with worry over his woman!

If he found her, he would marry her and keep her safe from all harm forevermore.

Guilt flooded his heart, for had he not already promised to keep her safe? And now she was . . . gone!

"I will find her," he whispered harshly to himself.

It was hard to believe she was gone. He knew he could not live without her. He could not believe that just when he had found the love of his life he should lose her.

No.

He would not allow it!

Theirs was a destiny to be shared for always.

Chapter Seventeen

As a virtue golden through and through,
Sufficient to vindicate itself
And prove its worth at a moment's view.
—*Robert Browning*

A warm nose probing and nudging Candy's cheek awakened her with a start.

Then her heart felt deep joy when the fire's glow revealed that Shadow was in the tepee with her, her eyes gazing into Candy's.

Candy flung her arms around Shadow's neck and hugged her.

A moment later, she wondered how Shadow had come to be in this tepee that belonged to Spotted Bear. Had the man gone and found Shadow after Candy fell asleep?

"You wonderful wolf," Candy murmured as she hugged Shadow, so glad that her wolf was unharmed.

Curious, Candy stepped outside with Shadow at her side, then stopped and gasped in dismay.

Spotted Bear was asleep beside the outdoor fire, but not alone. A pack of wolves were sleeping around Spotted Bear, some cuddling close to him.

All had their eyes closed but one.

Candy gazed incredulously at the beautiful white wolf that was gazing back at her with mystical luminous blue eyes. In them was no fear at all from Candy's presence.

Then as Candy stood rigidly still, the white wolf rose to his feet and came to Shadow. He nudged her side with his nose, which seemed to be a silent command for Shadow to make a choice: the male wolf or Candy.

When Shadow stood her ground beside Candy, the white wolf bared his teeth and let out a small growl. Then he returned to take his position beside the fire with the others.

By now Spotted Bear was awake.

He sat up and smiled at Candy, gazed at the sleeping wolves, then rose and led Candy back inside his tepee.

"Sit," he said softly, gesturing toward the pelts beside the fire. "I have a story to tell you."

Intrigued, still in awe of the wolves outside, Candy sat down beside him. As Shadow rested her head on Candy's lap, she listened to a remarkable story of survival—Spotted Bear's.

"After I was scalped and left for dead among the others who died that day at the hands of the Sioux, White Wolf and his pack came and dragged me away," Spotted Bear said. "I was barely conscious, but I knew the company I was in and was afraid. I had already lost too much blood to fight off the wolves. I expected to be their next meal. Instead, White Wolf and the others took turns cleaning my head wound by licking it. Eventually I fell into a deep sleep. When I awakened, I found a fish awaiting me. Although it was uncooked, I ate it ravenously, then crawled to a bush heavy with berries and ate their nourishment."

"This is incredible," Candy said as Spotted Bear paused long enough to slide another log onto the fire.

"After a few days of rest and healing, I was able to start a fire," Spotted Bear then said. "The wolves brought me slain rabbits, which I cooked over the flames of the fire, happily sharing the cooked meat with my new friends. I realized that all who knew me, my family, my warrior friends, even my chief, would never allow me near them again. I was a scalped man, a walking dead, a Ghost. My only friends now were wolves."

"And you stayed with them?" Candy said, marveling at the story and touched deeply by it.

She stroked her fingers through her wolf's fur, so glad that she, too, had been blessed to know the goodness of wolves.

"I stayed with the wolves and in time I was strong enough to build myself a better shelter and eventually this tepee. Eventually I was able to go on a real hunt," Spotted Bear said. He pointed to his bow and quiver of arrows. "I made these during my many idle hours. They have been good to me. They have brought down many a buffalo and deer. My knife helped me prepare the animals for food and hides."

He sighed heavily. "I have been a happy man with my wolf friends, and thus far no one has come near my home," he said. "Some of the wolves are always close by to protect me and scare away anyone or anything that might prove to be my enemy."

Candy was stunned by the story.

So much about it and the man was mystical.

How fortunate it was that she and Spotted Bear had become friends. She was relieved that he had brought Shadow into his life and treated her as a friend along with the other wolves.

Spotted Bear reached out and stroked Shadow's fur. "White Wolf led Shadow to this home, and I believe they have since mated," he said quietly. "So even when you return to my Wichita village with Shadow, do not expect her to stay long. She has followed the call of the wild and found her true place among my wolves. But know that you will be welcome anytime, for White Wolf now realizes that you are a friend and someone very important to Shadow."

Spotted Bear smiled. "I like the name Shadow," he said. "It fits this wolf's personality." He frowned. "But I cannot understand a name like Candy. Why did your mother and father give you such a name?"

Again Candy found herself explaining her name and wishing it were different.

"Return now to your bed of blankets," Spotted Bear said. "Sleep some more. Tomorrow I will take you back to your home among the Wichita, but I can go only so far. I cannot be seen with you. The Wichita might then see you as taboo since you had contact with a Ghost. I will point the way, then return to my own home."

"I am going to talk to Two Eagles about you and how wrong it is to treat you in such a way," Candy murmured.

"Thank you, but it would be words wasted. Take my advice—never speak of me to any red man," he said thickly. "Or you may find yourself shunned, too."

Candy was stunned that Spotted Bear could not trust Two Eagles enough to go home to his people.

"Two Eagles is now chief," she blurted out, only now realizing that she hadn't shared that news with Spotted Bear. "His father died a short while ago. Surely Two Eagles wouldn't send you away. He would be happy to know that you are still alive."

"Two Eagles is chief?" Spotted Bear gasped.

"Yes," Candy said. "So don't you see? Surely Two Eagles will welcome you home with open arms."

"It is sad that Two Eagles's father is dead, but I am glad that he is now chief, for he will be a good leader," Spotted Bear said.

"Spotted Bear, I don't think you heard what I said about Two Eagles surely welcoming you home," Candy persisted. "Because he is chief, you might be welcome now among your people. No man could have a kinder or more understanding heart than Two Eagles."

"*Ho*, Two Eagles is as no one I have ever known," he said. "But I would not want to put Two Eagles in the position of choosing between me and the rest of the tribe. Many would not want me in the village because of how they would see me—as a Ghost."

"But, Spotted Bear—" Candy said, reaching a hand out toward him. She knew there was no point in going on, for he did not even give her a look before standing and walking away from her.

She hugged Shadow, feeling very anxious to return to Two Eagles's arms. But at the same time, she would feel sad to leave this kind man behind, all alone, since she had not been able to convince him that he should return to his true home and people.

She remembered, though, that he was not really alone. He had a full pack of wolves to give him love. Because of them, he was alive.

Chapter Eighteen

Small in the worth of beauty
from the light retired.
—Edmund Waller

The clouds were heavy when Two Eagles rode from his village in search of Candy. Sitting tall in the saddle on his black stallion, and dressed today in warm buckskin, he looked around at how the clouds had dropped a thick fog over the countryside.

In the village, his people were lighting small fires before their lodges to chase the moist chill from their entranceways.

On mornings such as this, few ventured outside early. People would wait until the sun broke through the fog, and only then set out to work in the garden, or carry water from the river into their homes for the cooking chores that lay ahead.

But neither the fog nor the chill of the morning had stopped Two Eagles and several of his warriors from leaving to look far and wide for Candy. He sent warriors in different directions, to meet again at a designated place after a calculated time of searching.

It was many hours later when the sun finally broke through the clouds and sent its sparkling, warm rays down.

But the loveliness of the day did not help to lift Two Eagles's spirits. He was exhausted from having searched the long day through and still he did not have Candy with him.

He was beginning to believe that he would never see her again. Discouraged, he had just arrived at the meeting point of his warriors.

He watched as they began coming in from all directions, their faces masks of gloom because they did not carry good news back to their beloved young chief.

As they slowly gathered, Two Eagles still could not accept the fact that he might never see the lovely, sweet white woman again.

It would not be fair to either of them to have found one another and a love so promising, only to lose each other so soon.

He nodded to each warrior as he came and took his place among the others, waiting for them all to arrive before heading back to the village.

Then Two Eagles's eyes were drawn in a direction where no warrior had gone. Perhaps he was wrong to think that every inch of the land had been covered.

He started to turn his head to send one of his men searching in that direction, but stopped, his heart skipping a beat. He had caught sight of something that made joy fill his whole being.

It was Candy!

She was walking with her wolf at her side. They both had just come from around a bend in the path, where they had been hidden from sight by a thick stand of birch trees.

She seemed to have seen him at the same time he spotted her, for she broke into a hard run, waving at him. Shadow ran alongside her.

His heart thudding inside his chest, Two Eagles sank his heels into the flanks of his steed and rode hard toward her. When he reached her, he drew a tight rein and swept her onto his horse with him.

Tears of pure, sweet happiness swam in Candy's eyes as she wrapped her arms around his neck. "Thank you, thank you," she whispered as their lips touched in a sweet and wondrous kiss.

Then he framed her face between his hands as their eyes met and held. "Why did you leave?" he asked huskily. "Are you alright? Where did you and your wolf spend the night?"

Candy was uncertain what to answer. She longed to tell him to help Spotted Bear. But remembering Spotted Bear's warning that Two Eagles might turn away from her if he knew with whom she had spent the night, she kept the secret to herself.

"I was foolish to leave, I know that now, but I was so concerned about Shadow that I just had to go and look for her," Candy said softly. "You were immersed in your duties to your uncle. I . . . I . . . just couldn't ask you to help in my search."

"But you went on foot, and you seem to have gone very far," Two Eagles said. "Surely you knew it might be dangerous."

"Yes, I knew, but I had to go anyway," she murmured. "When I found Shadow, she was with a pack of other wolves. I thought they might attack, but thank God, they didn't."

She felt as though she was getting deeper and deeper into a lie she might not be able to explain away later if she ever got brave enough to mention Spotted Bear.

If Two Eagles knew that she lied this easily, might he lose respect for her?

"You are fortunate in many ways," Two Eagles said, brushing her lips with soft kisses. "But you are here, safe. That is what matters."

Very aware that his warriors sat on their steeds, witnessing their chief's attentions toward a white woman, Two Eagles met the gaze of each. Deliberately he hugged her to him, making clear his claim on her.

"I want to thank you all for taking time from your mourning to help search for my woman," he said firmly.

He saw varied expressions on their faces at his mention of Candy being his "woman." He hoped there would be few objections when the time came for him to announce that he would marry this white woman soon!

His warriors nodded and rode off, leaving Two Eagles and Candy momentarily alone.

Again they kissed; then he sank his knees into the flanks of his steed and soon joined his warriors. Shadow romped along beside Two Eagles's horse, occasionally glancing up at Candy, who in turn smiled down at her pet.

"It is good that you found Shadow," Two Eagles said, seeing that Candy looked often at her wolf.

"One of these nights, when the pack howls for Shadow, I am afraid she will disappear for good," Candy said.

She recalled how Spotted Bear had said that perhaps Shadow had mated with White Wolf. If so, would Shadow feel it was her duty to take her pups to their father?

Candy had to prepare herself for such a loss, yet she felt it would be wonderful for Shadow to have a family all her own, and a mate who endeared himself to her.

"All will be well with your wolf whether she turns to you or the wild wolves," Two Eagles said as the village came into sight. "She will choose the right road in life for her and be happy, and you should be happy for her."

"Yes, I will be, but I will miss her so if she chooses to live in the wild," Candy said solemnly.

"*Ho*, I know now just how much you would miss her," Two Eagles said, chuckling. "Since you went to such lengths to find her, I can tell just how much you love the wolf."

"When I care, I care deeply," Candy said, turning soft eyes up to him. "As I care for you."

She so longed to be kissed by Two Eagles, everything within her yearned for him.

She badly wanted a private moment with him, to tell him she loved him, but she knew that for now, all those feelings must be put aside. She knew that he could not yet have buried his uncle.

She deeply regretted causing Two Eagles such concern over her welfare when he was already filled with sadness over the loss of his uncle.

As they rode farther into the village, Candy was surprised to see relief in many eyes that she had been found. Hawk Woman, however, turned upon her a look of pure, deep-seated hatred, making Candy feel cold inside. Candy knew now that she had this woman to fear and wondered how the woman could be filled with such hatred for her so quickly.

Then Candy understood. The other woman's hatred had everything to do with Two Eagles. It was obvious that Hawk Woman wanted him all for herself.

Yes, Candy would have to be wary and watchful of this woman. She might be capable of anything if it meant she would get Two Eagles for herself in the end.

Two Eagles drew rein before his tepee. He dismounted, then lifted Candy from the saddle. She watched a young brave come and dutifully take his chief's horse away to the corral.

"Let us go inside," Two Eagles said, drawing aside the entrance flap. "Surely you are hungry, as is Shadow."

"I ate berries this morning," Candy said, deciding not to tell him that she had eaten a delicious roasted rabbit, too, which Spotted Bear had prepared for them before heading out.

After having traveled awhile on Spotted Bear's steed, a wild horse that he had captured and tamed, they had caught sight of some of Two Eagles's warriors in the distance.

Spotted Bear had said that it was best for Candy to go the rest of the way on foot. The warriors were surely out searching for her and would soon see her walking along and rescue her.

"Yes, food sounds good," Candy blurted out, hoping Two Eagles had not noticed her silence as she had thought about Spotted Bear.

She sat down beside the fire, which someone had kept burning for Two Eagles while he was gone.

She had to believe that someone was Hawk Woman, for even at this moment, she was entering the tepee with a platter of food.

Hawk Woman and Candy gazed at each other in silent battle, and Candy turned cold inside. She had never seen such hate as she now saw in the other woman's eyes.

"Thank you for bringing the food," Two Eagles said, not seeing the looks between Hawk Woman and Candy because he was leaning over the fire to add another log.

"If you need anything else, just ask," Hawk Woman said, her eyes glittering as she and Candy continued to glare at each other.

Two Eagles turned just to see Hawk Woman leave, but as he sat down beside Candy, he saw something in her eyes that he could not decipher.

It was an uneasiness, and he knew it had nothing to do with him. That only left Hawk Woman.

He wondered what had silently transpired between them during the short time he was not looking at them.

He hoped that Hawk Woman would do nothing foolish now that it was clear Candy was his chosen one.

"The food looks good," Candy said.

Shadow came and sat down beside Candy, her eyes on the meat on the platter.

Two Eagles grabbed a piece of venison and gave it to the wolf, who contentedly settled down on the mats and ate it as Candy and Two Eagles enjoyed their food.

A short while later, after the platter had been emptied of food, Candy stiffened when Hawk Woman called her name outside the tepee.

Candy and Two Eagles exchanged glances; then Two Eagles went to the entrance flap and held it aside.

He immediately saw that Hawk Woman was carrying two dresses and towels.

"What is it?" Two Eagles asked as Candy came and stood at his side.

"I am going for my bath," Hawk Woman said, giving Two Eagles a forced smile. "Surely Candy would like to take one, too, since she has been gone overnight. I have a dress and towel for her if she would like to go with me."

A warning shot through Candy. She knew Hawk Woman was up to no good, yet it would look ungrateful of her not to agree to such an offer.

Two Eagles gazed down at Candy. "Would you like to go with Hawk Woman?" he asked with an edge to his voice. Candy knew that he didn't trust her either.

Candy was torn. She did so badly want to bathe and have a different dress to wear. But could she trust the woman who offered such luxuries?

Thinking this might be the very time to set things straight between herself and Hawk Woman, Candy sighed. "Yes," she said. "I would love to go for a bath."

She smiled weakly at Two Eagles. "Will you be here when I return?" she asked softly.

"I will be here," Two Eagles said, glancing quickly at his uncle's tepee. The burial had been set for tomorrow.

For now, the shaman sat with his uncle, praying.

Two Eagles did not wish to disturb such prayers.

Shadow romped past Two Eagles and went with Candy and Hawk Woman to the river.

The two women walked on farther down the riverbank so that they would be far enough away from the village to bathe in privacy.

"This is very kind of you," Candy murmured while actually mistrusting every move Hawk Woman made.

Hawk Woman said nothing in return, just brazenly threw off her clothes and ran into the river.

Candy now saw behind Hawk Woman's latest scheme. Looking past this woman's bowlegs and fleshiness around the middle, Candy saw that she was otherwise well endowed where Candy wasn't. Hawk Woman had done this purposely to show off her buxom body; obviously she thought she had much more to offer her chief than Candy would ever have.

Feeling somewhat inadequate as she realized just how tiny her own breasts were in comparison with Hawk Woman's, Candy hesitated to take her clothes off. She feared the mocking look she would see in the other woman's eyes.

But being the stubborn person that she was at times, Candy jerked her clothes off and proudly pranced into the water, her eyes meeting Hawk Woman's in silent challenge.

She could tell that Hawk Woman was shaken by Candy's nonconcern over being less endowed than she; her plot was foiled.

Candy smiled wickedly at Hawk Woman, then bathed without another thought of inadequacy.

She kept an eye on Hawk Woman, though. She did not turn her back to the spiteful woman, and was truly glad when they both left the water and were clothed and on their way back to the village.

"I know that I should thank you for the dress and—" Candy began, but Hawk Woman interrupted her.

"I did not do this out of good feelings toward you," she hissed out.

"I know exactly why you did it," Candy said, smiling at Hawk Woman. "I'm certain you don't do many things without an ulterior motive. Hawk Woman, you are only making a fool of yourself by behaving in such a way toward me. Why don't you stop now before you are shamed further?"

Hawk Woman glared at Candy, then broke into a run until she disappeared into her tepee. As Candy rejoined Two Eagles, Shadow settled down at the back and was soon asleep.

"It is good that you are back safe with me after our long night apart," Two Eagles said tenderly as he drew Candy into his embrace. "Do not leave like that again. There are too many out there who would harm you."

"Yes, I know," Candy said softly, thinking there was someone inside the village who might be more of a threat than anyone outside it. "And, no, I won't do anything as foolish as that again."

She could not help thinking of Spotted Bear again. She badly wished to tell Two Eagles about him. She just couldn't imagine that Two Eagles, kind man that he was, could turn his back on one of his own people for such a reason.

Surely he would be glad to see that Spotted Bear was alive.

But she did not feel this was the right time to tell him. She had to wait for the right moment to repeat the story Spotted Bear had told her.

"I love you so much," Two Eagles said huskily, his hands at her waist, drawing her against him. "I would be no one without you."

She smiled into his eyes. She gently touched his face. "I have something that I have failed to say to you for too long now," she murmured.

"And that is?" he asked, searching her eyes, his pulse racing. Something deep inside him told him what she was about to say. It was something that he had been waiting for. The few words he hoped to hear would shape both their futures.

"I love you, Two Eagles," Candy murmured. "I love you so much."

She saw a look of total, undying love in his eyes, and something else—gratification to have finally heard the words that until now she had resisted saying.

But she *had* said them now, and would repeat those same words over and over again until the day she died.

She melted inside when he pulled her hard against him and kissed her passionately, then stepped away from her.

Her heart pounded as she watched him secure the ties at the entrance flap, which would keep everyone out of his lodge.

Then he came back to her, his eyes dark with passion, which matched how she felt, herself.

Her pulse raced as she became aware of a sensual craving in the pit of her stomach that she had never felt before. Slowly he began to undress her, and every place his hand touched sent an erotic shock to her heart. . . .

Chapter Nineteen

*All love that has not friendship for its base
Is like a mansion built upon the sand.*
—Ella Wheeler Wilcox

Candy found herself lost to Two Eagles, heart and soul, as he eased her down onto the soft pelts. He stretched out atop her, their bodies molded together as he cradled her close.

"Are you certain you are ready?" Two Eagles asked huskily as he searched her eyes with his. "I am the first with you and I want to be the last. But . . . are . . . you ready?"

Candy felt all bubbly, and the way he was looking at her created a small flutter deep in her belly. "I am ready," she murmured, gasping when his manhood touched her hot, moist entrance. She felt dizzy with a need that was new to her, yet a need that must be filled, and only by the man she adored.

And when she felt his fingers where no man's hands had been before, she could not deny the exquisite sensations that were blossoming where his hand caressed.

As he brought his lips to hers in a passionate-hot kiss, an erotic heat knifed through Candy's body, stabbing deep into her secret place. She sighed when she felt his manhood move slowly into her.

She clung to him and cried out against his lips when she felt a sudden stab of pain, a pain that changed quickly to something beautiful and sweet as he began his rhythmic thrusts, reaching deep into her.

His tongue brushed her lips lightly as he filled his hands with her breasts, kneading their soft fullness.

She had not been prepared for this intense pleasure; she wondered how she'd ever lived without it; without him.

But he was there now, giving her more loving and pleasure than she had ever known possible. The euphoria that filled her entire being was almost more than she could bear. When he leaned his head lower and swirled his tongue across a breast, sucking its nipple into his mouth, she couldn't think anymore. She was all feelings—wonderful, beautiful feelings.

She arched her back and clenched her fists as his body continued to move, sending his manhood deeper, thrusting, ever thrusting . . . his lips on hers again, kissing her with passion. She was liquid inside, and heat was spreading inexorably through her.

Frantic with his need of her, Two Eagles held her tightly against him, his manhood filling her, his strokes speeding up and going deeper and deeper into her warmth. Her inward flesh sucked at his, making him grow almost wild with the blaze of desire firing his insides.

He had never felt like this before. All women before Candy paled in comparison. He had never felt so alive. So needed.

His fingers caressed her breasts, and then he lowered his lips over one breast, his tongue flicking. He moved his hands to her back, making a slow, sensuous descent along her spine.

There was a stirring of fire within Candy, fanned to roaring flame by his caresses. A blaze of desire fired her insides. She reached out for him. He gazed into her eyes and felt her need.

His mouth closed hard upon hers, taking hers savagely in his. Her warm breath mingled with his as they clung, kissed, caressed, and he filled her with his heat over and over again in maddening thrusts.

Both drugged with passion, they reached that place of euphoria together, their bodies straining as his thrusts sank over and over into her, until they fell apart and lay on their backs, breathing hard.

After finally getting her breath, Candy turned on her side and gazed at Two Eagles, marveling at what they had just shared.

"My body . . ." she murmured. "I am stunned by how it can feel. It was so beautiful . . . such a splendid joy."

Two Eagles laughed softly. He reached a hand to her cheek. "My woman, your body, you, are beautiful," he said thickly. He pulled her closer. He kissed her. Then he gazed into her eyes again.

"Your passions were always there, lying smoldering just under the surface, waiting for the right man to awaken them," he said huskily.

"And there you are, the perfect man to awaken them," she murmured. She closed her eyes and shuddered sensually as his hand swept down her spine again, in soft caresses. "Yes . . . the perfect man," she sighed. "*My* man . . ."

"For always," Two Eagles said.

He swept her beneath him.

As he filled her again with his heat, she sought his mouth with a wildness and desperation she would never have believed possible.

She clung to him, their bodies moving rhythmically together, and again she felt the wonders of what his body could do to hers.

She shuddered, arched, and cried out against his lips, their climax almost instantaneous.

Candy marveled at it, finding it, ah, so wonderfully complete!

They clung for a while longer, then rolled apart, breathing hard.

She still felt as though she were floating above herself because the joy within her was so wonderful. This first time making love with a man had been so beautiful. Two Eagles had been so gentle and sweet. He had given her everything, even though he was a powerful chief who watched out for many people whose lives depended on him and the decisions he made.

This wonderful man not only also looked after Candy's welfare, but he loved her as no man ever loved a woman before. It was in the way he looked at her, the way he held her, and now . . . the way he made love with her.

"I see happiness in your eyes. I feel it when you touch me," Two Eagles said as he lay beside Candy, facing her.

He moved a hand slowly over her nakedness, savoring the softness of her skin. It resembled the petals of wild roses that he had found ofttimes in the forest.

"I didn't know someone could be this happy . . . this content," Candy said, quivering with ecstasy when he cupped one of her breasts and softly kneaded it.

When his thumb began circling her nipple in slow caresses, she closed her eyes in total bliss and sighed, then gasped with pleasure when he leaned over her and ran his tongue over the same nipple, then nipped it gently with his teeth. It was at this moment that Candy realized Two Eagles took much pleasure from her breasts, even though they were small in comparison with Hawk Woman's.

Yes, Candy's were small, but they were round and firm, and filled Two Eagles's hands when he cupped them.

"The night is long," Two Eagles said huskily as he leaned away and gazed intently into her eyes. "I do not want to spend it sleeping."

Candy opened her eyes and gazed into his. "But

tomorrow you have much to do," she murmured, gently touching his cheek. "Your uncle—"

"*Ho*, my uncle," Two Eagles said, rolling away from her and resting on his back as he gazed through the open smoke hole overhead.

The stars filled the dark heavens tonight with their twinkling sequins, and the moon was now full and bright.

Somewhere close by in the trees an owl spoke to the night with its soft hoots, another one responding from a nearby tree.

"*Nahosah*, tomorrow, I will say my final good-bye to my uncle," Two Eagles said. "The sadness I feel runs so deep."

Then he turned to Candy again and took one of her hands in his. "That is why I do not want to spend the night sleeping," he said thickly. "With sleep come dreams, and I do not want to dream of things that disturb me, not when I can spend my waking hours with the woman I love."

"Then I shall stay awake with you," Candy said, bringing his hand to her lips and gently kissing it.

"We can talk, then make love, then talk again," Two Eagles said, smiling into her eyes.

"There *are* some things I would like to ask you," Candy murmured as she slid her hand free of his. She reached that hand to the scar beneath his lip. "Like . . . this scar. Was it made during an act of bravery?"

He smiled, then took her hand and held it as he described a day in his youth that he had shared with a very special friend, a man who was also chief, but for another band of Wichita.

"I wish that I could say I did earn the scar through bravery," he said, in his mind's eye reliving the moment that had left its imprint on him for eternity. "But I did not earn it in an honorable way, but instead through carelessness."

"Truly?" Candy said, searching his eyes. She was surprised to hear this man had ever done anything careless in his entire life, even when a boy. "How did it happen?"

"My best friend, Proud Wind, and I were on our very first hunt. We were young braves who had not yet gained the title of warrior," he said, remembering the pain that had come with that carelessness, a pain he hid from his friend so that he would not be seen as weak. "We were packing buffalo meat on an unbroken horse when it suddenly reared away and then kicked me with both hind hooves."

"Oh, *no*," Candy said, flinching at the very thought.

"With a broken jaw tied to keep it in place, I had to drink soup for more than a moon," he said thickly. He visibly shuddered at the thought of those many bowls of soup. "I now despise soup . . . all kinds!"

Candy scooted closer to him and brushed a soft kiss across the scar, then smiled into his eyes. "If I had been there that day, I would have helped get your mind off the pain," she said, softly giggling.

"Just looking at you would have been enough to make me forget everything but you," Two Eagles said, his eyes twinkling. "Even as a young brave I would have known how special you were to be to

171

me when we were old enough to know what pure love was."

"Pure love," Candy said, sighing deeply. "Yes, what we have is pure love."

Then she reached for his hand and gazed at the tattoo on the back. It was a small design resembling a bird's foot. "I have never seen such a tattoo before," she murmured. "Can you tell me about it?"

"The tattoo was placed on my hand immediately after I killed my first bird. I was a small child with a new bow and arrow," he said, pride in his eyes. "All young braves are marked in the same way for the same reason."

Then he saw her gaze move to the tattoo on his right arm.

"The tattoo on my right arm, that mark in the form of a small cross, is a symbol of the stars and represents a well-known mythical hero among the Wichita. He is called Flint-Stone-Lying-Down-Above, which in my language is spoken as *Tahanetsiciha-didia*, the guardian of the warriors."

He took her hands in his. "How do you feel about the tattoos? I have never seen them on any white man or woman," he said, searching her eyes.

"As far as I know, white women do not wear tattoos at all, and I have rarely seen tattoos on white men. Those who do wear them are seen as unsavory sorts," Candy said.

"I understand the meaning of unsavory," Two Eagles said. "Do you see me as unsavory for having tattoos on my body?"

"No," she quickly said. "Not at all. I understand

now why you have them, and I find them intriguing, even honorable."

He hesitated, then said, "The women of my tribe are also tattooed."

Stunned at this knowledge, Candy could only gasp. "Truly?" she asked. "I . . . I . . . haven't seen any on the women."

"Do you think it unsavory for the Wichita women to wear tattoos on their bodies?" he asked a little guardedly.

"Heavens, no," she rushed out, realizing that her shocked reaction had disturbed him. "Truly, I do not see any of your women as unsavory. There must be a reason for the women to be tattooed."

She paused, then with wide eyes gazing into his, asked, "Why do they have tattoos, and . . . where?"

He slowly traced a finger around the nipple of one of her breasts. "This is where you will wear your tattoo after you become my wife," he said, watching for her reaction.

Candy's breath caught in her throat at the thought of being tattooed, especially on her breast.

Chapter Twenty

Her eyes as stars of twilight fair;
Like twilight's too, her dusky hair;
But all things else about her drawn
From May-time and the cheerful dawn.
—William Wordsworth

But soon all of her concerns about being tattooed melted away as Two Eagles bent low and licked slowly around her nipple, causing reborn sensations of bliss to float in warm waves through her blood. She closed her eyes in ecstasy, only opening them again when his voice broke through her passion.

"Let me explain more about the reason why the women's breasts receive a tattoo," he said softly. "Three concentric circles are tattooed around one nipple of each Wichita woman. These concentric rings prevent the women's breasts from becoming pendulous in old age."

Candy recalled something her late grandmother

had complained about more than once to her mother, when they had no idea Candy was listening. She decided to share this with Two Eagles.

"I remember my grandmother complaining to my mother, when she didn't know that I was listening, how she hated her breasts. She said that they hung like long melons down almost to her belly."

Candy lowered her eyes, then gazed into Two Eagles's again. "To be truthful, I have always dreaded this happening to me," she said softly. "Now it won't if that myth about the tattoos is reality."

"It is no myth. Will you accept being tattooed?" Two Eagles asked, again searching her eyes.

"If that is part of what is required of me to be your wife, yes, I will accept my tattoo," she murmured.

"There is something about you that I have wondered about, too, but have not asked," Two Eagles said, lifting her so that she sat on his lap facing him. They were both comfortable with their nakedness in each other's presence.

"And that is?" she asked, twining her arms around his neck, oh, so in heaven as she fell more and more in love with him as each moment passed.

"Your name," he said. "I have always wondered about the strangeness of it, but never voiced my curiosity aloud."

Candy sighed. "Most people wonder about it when they hear my name," she said softly. "My mother's best friend, whose name was Candy, was one reason I was given this name, and then my mother said that I reminded her of the sweetness of

176

candy when I was born. I was so tiny and always smiling, so even when my father protested against the name, my mother would not allow me to be named anything else. I have been embarrassed by my name all my life."

She swallowed hard, then said, "When I reached school age, I began calling myself by another name, but when my mother discovered this, she went into a fit of rage and I had no choice but to resume being called by the dreadful name Candy."

"By what name did you call yourself?" Two Eagles asked, intrigued anew by this strong-willed woman who had had the courage to give herself another name, if only for a short while.

"Nancy," Candy said, smiling. "I called myself what I had named my first doll."

"That is a nice name," Two Eagles said. "Would you prefer that name now that you are no longer with your mother? Or would you like a new name? If so, I will rename you."

"Would I . . . like . . . a new name?" Candy stammered, her eyes widening. "Yes, oh, yes, I would. Do you have one that you have chosen for me? What name do you see me as?"

He placed his hands at her waist and drew her even closer to him, yet leaving enough distance between them so that they could still peer into each other's eyes. "My woman, I noticed how delicately beautiful you were the first time I saw you— so beautiful you reminded me of a butterfly's wings," he said. "I would like to call you Painted

Wings, since all butterflies' wings seem to have been created by an artist."

"Painted Wings . . ." Candy whispered, in awe of the lovely image. She smiled into his eyes. "Oh, yes, I adore that name."

She flung herself into his arms. "I will love being called that," she murmured, then leaned away from him and gazed into his eyes once again. "But you must understand that it will take time for me to get used to it."

"I understand," he said. "For now, I shall think of you as Painted Wings but I will not call you that just yet. You tell me when you wish to be addressed that way by me, and everyone else."

Candy still couldn't get over how understanding he was about everything.

But there was one problem. No matter how lovely she thought the name Painted Wings, she felt it might be hard to adjust to being called an Indian name. Perhaps after she was married to him, and felt more Wichita, she could feel like the Painted Wings he had named her.

They stretched out beside each other again near the fire on the rich, thick pelts and talked of so many things that thrilled Candy's heart. The more she was with him, the more she adored him.

It still surprised her that she could lie nude with a man and not feel uncomfortable or bashful.

Just like making love with him, being naked with him was so natural . . . so right!

Suddenly Candy recalled something that even now seemed too strange to be real.

178

She turned on her side and faced Two Eagles. "You would not believe what I saw while I was looking for Shadow," she blurted out, then told him about seeing the three buffalo kill two huge bears, when she would have thought that bears, with their massive claws and teeth, would have been the victorious ones.

"I understand how that can happen," he said. "For it is now the Moon of Strawberries, when bears are seeking green sedges, or roots, anthills, and berries, and when buffalo sharpen and polish their horns for bloody contests among themselves. They fight over the female buffalo that they want to mate with. Those horns and that fighting spirit are enough to overpower any other animal."

"That is so interesting," Candy murmured, impressed that Two Eagles seemed to know so much about so many things.

She could hardly wait for him to teach her about such things, and especially about the ways of his people. She wanted to learn to adjust to living with them, for she never wanted Two Eagles to be disappointed in her.

"I have wanted to ask you about something but felt that I shouldn't," Candy said.

"Never hesitate to ask me anything," he said. "Asking is learning. I will gladly teach you my people's customs. One day, you will know as much as myself."

She blushed. "I doubt that," she said, then gazed into his eyes. "Outside, there are five poles that project from one side of your entranceway. Why are they there? Is there a meaning to them?"

"There is much meaning," he said. "Four of them represent the four world quarters, or gods, while the upward peak is symbolic of Man-Never-Known-On-Earth, or *Kinnekasus,* the Creator."

He gestured toward the entranceway. "And the door of all homes of my people is placed on the east side so that the sun may look into the lodge as it rises, while the small circular opening overhead is placed there not only for smoke to escape through, but also so that the sun may look into the lodge at noon, and at night, the star gods are thought to pour down their strength into our homes."

He then gestured toward the fire pit. "The fire's place in all my people's lodges is considered sacred," he said. "There offerings are made, food is cooked, and medicine is heated. We Wichita people view our home as a miniature of the universe itself."

"There is so much to learn," Candy murmured.

"You are like a newborn babe, who learns something at each new sunrise," he said. "When you give birth to our first child, who will then learn as you learn now, you will be the teacher while I, the father, will be busy at my chieftain duties."

"It is all like a dream, my life now, in comparison to how I lived before I met you," Candy said softly.

She knew now why her father had been stationed at Fort Hope. It was to fulfill her destiny . . . to find Two Eagles and fall in love.

"My woman," Two Eagles said huskily as he

wrapped his arms around her and drew her beneath him. They made love again as Shadow slept soundly beside the warmth of the fire, one ear lifting to the sound of wolves suddenly howling in the distance.

Chapter Twenty-one

Love not me for comely grace,
For my pleasing eye or face,
Nor for any outward part,
No, nor for my constant heart.
—Anonymous

Billowy white clouds skipped across the blue sky overhead as Candy stood in the shadows of a tall birch tree a few feet away from the Wichita people, who were conducting the burial ceremony for Short Robe. He was dressed in his most colorful clothes. He wore yellow streaks beneath his eyes so that he would not lose sight of the sun on his journey now that his soul had departed to the land of ghosts.

Candy was only observing the burial of Short Robe, not an actual participant. Two Eagles had asked her to join the funeral rites with his people, but had not asked her to stand next to him. She understood. Until she became his wife, her place was not at his side during such important functions. He had not told her this; she just felt it.

She had walked slowly with the people through a forest of birch and cottonwood trees as Short Robe was carried on a travois for his last journey on earth. After a time, they came to a clearing where a grave had been dug for his burial.

Candy looked even now at the many mounds of earth dotting this otherwise flat stretch of land. The wind sang low in the branches of the tall pines all around them.

The graves were not marked as white people marked theirs, with names engraved on stone. Instead there were only uncarved stones placed over the graves.

She wondered how the families of the deceased remembered which grave belonged to whom, since there were no identifying markers except the stones. She could only conclude that they knew without needing markers.

Another thing that puzzled her was the size of the hole that awaited Short Robe's body. It seemed large enough to hold several deceased, not just one.

She looked slowly at a lovely mare that stood close to the grave. It held no saddle on its back, nor reins. A lone rope hung around its neck, but not an ordinary rope. This one was decorated with feathers and flowers, obviously ornamented thus for the burial ceremony.

She glanced again at the large grave, and then back at the horse that stood dutifully close to the dead warrior it had belonged to.

A chill went down her spine as she guessed why the grave had been made so large. She had heard that some Indian warriors were buried with their favorite steed!

Was this horse going to be destroyed, then placed in the grave with Short Robe?

The shaman, Crying Wolf, was kneeling beside the fallen loved one who lay on the travois, chanting Short Robe's deeds as a warrior.

When Crying Wolf was finished, everyone began a low chant as Short Robe was lowered into the grave.

Soon his bow, his quiver of arrows, his lance, and war knife, were placed in the grave with him.

What happened next was so sudden, so shocking, yet a necessary part of the burial rites. A warrior stepped up to Short Robe's horse and shot it, killing it instantly.

Many men then went to the horse and with great ceremony lowered it into the grave beside Short Robe, so that they would make the long journey together, as they had traveled while Short Robe still had breath in his lungs.

Shaken by what had just happened, Candy turned and looked away just as the warriors knelt beside the grave, and with their hands started pushing earth into it.

Candy saw that Two Eagles was among those who filled the grave. When it was done, they placed stones over the thick mound of earth.

Candy waited until she saw the people head back toward their village. Then she fell into step after they had all passed her by, even Two Eagles. He and the shaman led the procession.

She had felt his eyes on her as he had walked past, but she knew why he hadn't stopped to see if she was alright.

He was still involved in the burial process, which would not end until all his uncle's personal possessions were taken care of.

Two Eagles had told her that after the burial, everyone would return to the village, where they would stand back and watch as Two Eagles took his uncle's belongings from his tepee. Before burning Short Robe's tepee, which was the custom after someone died, he would hand out all of his uncle's possessions to those who were no kin to him, for it was the rule that no Wichita could benefit from the death of a family member.

After arriving at the village, Candy went straight to Two Eagles's lodge, which now was also hers, and stood outside. She watched as Short Robe's belongings were handed to those who stepped up and voiced a need for them.

This process took a while; then Candy watched Two Eagles light a torch in the flames of the huge outdoor fire, and go back to his uncle's tepee to set it ablaze.

Everyone was quiet as they watched the leaping flames reach heavenward. The buckskin covering was soon gone, leaving only the remains of the lodge poles blazing red with fire. One by one, they crumbled to the ground, until all that was left of the tepee was simmering, glowing ashes.

Then the mourners solemnly turned and began making their way toward their own homes, the children quiet, too, for they had loved this old man who shared so much with them.

But there was one person who did not go directly to her lodge. Hawk Woman was walking toward Candy, a look of open and utter contempt in her eyes. Before Candy could get inside the tepee, Hawk Woman came up to her and gave her a hard shove while no one was looking.

Candy fell awkwardly to the ground, shaken by the fall but not hurt, except for her pride. She looked up at Hawk Woman who stood over her, her eyes snapping angrily.

"Why did you do that?" Candy asked as she slowly pushed herself up.

She received no response from Hawk Woman. Candy had never had an enemy before now, but knew for certain that this woman was the worst kind of enemy anyone could have.

It was evident that Hawk Woman wasn't about to respond to Candy's questions. She had come to do what she had wanted to do ever since she realized that she had lost Two Eagles to Candy.

Hawk Woman gave Candy a strange sort of sneer, then stomped away to her own tepee.

Candy looked over at Two Eagles. He had not seen what had happened to her. He was too involved in trying to make a group of children understand why someone like Short Robe had to die, that everyone had their time for dying.

Even now Two Eagles was embracing one child

after the other. Their parents had already gone into their lodges, the sound of soft chants and prayers wafted from the smoke holes of each, proving that the mourning might continue throughout the night.

Candy badly wanted to tell Two Eagles about this incident with Hawk Woman, yet she knew that he already had much on his mind; he didn't need to be bothered with the acts of a spiteful woman.

But Candy, herself, would be more watchful. She would not allow Hawk Woman ever to get the better of her again.

She wondered what else the woman's scheming mind might conjure up in order to harm her.

She gave Hawk Woman's tepee one last look, seeing the entrance flap tied closed, then sighed heavily as she turned and hurried inside her own. She found Shadow snoozing restfully beside the lodge fire, which had burned down to low embers.

Candy was always relieved to see Shadow after being away from her, even if for only a short while. She knew that, more than likely, Shadow would leave one day and never return. Candy had to keep reminding herself it was the natural thing, for her wolf was born in the wild and had instincts that told her that was where she truly belonged.

But even knowing those things did not make the thought of eventually losing her pet any less painful.

Sighing heavily, Candy placed several logs in the fire pit, where the glowing coals soon took hold and created a softly burning fire which cast dancing shadows over the inside walls of the tepee.

This relaxed Candy so much that she soon forgot

Hawk Woman. She stretched out on the pelts beside Shadow, snuggled close to her wolf, and soon drifted off into a restful, sweet sleep. She didn't even hear Two Eagles when he came in and joined her, soon falling asleep himself.

Hawk Woman crept up to Two Eagles's tepee, parted the entrance flap that he had forgotten to secure, and gazed inside at Two Eagles and Candy as they slept.

A keen jealousy knifed through her at the sight of Two Eagles lying so close to Candy, his arm resting over her.

A low hiss came from Hawk Woman as she dropped the flap, then went to the river and waded in, hoping that the shock of the cool night air against her wet flesh would help her forget the desire for vengeance that would not leave her.

Somehow, somewhere, she would get rid of Candy, and then it would be just Two Eagles and Hawk Woman again, both free to love, and eventually marry.

"I will have him," she whispered harshly to herself, her body shivering as she ran from the water. The coldness had not banished any of her thoughts.

She now knew that nothing but finally achieving her goal would ease her mind. Nothing but revenge would let her live as she had before Candy arrived with her sweet, syrupy voice and petite body.

In the moonlight, Hawk Woman gazed down at her own body, hating her thick waist and bowed legs, but proud of her large breasts.

Growling, she yanked on her dress and ran to her tepee. Inside, she changed into a dry robe, then threw herself onto her bed of blankets and sobbed until she finally found some solace in sleep.

But even then she couldn't find the peace she hungered for. In her dream she saw Two Eagles making love with Candy. She could even smell them.

She awakened with a start, her body wet with perspiration.

"I must achieve my goal soon or lose my mind," she whispered to herself.

Hawk Woman had already lost too much that was precious to her. Rarely did she allow herself to think about her losses, or her life when she'd been called Sara Thaxton. It was just too painful to recall the daughter that she had left behind.

Penelope. Precious Penelope!

"No," she cried in a soft whimper. She could not think about her. The moment she had given birth to the baby, Albert Cohen had taken her from Sara's arms. He had hated Sara so much, he had denied her her very own child and had given her to another woman to feed from her milk-filled breasts, even though Sara had had more than enough to fulfill her child's needs.

Penelope had never known that Sara was her mother.

"Oh, my baby," she cried, her body feeling so empty.

Chapter Twenty-two

As sometimes, in a dead man's face,
To those that watch it more and more,
A likeness, hardly seen before,
Comes out to someone of his race.
—Alfred, Lord Tennyson

Candy was fighting off her nervousness as she rode on a beautiful white mare beside Two Eagles's black stallion.

Two Eagles sat alert and silent in his saddle. His jaw was set, his muscled shoulders tight beneath his fringed buckskin shirt, his eyes directed straight ahead. She knew this journey was a painful one for him, but he was determined to visit the other band of Wichita whose lives had been touched by Candy's father.

She glanced at the large buckskin bag that hung at the right side of Two Eagles's steed. Just thinking about what was inside the bag made her shiver.

It was the severed head her father had kept as a trophy!

Dressed in a lovely beaded doeskin dress and moccasins, her golden hair waving about her fringed collar, Candy rode as straight-backed and rigid as Two Eagles. She dreaded what was to happen today, only one day after Short Robe's burial.

Two Eagles had awakened her early this morning and told her of the mission he must undertake today. It was the day that he would be returning the head of Chief Night Horse to the Raven band, their neighbors.

When she had told him that she would rather not accompany him there, Two Eagles had said that he thought it best that she go with him, because she would soon be his wife. He wanted the Raven band to understand her importance to him, especially since they would know who her father was.

Two Eagles had said that it was best to make it clear that no matter what guilt lay on the shoulders of Candy's father, none of it rested on hers.

Despite his words, Candy felt a tightness in her chest, and knew that she was experiencing terrible dread. What if the people of the Raven band did not see Candy in the same light as Two Eagles?

Perhaps they would not even allow her to leave their village alive with Two Eagles. Perhaps they would make her pay for the sins of her father, as Two Eagles had started out to do.

Oh, she was so very afraid to mingle with other Indians, especially those her father had so terribly wronged. Might not this band of Wichita want *her* head after learning who she was?

Yet she had been afraid to stay behind, for Hawk Woman's hatred was becoming ever more obvious, and Candy didn't want to burden Two Eagles with worry for her. He already had the weight of the world on his shoulders.

And she had seen the seriousness with which Two Eagles had told her that he wanted her to go with him, so she had agreed.

She sighed heavily as she again tried to compose herself for what was to come. It seemed they had been traveling for hours, but in truth they hadn't. It just felt as though every step her horse took was bringing her closer to her death!

But she knew that was not so. Two Eagles would never have brought her today if he had thought for one moment he would be placing her in danger.

She looked quickly heavenward when she heard the call of a red hawk and saw its mighty outline against the ocean of blue sky. It soared with wide-spread wings overhead.

And then she saw another hawk join the first. Their red wings flashing in the sunlight, they dove downward and then just as quickly floated away again on the sweet breeze of the morning.

Candy knew that the Wichita saw such things as omens. Was this sighting an omen? If so, was it good or bad?

"We are almost there."

Two Eagles's voice broke through Candy's preoccupation with the hawks. She tore her eyes away from their loveliness.

At once she noticed something else. A flock of birds had congregated on a nearby hilltop, seemingly undisturbed by the presence of humans on horses so near them. And they were behaving very strangely. They were huge, each one weighing about seven pounds, she guessed.

Two Eagles saw her fascination with the birds. "Those are male sage grouse," he said. "They are involved in a mating ritual."

"They are fascinating," Candy said, her eyes widening as each bird spread its long, spiky tail feathers, then inflated the air sacs beneath their white breasts. The morning air was filled with loud plopping sounds. There were at least a dozen male birds involved in the ritual.

"They are displaying together in a *lek*, a mating ground, advertising themselves to shy, camouflaged females waiting somewhere nearby," Two Eagles said. Then his eyes were drawn elsewhere, and he grew silent again.

Candy saw him looking at something besides the birds. She followed his gaze and saw a huge village of tepees up ahead, surrounded on three sides by birch and cottonwood trees; a meandering stream ran snakelike behind the dwellings.

Smoke spiraled lazily from the smoke holes of the lodges, and many beautiful horses munched on thick grass in a corral at the far side of the village, close to the creek.

Candy heard the steady throbbing of drums coming from the village, and wondered if those drums were being played because of Two Eagles's arrival. Was it a good sign that they played so constantly and rhythmically? Or . . . bad?

Candy flinched as though shot when she saw several warriors ride out of the village, heading toward Candy, Two Eagles, and his warriors.

"Two Eagles, I am so afraid," Candy said as the warriors came ever nearer.

Two Eagles sidled his horse closer to hers and reached a hand out to gently touch her arm. "My woman, you should never be afraid of anything while I am with you," he said gently. "Do you think I would put you in danger? These people are my friends; they were friends to my father and grandfather before him. They would never harm anyone who rides at my side."

"But I'm not just anyone," Candy said, gulping hard. "I . . . am . . . a white woman, the daughter of the most hated colonel of all."

"You might be his daughter, but your heart is yours, and it is a kind heart. You have been good to the Wichita," Two Eagles said, smiling at her. "Especially to this Wichita chief."

Candy blinked tears from her eyes and smiled softly at him. "Yes, especially to this Wichita chief," she murmured. She looked straight ahead again as he dropped his hand away from her and drew rein along with his warriors as the riders came up to them and stopped.

"It is good to see you again, Chief Two Eagles," one of the Raven band warriors said, placing a knotted hand over his heart. "Come. My chief awaits your arrival."

Candy saw how the warrior's eyes lingered on her, and then turned to the bag that hung on Two Eagles's horse. Surely he had guessed what lay within it, because Two Eagles had sent a scout ahead to explain.

She believed the scout had also prepared these people for the arrival of a white woman who would be accompanying Two Eagles and his warriors.

She wondered if they had been told who she was, and why she was there, and if they knew she would soon be the wife of Two Eagles.

Her heart pounded as Two Eagles said nothing, only nodded to the Raven band warrior.

Candy got as close as she could to Two Eagles's steed as they rode behind the Raven band's warriors until they reached the village.

All activity stopped at the village as everyone, women, children, and men alike, gazed in wonder at the woman riding at Two Eagles's right side. She was wearing a fringed buckskin dress, yet her skin was white, her hair golden.

Candy wasn't sure what to do when she saw Two Eagles nodding a fond greeting to everyone, with smiles and nods of welcome coming back to him.

So she forced herself to smile, praying to herself that the quivering of her lips could not be seen. Her fear continued to build when she saw the huge tepee that Two Eagles was heading toward.

She knew it had to be the chief's lodge because it was the largest tepee in the village.

All of the Raven band warriors broke away, leaving Candy and Two Eagles alone with his warriors.

When they reached the large tepee, Two Eagles nodded over his shoulder to his warriors, who slid from their saddles and stood beside their horses, surely having been instructed to stay there until Two Eagles was finished talking with the Raven band's chief.

Candy stiffened when the chief stepped outside. He appeared to be the same age as Two Eagles, and wore only a breechclout and moccasins. His coal-black hair fell in a long braid down his muscled copper back. She knew this had to be Proud Wind, the son of the older chief whose head was being returned to its rightful place today.

He came and extended a hand up to Two Eagles, who accepted it. Then as Proud Wind stepped back, Two Eagles dismounted and embraced him.

When they stepped away from each other, Two Eagles turned and smiled up at Candy. "Proud Wind, this is my woman, Painted Wings, who will soon be my wife," he said, pride in his eyes. "Painted Wings, this is my best friend from my youth, Proud Wind."

Candy was not surprised to be introduced as Painted Wings, for surely that name would make her more acceptable to Proud Wind.

Proud Wind stepped closer and smiled up at Candy, too. "It is good to know the woman who will be my friend's wife," he said, nodding.

"I am proud to know you," Candy said. Then as

Proud Wind stepped aside, Two Eagles approached Candy's mare and helped her from the saddle.

She stood beside Proud Wind as Two Eagles went to his horse and removed the bag. He did not yet open it or offer its contents to Proud Wind.

Proud Wind gestured toward his entranceway. "Come inside and rest beside my fire with me," he said, his eyes glancing anxiously now and then to the bag.

He held the entrance flap aside as Two Eagles and Candy went inside, then followed them in.

Candy was impressed by this chief's lodge, as she had been by Two Eagles's. All of the inside cover was painted with what looked like war exploits, and she was curious as to their meaing.

Was he a war chief while Two Eagles was not? Was that why Proud Wind's father had been treated so inhumanely?

She was also impressed by his show of weapons, which stood against the buckskin covering at the far back of the teepee.

Soft-looking, colorful mats were spread across the floor, and close to the fire soft pelts lay in abundance.

And, just as she had seen no signs of a woman living in Two Eagles's lodge when she had first entered it, she saw no such signs here. It seemed that this young chief had yet to find a woman he wanted to marry.

"Sit," Proud Wind said, motioning with a hand toward the plush pelts. "It is good to have your company."

Two Eagles smiled and nodded. Still holding the

bag rigidly between his hands, he sat down. He rested the heavy bag on his lap as Candy sat down close beside him.

Proud Wind sat across the fire from them, his legs crossed, his hands resting on his knees. "I am sorry about Short Robe's passing," he said gently. "I remember him well from our youth. He was a masterful hunter who taught us many skills."

Two Eagles smiled mischievously. "You were more of an astute student than I," he said. "That is proved by which of us has a scar from carelessness on his face."

Candy looked quickly at Proud Wind, realizing that it had been he who had been hunting that day with Two Eagles.

That proved just how old their friendship was. Perhaps that was why he had so easily accepted Two Eagles's woman even though her skin was white.

She had to wonder, though, if he knew who her father was.

If not, how would his impression of her change once he learned the truth?

She sat rigidly still as they talked of old times at length. All the while Two Eagles held the bag steady on his lap, with Proud Wind casting it occasional, nervous glances.

Suddenly Proud Wind rose and came around to stand beside Two Eagles. His hand trembled as he reached out toward his friend. "It is time," he said thickly.

Two Eagles rose slowly to his feet, his eyes wavering as he handed the bag over.

No one said anything as Proud Wind rested the bag on the floor, then slowly opened it.

Candy scarcely breathed as she watched Proud Wind reach inside the bag. She was aware that Two Eagles was tense, too, because his own breathing was shallow as the jar, still wrapped in a maroon cloth, was lifted from the bag.

Chapter Twenty-three

Two souls with but a single thought,
Two hearts that beat as one.
—Frederick Halm

"Uncover it for me?" Proud Wind said as he gave Two Eagles a sorrowful glance.

"Are you certain . . . ?" Two Eagles asked, getting to his feet and then sinking on his haunches beside his friend.

"It must be done," Proud Wind said. "Then I will place it where it belongs. My father will finally rest in peace."

Candy could not watch. She turned her eyes away and closed them, but she heard the gasp of horror and knew that the head inside the jar had been revealed to Proud Wind. He let out a heartrending cry.

Two Eagles saw, heard, and felt his friend's agony.

He rose to his feet and reached for Candy's hand, prepared to leave.

But Proud Wind stopped them. He had placed the jar at the far back of his lodge and covered it again with the cloth; then he embraced Two Eagles.

"Thank you for again proving yourself the friend you have always been," he said. "You have done all that is possible to right this terrible wrong. My father smiles from the heavens at you. So does my mother, who has walked the long road to the hereafter, too."

"It was from my heart that I did this," Two Eagles said, easing himself from Proud Wind's arms. He looked over at Candy, then into Proud Wind's eyes. "I wish to tell you everything about my Painted Wings. I feel that it is best for you to know."

Candy felt that she might faint, for she now knew that soon her whole identity would be revealed to Proud Wind.

Proud Wind gave Candy a curious gaze, then nodded and motioned with a hand for them to sit again.

He sat across the fire from them as Two Eagles began his tale of how he had rescued the jar from the colonel's office, and then how he had found Candy fleeing the massacre.

He explained how he had taken her home as his captive, and then how it had all changed, so that now they were in love.

"She is nothing like her father, who did this to Chief Night Horse," Two Eagles quickly interjected. "She is a good woman with a pure heart, a woman who will soon be my wife."

Candy could tell that Proud Wind found it difficult to hear all this about Candy, yet he said nothing, only sat stoic and thus far unresponsive, his arms folded across his bare chest.

Candy's hopes waned when she saw from Proud Wind's expression that he might never understand Two Eagles's choice in women. She only hoped that he would never voice his sentiments aloud to his friend.

Taking advantage of a pause in the conversation, Candy leaned forward and said, "I apologize for all the wrongs my father did to you and your people. I also apologize for those men who followed his command. I am sincere in my apology. I truly wish to be your friend, as Two Eagles has been your friend."

When Proud Wind still said nothing but merely sat quietly gazing back at her, Candy felt that she had not made a good impression. She wondered now what the future held for these two powerful young chiefs—and for herself. Would Two Eagles choose his friendship with this chief over his love for her?

She prayed it didn't come to that.

"We will return home now," Two Eagles said, feeling a strange emptiness in the pit of his stomach. His friend had obviously not accepted this woman who would be Two Eagles's wife. "I wish you much happiness, my friend, and again, it is with a sorrowful heart that I mourn the death of your father."

Two Eagles rose to his feet and reached a hand down for Candy. She took it, glad that this meeting was coming to a close, yet sad that the outcome was so bleak.

She rose to her feet slowly. In the next moment, she was stunned speechless when Proud Wind suddenly came and whisked her into his arms for a gentle hug.

"I accept your apology," he said thickly. "I am sorry it took me so long to make up my mind, but I have never felt opposing emotions as those I have known today."

He stepped away from Candy and peered intently into her eyes. "I truly forgive you for having a father such as Colonel Creighton," he said solemnly.

Two Eagles was relieved to see his close friend finally accept his future bride. Had he not, Two Eagles would have lost a friend, for he would not tolerate anyone being cold to his woman, not even a man Two Eagles counted as his brother.

"Thank you," Candy said, flinging herself into Proud Wind's arms. "Oh, thank you so much."

Proud Wind embraced her again, then stepped away and turned to Two Eagles. "We should not wait so long before seeing one another again," he said, then hugged him. "I appreciate such a friend as you. Thank you for . . . for . . . bringing back to me what I sorely wanted."

"Come soon to my village," Two Eagles said, clasping hands with Proud Wind. Then they all left the tepee.

Smiling, Two Eagles, Candy, and the warriors rode from the village.

They traveled for a while, then stopped to drink from the river.

While there, Two Eagles showed Candy how his

204

father had taught him to search in the sand along the river to find places where rats had hidden caches of ground beans. He and his father had stolen the ground beans from those caches to eat them.

"You actually ate what you took from a rat's house?" Candy said, shuddering at the thought.

Two Eagles laughed at her reaction. "*Ho*, we did, often," he said.

Candy marveled over what he had told her, realizing that she might hear many more things like this now that she was living in a much different culture from her own. Smiling, she mounted her horse when Two Eagles got on his and rode onward.

The weight of the world seemed to have been lifted from their shoulders now that they were past the ordeal of returning Night Horse's head to his son.

Two Eagles felt as though he could begin truly living the rest of his life. And how happy he would be now that he had found the woman he was destined to love.

Chapter Twenty-four

Nay, answer not, I dare not hear,
The words would come too late,
Yet I would spare thee all remorse,
So comfortable my fate.
—Adelaide Anne Procter

While Two Eagles and Candy were gone, the women of the village had decided it was time for the village's annual corn roast. They had waited to actually begin cooking until Two Eagles returned, so he could give his permission for the roast.

Although it was soon after Short Robe's death and burial, Two Eagles knew that his uncle would want him and his people to go on with the business of living.

The day after their visit to the other Wichita village, the annual corn roast would begin.

Candy was already awake this morning but leisurely lying at Two Eagles's side. He was still asleep. Suddenly she heard a woman shouting outside.

Two Eagles was quickly awake.

"Who is that?" Candy asked, rising and quickly dressing, as did Two Eagles. "What is she saying?"

"Come outside with me," Two Eagles said, reaching a hand out for her. "This is the beginning of a very good and satisfying day for my people."

They went to the entrance flap and Two Eagles held it aside just as the woman called out again. This was a yearly ritual before the corn harvest could begin,

"The corn is ripe! The corn is ripe!" Bright Sunshine shouted again as she ran toward Two Eagles's lodge, carrying an ear of corn.

When she reached Two Eagles, Bright Sunshine held the ear out to him. The people of the village had come from their teepees to watch.

"The stalks are heavy laden with ears, and near the bottom are many suckers," Bright Sunshine announced, knowing that was what must be said to prove their crop was good this year. "Is it not a good day for roasting?"

Candy saw the woman stand there, anxiously watching, as Two Eagles examined the ear of corn. Then he nodded, smiled, and handed it back to Bright Sunshine.

"*Ho*, it is a good crop," Two Eagles said. "And today is a good day for roasting."

Candy saw the anxiousness leave the woman's eyes and the broad smile she gave her chief.

She watched as Bright Sunshine was joined by

many other women. Then they all went into the garden together. They carried on their backs bags made of scraped hide into which they would toss the ears of corn as they gathered them.

"Should I join the women?" Candy asked as she and Two Eagles went back inside his tepee.

"No, no one expects you to," Two Eagles said, drawing her into his embrace and hugging her. "They will be back with the corn before you could even get there to help them. This is a day they all look forward to. They will pick the amount of corn they need quickly so that the roast can soon begin."

"How are you feeling today?" Candy asked, searching his eyes. "The last two days have been quite trying for you."

"I have learned how to endure hurts," he said thickly. "After losing my mother and father not so long ago, I learned what strength it took to accept such things. Losing my uncle was hard, yet I will endure it."

He framed her face between his hands. "I have you to help me through my hurts, trials, and tribulations," he said. "Together we can get through anything."

"Yes, together," Candy murmured, her breath stolen away when he pulled her hard against him and kissed her so passionately, she felt she might swoon.

Then he lifted her into his arms and took her back to their bed and laid her down on it.

She watched him remove his clothes, then giggled when he knelt beside her and removed hers.

"I feel shameful," she murmured. "The other women are working, yet I—"

"Yet *you* will keep their chief busy doing things he hungers to do before he resumes his duties to his people," he said, tossing her clothes aside. "My duties first today are to *you.*"

"Your duty?" Candy murmured, laughing softly. "Am I a duty?"

She gasped with pleasure and forgot her question when he lowered his lips to a breast and flicked his tongue over and around the nipple.

Matching passion with passion, he brought his mouth down on hers and pressed a warm kiss to her parted lips.

Her body pliant in his arms, Candy gasped when he slid his manhood into her and began his rhythmic strokes, every thrust promising rapture.

Very aware of her warm flesh around his swollen, throbbing member, he moved and slid and quietly groaned. He reached a hand down between them and stroked the soft golden patch of hair between her thighs, eliciting a moan of ecstasy from her when his fingertips found her tiny bud of pleasure and caressed it.

"My love. . . ." Candy whispered against his lips. "What you are doing to me—"

"You feel it," he whispered back. "You feel all of it."

"Yes, oh, yes," she said, giving a cry of sweet agony when he slid his lips downward, across the hollow of her throat, and then brushed his tongue across the smooth, glossy skin of one breast.

She clung to him as he kissed the nipple, sucking it, then flicking it with his tongue, all the while his heat was moving in even strokes within her.

Candy was almost mindless with pleasure as she was suddenly overcome by an almost unbearably sweet pain. The fire was burning higher and higher within her.

Two Eagles paused for a moment, then again pressed endlessly deeper within her. His shoulders swayed with his own passion. Beads of sweat broke out across his brow.

Aflame with spiraling need, Candy moved her body sensuously against Two Eagles's, very aware of how their naked flesh seemed to fuse, their bodies sucking at each other, flesh against flesh, in sensual pleasure.

Candy's breath was ragged as surges of ecstasy welled within her. She felt his body tremble, and just as she reached that wondrous peak of ultimate passion, he held her, and they both went over the edge into total ecstasy.

Breathing hard, they fell away from one another.

"Will all mornings begin like this after I am your wife?" Candy asked, still feeling a sensual tingling at the juncture of her thighs, where he had fed her hungers with the wonders of his body.

"Is that what you would want?" Two Eagles asked, slowly running a hand across her belly, then caressing her love bud with a finger, eliciting a guttural moan from deep inside Candy.

"It would be all I need to exist," Candy said

huskily, her heart throbbing hard as she felt the pleasure rising again where he still caressed her.

"You would need no food, no water, no—?" he began, but she interrupted him by sealing his lips with a finger.

"I would need nothing else but you," she said, feeling the heat rush to her cheeks as pleasure spread within her.

She reached down and took his hand away.

Then she placed her hand around his manhood, which was grown again to its full size, hot and throbbing against the palm of her hand.

Oh, so wanting him again, she guided him inside her, her legs spreading out more widely in order to allow him to move further inside her this time.

"It is so wonderful," she sighed, closing her eyes as he kissed her hard, his body moving rhythmically against hers until again they reached that plateau of pleasure that only those who were truly in love could experience.

Again they lay together, filled with love and devotion for one another. Then Candy looked toward the entrance flap when she heard the commotion of the women returning from the fields.

She gazed up at Two Eagles. "So soon?" she asked, an eyebrow arched. "Did they harvest the corn this quickly?"

"They only brought back what will be required for today's roast. They will return another day and complete the harvest," he said, smiling into her eyes. "That day the women will gladly accept your help, for there is much corn to be taken from the fields for storage for the long winter ahead."

"I will gladly do anything that is asked of me, for I want to be fully accepted by the women of your village," she murmured. She blushed. "And, of course, the men."

"You have already been accepted," Two Eagles said. "By everyone."

But even as he said it, he knew there was one person who resented Candy's presence: Hawk Woman. He knew he had to deal with her, one way or another, soon.

They quickly dressed, then left the tepee together. Shadow was now awake and walked beside them.

Candy gasped at the amount of corn the women had harvested so quickly. They were in the center of the village now, near the huge outdoor fire that still burned.

Each was emptying her bag, dumping the corn into one big heap. The pile soon became so high that it looked as if wagons had been used to haul it instead of the simple carrying bags.

"The next step is to build a long, narrow ditch with mud embankments along each side against which to lean the corn," Two Eagles explained.

"And then what?" Candy asked, truly curious as she watched the women dumping the last of their corn on the pile.

"They will build a big fire and throw the ears into it," Two Eagles said. "The women will take turns reaching their hands in and out of the flames to turn the ears over. They are skilled at doing this, and no one ever burns herself. When the wood burns down, the naked ears are left to roast in the coals. Sometimes the ears roast all night, as this gives them a delicious flavor, but today the women will just leave the corn in until the sun begins lowering in the sky. Then whatever husks remain on the corn will be removed and the women will proceed to cut the kernels from the cobs. For this purpose they will use a clam shell, but kernels from small-grained ears are removed with a knife."

"It sounds so tiring," Candy said. "Are you certain they don't want me to help them?"

"They are very practiced at this, so they would not consider asking you to join them now. But soon, when the full crop is to be gathered, they will welcome you at their sides," Two Eagles said. "But as you can see, today they are doing fine without you."

Candy saw some of the women spreading large hide covers over the ground, then pegging them down tight until they were smooth. "Why are they doing that?" Candy asked, glancing up at Two Eagles.

"The kernels of the roasted corn will be spread out there," he said. "The blue corn will be separated into three groups by size, small, medium, and large. Then they will be winnowed and put into sacks made of tanned hide. After each sack is full, the women will beat upon it with a long stick to make sure that the grains are settled compactly into the bag. They will place a lid inside the bag and pull the drawstring closed. After all the bags are filled, there will be a big pile of them."

Candy had heard everything Two Eagles had said, but her eyes had been drawn elsewhere, to where children stood in a circle around another cluster of plants that grew where no tepees had been built.

"What are they doing?" she asked. "They seem to be having so much fun, but all I see beside them are plants. I believe those are bullhorn plants, aren't they? I've seen them, but never went close to really look at them. The thorns looked very sharp. I'm surprised the children aren't being cut by them."

"Come and see," Two Eagles said, taking her by the hand and leading her toward the children. "The children are enjoying one of their favorite sports."

"Sport?" Candy said, arching an eyebrow. "How can that be called a sport?"

"You will soon see," Two Eagles said, chuckling.

When they reached the children, they stood to one side, yet close enough to witness what they were doing.

"There are so many ants," Candy said, shuddering, for she despised the tiny crawling creatures. The children, however, were somehow amusing themselves with them.

"Ants live in the huge hollow thorns of the bullhorn plant, and one need only touch a leaf or stem and ants will rush to defend the plant," Two Eagles said.

Candy watched as what seemed an army of ants rushed out after one child touched the plant. Then the ants went back into hiding, only to reemerge as another child touched the plant.

The children seemed endlessly amused by this game, giggling as again and again they caused the ants to emerge, to attack whatever was disturbing their home.

Two Eagles and Candy watched awhile longer, then went back to their lodge, where food awaited them.

While they had been gone, someone had come and brought them a large tray of vegetables, fruit, and meat. They were both famished after having made love twice in such a short time.

As Candy ate, she became immersed in thought, wondering where Hawk Woman was today. She had not been with the women who had gone for the corn, nor had Candy seen her outside her lodge.

She gazed in wonder at the food.

Had Hawk Woman brought it?

Was it even safe to eat it?

Then she realized just how foolish it was to suspect such a thing, for Hawk Woman would not harm her chief. Candy resolved to enjoy the food with Two Eagles, smiling as the man she adored fed Shadow a piece of meat.

She was concerned about her wolf.

Shadow had been acting differently, of late. She was quiet, not romping around outside as she had always done at the fort.

Shadow slept most of the time now.

Candy recalled Spotted Bear's belief that Shadow might have mated with White Wolf. If so, Candy wondered how soon the pups might be born.

"I'm concerned about Shadow," Candy said. "Have you noticed how she sleeps most of the time?"

"It is a sign of contentment," Two Eagles said, stroking Shadow's thick fur. He smiled at Candy. "She will be alright," he said softly.

Candy returned his smile, then her mind drifted back to Spotted Bear. Often she had wanted to tell Two Eagles about having been helped by Spotted Bear, and how lonely he was, with only wolves sharing his life.

Some day she wanted to get the courage to tell Two Eagles her secret about the man who now saw himself as a Ghost. Oh, surely Two Eagles would take pity on him and bring him back into his world.

Yet there was the chance that Two Eagles might be offended that Candy had spent time with Spotted Bear, a man banished from their people. He might be even more angry that she had kept the truth from him.

"You are in such deep thought," Two Eagles said, placing a finger beneath Candy's chin and bringing her eyes around to meet his. "Do you have something you wish to talk about?"

Feeling as though he had read her thoughts, Candy almost blurted out the truth to him, but she couldn't take the chance. She wanted nothing to spoil this happiness that she had found with him. Having Hawk Woman to worry about was enough!

"I still can't help worrying about Shadow," she said, hiding the truth.

"Whatever will be will be," Two Eagles said. "You live your life, Shadow will live hers. It will be for her to choose and for you to accept."

"Yes, I know," Candy murmured, nodding.

She smiled as Two Eagles brought a piece of apple to her lips.

She opened her mouth and let him feed it to her. Deliciously sensual feelings swept her all over again, and she wanted nothing now but his arms around her.

She ate the piece of apple, then reached her hands to his cheeks, bringing his mouth to hers. "You taste much better than the apple," she whispered against his lips.

He shoved the platter of food aside and swept his arms around her. He lifted her and carried her back to their bed.

Again they made soul-satisfying love.

Chapter Twenty-five

The sacred fruit forbidden!
Some cursed fraud
Of enemy hath beguiled thee.
—John Milton

Several days had passed and the harvest was completed. Everyone was pleased, because it had been a very fortunate planting season.

Candy was with Two Eagles taking a leisurely ride on their steeds in the early evening. Candy was feeling especially happy that she had participated in the harvest.

She now knew not only how to harvest corn, but also beans and pumpkins.

As she rode in the shade beside the river with Two Eagles, where tall cottonwoods stood like sentinels over the water, she recalled what she had done to help. She wanted to fix it in her memory until the next harvest season, for she never wanted to disappoint Two Eagles by failing in her duties as his wife.

After harvesting all the corn and preparing it for storage for the winter, the women had picked the beans. Still in their pods, the beans had been spread out upon a hide pegged to the ground. When the beans had dried, they were beaten with a stick to release them from the pods. Finally the beans were winnowed and then packed in bags.

After the pumpkins had been harvested, all the women sat down together in the shade of trees. Each woman took several pumpkins from the pile and prepared them in the traditional Wichita way.

The first step was to peel the pumpkins. Then some were cut spirally into strips from top to bottom, while others were cut into rings and hung on a cross-pole to dry.

After the whole pumpkin had been stripped, there was a disc left at the bottom, which was known as the "Sitting One."

The pumpkin pieces were then left to dry for about a day. Afterward, the women gathered again to complete the process. The pumpkin strips were braided and formed into mats, which were left out in the sun to dry.

Two of these that Candy had helped to make lay even now in Two Eagles's tepee, a reminder of how much she had already learned. She was eager to prove that she was worthy of being a Wichita chief's wife.

There were other, less pleasant memories of the past days, too. Hawk Woman had not worked in the communal garden with the others. Instead, she had strutted around the village with her hands and clothes clean, her golden hair hanging down long and beautiful to her waist.

"What makes you frown?" Two Eagles asked, bringing Candy back to the present.

"I'm sorry," she said, laughing softly. "I did not mean to think so hard on things. I *am* enjoying riding with you on this beautiful evening, but I couldn't help thinking proudly of all that I managed to learn these past several days while helping with the harvest."

"I would have preferred it if you had not gone away from the village without me there to protect you," Two Eagles said, his voice drawn. "But I understand your need to prove to the people of my village that you are not the sort to sit by and watch while others do the work."

"No, I would not want to get the reputation that Hawk Woman has," Candy blurted out, her eyes wavering when she realized what she had said. The spiteful words had crossed her lips before she thought them over.

"You mean because Hawk Woman did not join the harvest," Two Eagles said, drawing rein.

Candy followed his lead by stopping her horse, too. She gazed into his eyes, hoping that he would not think less of her for criticizing Hawk Woman.

"Yes, I still cannot help being curious about how Hawk Woman can sit idly by while the other women work so hard," Candy murmured. Her eyes lowered. "Even I."

221

She was not about to mention her hair, how she had been forced to have hers cut while Hawk Woman's hung so beautifully down her back.

She might have already said too much about the woman; she didn't want Two Eagles to think she was jealous.

Two Eagles dismounted as Candy slid from her saddle. He came and took her reins, then tied both horses to the low limb of a tree.

"*Suk-spid*, come. Come and sit with me beside the river," Two Eagles said, taking one of Candy's hands. "I have brought you here to share an unusual sight with you."

His gaze moved approvingly over her; how sweet she looked in a new dress that one of the women had made for her. Many of the women had brought dresses for Candy since she had none of her own.

That was one of the next things she would learn to do—sew her own clothes and learn the fancy beadwork that would decorate them.

She had proven to be an astute student of all that was shown her, so he knew that the ability to sew clothes for the two of them would come quickly, too.

Two Eagles found a soft, velvety cushion of green moss and sat down on it with Candy beside him. The lowering sun was sending streamers of light down through the leaves overhead. Not far away a wood thrush sang its lovely song.

"What do you want to show me?" Candy asked, searching his eyes.

He gestured outward, across the water. "Follow my eyes and see what I have marveled over so often," he said, now looking at a sand dune in the center of the river.

Candy looked where he was pointing and gasped. "What sort of island is that?" she murmured.

"It is no island," he said, dropping his hands. He raised his knees and wrapped his arms around them. "It is what is called a sand dune."

"In the Kansas River?" Candy asked. She looked quickly over at him. "How did it get there? It is so beautiful."

As he began explaining, she gazed again in wonder at the sand formation in mid-river.

"This has been here for as long as my people have made their home on this land," Two Eagles said. "It is there because of war between wind and land. Trees that once grew in the lee of the dune have now been entombed by it as the wind shifted the sand. They are called Ghost Trees because they still stand there, dead but not decomposed."

"But there are huge cottonwood trees there, very alive," she said. "Surely some are fifty feet tall."

"But you will notice that most of their height is hidden under the sand," Two Eagles said. "When their limbs were enshrouded by sand, they shot down roots and new trees sprouted."

"I see so many other things," Candy murmured. "Plants that one wouldn't normally see in Kansas."

"I have gone there by canoe, and, yes, there are a wide variety of wild plants, their seeds planted there by the wind," he said. He looked over at Candy. "There are many other things there to marvel over, too."

"Tell me," Candy said.

"I have seen a prickly pear cactuses cozy up to arctic bearberry," he said. "Southern dogwoods bloom just down the dune from northern ash pines."

Candy's eyes widened when several great herons and eastern woodpeckers took flight from the sand dune. "It seems to be a paradise," she murmured.

When Two Eagles did not respond but instead looked solemnly at her, she wondered what had caused the change.

"What is it?" she asked softly.

"I brought you here, alone, to tell you something else," he said. "I believe it is time to explain to you how Hawk Woman came to be among my people, and why she must be protected at all times from being seen by white people." Two Eagles took Candy's hand and held it on his lap. "While she is safely inside the boundaries of my village, where no white man can come without permission, I feel the woman is safe enough. She only leaves the village long enough to bathe, and the sentries posted at strategic points keep all the women safe by the river. I am the one who made the command that she not work in the fields with the rest of the women. She must be guarded against the man who would probably kill her if he ever found her."

"Who is this man that Hawk Woman fears so much?" Candy asked.

"When I found Hawk Woman, she was called by the name Sara Thaxton," Two Eagles said. "She was dehydrated, sunburned, and terrified. She knew not

224

that I was a friend, even when I told her in her own language that I was."

"But you brought her to your village anyway?" Candy asked, searching his eyes.

"Not until she felt comfortable enough to tell me what had happened to her. Only then did I bring her to the village," Two Eagles said, nodding.

"What had happened?" Candy asked.

"She had been part of a wagon train," Two Eagles said. "She became the lone survivor after Sioux renegades attacked and killed everyone and burned the wagons."

"But how could she have survived if everyone else had been killed?" Candy asked.

"Just like you, she managed to escape," Two Eagles said. "She was trying to find a safe shelter when two wagons happened along, one driven by a man named Albert Cohen, and the other by a woman he introduced as his wife."

"But she ended up being saved by you," Candy said. "How? What happened to that man and his wife?"

"Before I found her, she had been forced to travel with Albert Cohen and his family," Two Eagles said. "At first she was happy they'd found her, but when she discovered who was inside the two covered wagons, she became alarmed. There were eight women and several children, and she was told that those women were his wives, and the children were borne of those wives and were all his, too."

"The man had eight wives?" Candy gasped, her eyes widening.

"He professed to have eight wives," Two Eagles said, nodding. "You see, he explained to Hawk Woman that he was of the Mormon faith, whose belief it was that a man should take several wives to bear him many children."

"Yes, I have heard of this practice," Candy said. "So what then did Hawk Woman—I mean Sara Thaxton—do?"

"She was mortified by this man who had such power over women. Hawk Woman then asked why he and his family traveled alone, and not with other Mormons," Two Eagles said. "He explained to her that he had been banished from the Mormon people for something he had done, but he refused to tell Hawk Woman what that was."

"So it was then that she fled?" Candy asked.

"She didn't want to travel with him, but she decided that she had no choice until someone else came along that she could ask for help," Two Eagles said. "But she soon realized that she was there to stay, that he was not going to let her leave, and after one night of forced sex with the man, she managed to flee into the night. She was alone for many days before he found her again. And then she was with him for six winters before she found a way to flee again, this time successfully."

"And so that is why she is here now," Candy murmured.

"I felt compassion for the woman at what she had been forced to endure and offered to protect her from Albert Cohen if she wanted to live among my people," Two Eagles said. "She agreed, and as a part of the plan to protect her, she left behind forever the name she was born with. She became Hawk Woman. I gave her that name because the day I found her, several hawks had been circling overhead as though protecting her."

"And so you took over the chore of protecting her," Candy said. "Like you vowed to protect me."

"It is not the same at all," Two Eagles said. "Soon after she became a part of my people's lives, it became known to me that she was in love with me, but I felt nothing but pity for her and could never return her love. She has tried everything within her power to make me love her, but the longer she is among my people, the more embittered a woman she proves herself to be. I can never return her attention, or love. But I had vowed to keep her safe . . . and I never go back on promises."

"And so that is how she remains at your village, still protected, even though I have seen that she is not liked by those who know the true person she is," Candy said. She was glad that he had shared this story with her, for she felt better now about her situation. Candy now knew that Two Eagles would never abandon his love for her to pursue the other woman with the long, golden hair.

She also knew that she must continue to be wary of the woman, but she would not share Hawk Woman's antics just yet with Two Eagles. Candy felt that she could take care of herself.

"Do you think the man is looking for her even now?" Candy asked.

"She believes he is not the sort to easily give up a

woman he considers his wife," Two Eagles said stiffly. "A woman he feels he might have impregnated again, for he would not want to risk losing a son, if a son was born of their union."

"Impregnated *again?*" Candy gasped.

"*Ho.* Hawk Woman had a daughter by the man," Two Eagles said. "She named her, but never was she able to mother her. To make Hawk Woman pay for escaping the first time, the man took the child from her the moment she was born. She never had a chance to mother her baby. When she fled, it was to flee not only the man, but also the hurt of not being allowed to have her child."

"How horrible," Candy gasped. "Now I see why she is such a bitter, cold woman. I can't help but pity her."

"Do not waste pity on her," Two Eagles said flatly. "Except for the kindness she showed my uncle Short Robe, she otherwise has no warmth inside her. And I feel it has nothing to do with having lost her child. People like her are usually born that way, not shaped by tragedy."

"And so you do believe the man is looking for her?" Candy asked, reaching a hand to her cropped-off hair. If this man happened along and saw her from a distance, might he not think he had found his lost wife?

"We do not risk that possibility," Two Eagles said. "That is why she seems to be getting special treatment. It is only because she might still be in danger, for I feel that if he found her, he would kill her. And although she is a cold and unlikable woman, she deserves to live as much as you and I."

He looked over his shoulder into the distance, then gazed into Candy's eyes again. "And one day that man might find her," he said, frowning. "More and more white people are occupying land close to my people's village," he said tightly.

"Father was talking about that. He said that although he wanted to leave Fort Hope, he felt that some soldiers should stay to protect the settlers who are coming in so quickly," Candy said.

"Those people who are making homes in this area are brazen," Two eagles said bitterly. "I have not yet told you this, but tomorrow I will leave the village for a while to have council with another Wichita band. They have requested my help. They are having problems with a white family that recently moved into the area. The children of this white family have been caught stealing wood from outside the lodges of this band. I am meeting with their chief to offer advice."

"Could this family possibly be . . . that of the man who is searching for Hawk Woman?" Candy asked, suddenly feeling threatened, herself, by Albert Cohen.

"That is one reason why I am getting involved," Two Eagles said flatly. "I am going to see whether or not this man has one wife, or . . . many. If he has many, and he does not travel with others of his faith, I will know it is he."

"Good Lord," Candy said, paling. "I don't think I want to go with you this time. Is that alright?"

"I would not want you to go," Two Eagles said, twining an arm around her waist and drawing her closer to him.

He was aware again of the nearby wood thrush and its lovely song. "Do you hear the birdsong?" he asked, searching overhead for the creature.

"Yes, I know this bird," Candy murmured. "It has been called a Shakespeare among birds."

"Shakespeare?" Two Eagles said, lifting an eyebrow. "What is a Shakespeare?"

"It is the name of a man who wrote many beautiful poems and plays," Candy said, looking quickly overhead when she heard the stirring of leaves. The bird began singing even more loudly on a closer limb, but Candy couldn't see it. She didn't really need to. The wood thrush's true beauty was in his enchanting voice.

Suddenly she and Two Eagles realized there were two wood thrushes. They seemed to fire off notes at each other, each defending his portion of the forest.

Their weapons were their voices, their melodies their ammunition, each seeking to wound the other's pride, but their sweet fluting pierced only the evening's silence.

And then she saw one of the birds. He was pouring out his song from the middle of a low limb that was draped with leaves. He had a brown back and a speckled breast.

"Do you see him?" Candy asked as she found Two Eagles looking in the same direction.

"*Ho*, he is a part of the ancient magic which lives in these woods," Two Eagles said softly.

"That is so beautiful," Candy murmured. "And just listen. He sings more enchantingly than any other bird I know. Lyrical, liquid, and loud, his voice has beauty and depth to match nature's own loveliness."

They both went quiet as they continued to listen. Each song of the bird consisted of several phrases, variations on his basic "ee-o-lay" theme; the notes sounded like a flute, but richer, not airy.

The sun had shifted lower in the sky. An orange haze now filtered through the trees from where the wood thrush still sang. To gaze on this pleasant light, to be bathed in it, to see the trees reaching high into the air, their leaves hanging motionless, and to hear the ageless song of the bird rising above it all, put Candy in a state of almost hypnotic serenity.

"Soon the moon will replace the sun in the sky," Two Eagles said, drawing Candy from her reverie. "The moon is the special guardian of Wichita women, for the moon is a woman and possesses all the powers that women desire. It was the moon who taught the first woman on earth and gave her power. She instructs women as to the time of the monthly sickness, informs them when they are pregnant, and when the child is to be born. She has told them that after birth the child must be offered to her by passing the hands over the child's body and raising it aloft to the moon. At that time the moon is asked to bestow her blessings upon the child, that he or she may grow into power rapidly, for she, herself, has the power to increase rapidly in size."

Two Eagles took Candy's hand. "She also leads

lovers into each other's arms," he said huskily. "But I need no guidance from the moon at this time."

He pressed his lips to Candy's, and with his arms lowered her gently to the ground.

"I will never need anything but you," he whispered against her lips, his hands already up inside the skirt of her dress, his fingers teasing where Candy was already trembling and warm with want of him.

They made leisurely love as the sun swept lower in the sky and the wood thrush flew away, leaving silence in its wake, except for Candy's and Two Eagles's soft moans of gratification.

Chapter Twenty-six

I cry your mercy-pity-love-aye, love!
Merciful love that tantalizes not.
One-thoughted, never-wandering, guileless love,
Unmasked, and being seen without a blot.
—*John Keats*

It was mid-morning. The sun cast its golden glow down the smoke hole into the flames of the fire as Candy sat there, feeling alone, even vulnerable, while Two Eagles was away at the neighboring village.

She was recalling why Hawk Woman was being sheltered in Two Eagles's village. He was protecting her from a white man who had wronged her. If this white man had heard that Hawk Woman was in this village, wouldn't he have made his home close by in order to eventually reclaim her?

And would not a man like him force his children to steal wood?

Candy looked over her shoulder at Shadow's

empty bed. Her wolf had sneaked away in the middle of the night, crawling beneath the tied entrance flap. She was still gone. Every time Shadow left her now, Candy wondered if she would ever see her again.

She looked at the entrance flap as the wind caused it to flutter. For a moment she hoped it was Shadow returning.

But her hopes waned as the wind fluttered it again.

She pushed her half-eaten platter of food aside. With so much on her mind, her appetite was gone. Although she knew that Two Eagles was a strong leader who knew this land well, she could not help worrying about him every time he left the safety of his village.

And now she had to accept that he would be gone longer than anticipated. Only moments ago a warrior had come and told her that Two Eagles would be delayed long into the night, and not to worry. Things had not yet been settled at council, and Two Eagles would not leave until it was done. He gave his heart and whatever else he could to help those who sought his assistance.

Suddenly the entrance flap fluttered again. Thinking it was the wind once more, Candy paid no heed to it.

But when she heard Shadow panting, she knew that it wasn't the wind, but her pet finally coming home.

Candy opened the entrance flap to let her in and reached her arms out for Shadow. "Where have you been?" she said. "And for so long. You had me worried, Shadow."

Shadow didn't seem interested in Candy's cuddling at the moment. She was obviously agitated about something as she pawed at Candy's arm, whined, then ran back to the entrance flap. She paused there, looking back at Candy with what seemed to be a pleading expression.

Candy now realized that her wolf wanted her to follow her.

Two Eagles came suddenly to Candy's mind. Might he be in some sort of trouble? Would Shadow know to come for Candy if he was?

Or could it be Spotted Bear? It would make more sense that Shadow would be concerned about him, for he was alone, with no one to help him if he was in trouble.

Yes, it must have something to do with Spotted Bear, a man alone in the world. But even if Spotted Bear was in trouble, what could Candy do about it?

Candy rose and went to Shadow. She knelt down before her and reached a hand out, but Shadow avoided her touch. Instead she paced nervously back and forth before the entrance flap.

"You are certainly agitated about something," Candy murmured, again seeing the pleading in her wolf's eyes. "Shadow, what should I do?"

When Shadow ran from the tepee, then came in again, her eyes peering intently into Candy's, Candy knew that she had no choice. She knew what she must do. She had to follow Shadow. She had to go and see if something had happened to Spotted Bear.

"I have no choice," she said, walking quickly to the back of the tepee. She would follow Shadow and see what was wrong. But she would not leave the village without weapons this time. If Albert Cohen was anywhere near the area, she had to protect herself.

She sheathed one of Two Eagles's knives at her waist and grabbed a rifle. She checked the firearm to see if it was ready for firing, smiling when she saw that it was.

She went to the entrance flap where Shadow waited for her, a part of her warning her of the dangers she might be placing herself in, while another part thought of Spotted Bear and the trouble he might be in.

In a way, it was fortunate that Two Eagles was gone. Candy would have time to go and see about Spotted Bear without anyone knowing, especially if she went this time on a horse. She might even get back home before Two Eagles returned.

If Two Eagles arrived home before she did, she would just have to face what he might do when he discovered where she had gone.

This time, if he asked, she would tell him the truth about Spotted Bear and her association with him.

Knowing that she had the freedom now to come and go as she pleased, Candy rushed from the tepee, the rifle in her right hand.

She stopped and looked slowly around her. Thus far no one had noticed her. The women were busy with chores, as were the men. And the children were engrossed in play and noticed nothing except their friends.

Candy glanced over at Hawk Woman's tepee. She had been hiding inside it ever since she'd heard about the new family of white settlers that had moved into the area. She had truly become alarmed when she learned that the children of the family were brazen enough to steal wood from an Indian village. The children the Mormon family had been that brazen, forced to behave so by a father who stopped at nothing to get what he wanted.

With all these things swirling inside Candy's mind, she hoped she would not regret leaving the safe confines of the village.

"Let's go," she said, giving Shadow a quick pat. "You lead. I'll follow."

She hurried to the corral and saddled the horse that was now hers.

Soon she was riding from the village, ignoring the eyes of the sentries on her.

Letting Shadow lead the way, Candy was soon certain that he was taking her to Spotted Bear's home.

"I hope I'm doing the right thing," Candy whispered to herself. She sucked in a nervous breath as she sank her moccasined heels into the flanks of her horse.

She would worry about the possibilities of what might happen to her later. She owed Spotted Bear. He had saved her from harm when he found her lost and scared. She must do what she could to help him if he was in trouble.

She nudged her steed with her knees, urging the mare to a faster pace. She did not think any more about herself and what might happen as a result of her actions today.

She could only envision Spotted Bear and how pitiful he'd looked after being scalped and left for dead.

And now?

Was he ill?

Or had he been injured?

She would soon know, for she was seeing many things that looked familiar to her now. She was close to where Spotted Bear made his home.

Finally she was there.

As she rode up to the tepee nestled deep in a thicket of cottonwood trees, she saw the pack of wolves lying outside his entrance flap.

They all jumped up and gazed at her, then went and snuggled close to Shadow, whom they were obviously welcoming in a loving way.

Candy felt absolutely safe among the wolves, even the white wolf, as she hurried inside the tepee and found him lying almost dutifully at Spotted Bear's side. Spotted Bear lay on a thick cushion of pelts beside his fire pit, but the wood had burned all the way down to gray ashes.

"Lord," she whispered to herself when she saw how flushed Spotted Bear's face was, and how relieved he was to see her.

She could tell that the man was burning up with fever.

She immediately knew that he needed medicine, yet how could she get it for him?

"How . . . did . . . you know that I am ill?" Spotted Bear asked, reaching a trembling hand toward Candy.

She took it, flinching when she felt the heat of his flesh against hers. "Shadow came for me," she said. "She sensed how ill you were and . . . came . . . for my help."

"Leave," Spotted Bear said thickly, his brown eyes pleading with her. "Do . . . not . . . involve yourself . . . in my life. It . . . would . . . not be good for you. You already . . . know . . . that. I explained it to you."

"But I can't leave without helping you first," Candy said, holding his hand.

"Leave," he insisted, trying to raise himself up on an elbow but collapsing back down to the pelts, too weak to do anything but lie there. "Return to the village . . . to Two Eagles. If he or any of my people ever learn of your . . . acquaintance . . . with me, you will be turned away . . . shunned."

"I can't think about that now," Candy said softly. "I can't . . . I won't . . . leave you without doing what I can for you."

She leaned down closer to him and looked him square in the eye. "Let's chance it, Spotted Bear," she blurted out. "Return home with me. I see no other way, because I know nothing about what to do for a fever such as you have. Please return to your village with me. Two Eagles is not the sort to be cruel, especially not to someone of his own band . . . someone he thought was dead."

"I . . . am . . . so ill . . ." Spotted Bear said, his voice breaking. "I believe I *will* die without proper care, but I . . . can't . . . ask this of you. Your life could be ruined because of me."

"I am willing to chance it if you are," Candy said, but inside she was terrified at the thought of losing Two Eagles. Without him, her life would be meaningless.

"You . . . would . . . do this for me?" Spotted Bear asked, tears filling his eyes.

"Yes, and I *am* going to do it," Candy said determinedly. "I must take you for help."

She looked toward the entrance flap when she heard her horse whinnying, then gazed into Spotted Bear's feverish eyes again.

"But how can I get you to the village?" she wondered. "You are too ill to travel on the horse."

"I . . . will . . . instruct you how . . . to . . . make a travois," Spotted Bear said.

He grabbed her hand. "Are you certain you want to risk everything for this . . . weak . . . sick man?" he asked, desperation in his voice.

"I don't believe I will be risking anything," Candy murmured, yet deep inside herself she knew there was a chance that she was.

If Two Eagles didn't understand, she could lose him.

"Time is wasting. You need to get help as soon as possible," Candy said firmly. "Now tell me how to make that travois."

She carefully followed the instructions he gave her, and soon the travois was ready for traveling.

She attached it to her horse by two long poles on

each side, which would be dragged behind her steed, with Spotted Bear secured safely on it.

"Can you make it out to the travois?" Candy asked, not sure if his legs would hold him up. "You are so weak."

"If I . . . have . . . to crawl, I will," Spotted Bear said, tumbling sideways from his bed of pelts. He paused and gazed up at Candy. "Your whole life could change . . . because . . . of me. This is the time for you to change your mind."

"I'm taking you home," Candy said, her voice breaking. "So come on. I'll help you to your feet. I'll get you outside to that travois, one way or another."

She felt his weight tugging against her as she grabbed him by the waist until he finally made it to his feet.

She had to half drag him because it was impossible for someone as tiny as she to hold him up.

But finally she had him secured on the travois and wrapped snugly in a blanket. Then she mounted her mare and headed back in the direction of Two Eagles's village. The wolves, among them Shadow and White Wolf, ran alongside the travois.

Candy and her entourage traveled steadily until she knew that the village was just up ahead. Then the wolves, except for Shadow, suddenly scampered away and were soon hidden in the trees at Candy's far right side.

Candy understood their need to hide when they had sensed the nearness of other humans. Now she, too, saw riders in the distance. They were riding ahead of her, going in the same direction she was traveling. It was Two Eagles and his warriors making their way back home after many hours of council at the other Wichita village.

They were moving in a much more leisurely fashion than Candy, who was riding as fast as she possibly could with the travois being dragged behind her. It was apparent that Two Eagles wasn't aware yet of her presence behind him.

She drew rein and stopped. Her heart pounded inside her chest, for she was suddenly afraid of the consequences of what she had chosen to do.

If she lost Two Eagles's respect and love, oh, what would she do?

She gazed over her shoulder at Spotted Bear. She saw that his face was beet red with fever and he seemed unconscious.

She knew that he was worse!

She looked ahead at Two Eagles again.

Neither he nor his warriors knew yet that she was there, behind them.

She saw Shadow gazing up at her as though questioning her reason for stopping.

"Yes, Shadow, I know what I must do, and I will," Candy said, her voice filled with sudden determination. She pointed at Two Eagles. "Go! Go, Shadow! Go and get Two Eagles! Now! Hurry!"

Shadow paused, then took off at a hard run.

Candy fought off fear as she saw Two Eagles suddenly stop and wheel his horse around. Everything inside Candy went cold when she saw Two Eagles look at Shadow, then past the wolf, at her.

Suddenly Two Eagles slapped his reins against his

horse's rump and rode hard toward Candy. Shadow ran alongside him.

A part of Candy was, oh, so afraid of Two Eagles's reaction to what she had done, while another part of her trusted his love for her and believed that he would understand her decision to risk everything to help save this ailing, lonely man.

Chapter Twenty-seven

All was gloom, and silent all,
Save now and then the still foot-fall
Of one returning homewards late,
Past the echoing minster-gate.
—John Keats

The other warriors stayed their ground as Two Eagles rode up to Candy and drew rein beside her.

He gazed questioningly into her eyes, and then looked down at the ailing man on the travois. He gasped and quickly dismounted, then knelt beside the travois.

"Spotted Bear?" he said, in his voice a deep caring.

He was stunned not only that Spotted Bear was with Candy, but also that he was alive.

He could see where the wound from being scalped had healed, but he could hardly believe his eyes.

Two Eagles's voice brought Spotted Bear out of his

semi-coma; his cousin's voice had reached into his consciousness.

He held a shaky hand toward Two Eagles. "Cousin," he said, his voice dry with fever.

Then he looked up at Candy, who still sat on her horse, tense with fear of how Two Eagles was going to react.

He then gazed at Two Eagles again. "Cousin, please do not turn the woman away for . . . having helped . . . me, a Ghost," he pleaded.

Two Eagles gazed up at Candy as she slowly dismounted.

When she stood on the ground a few feet from the travois, he saw the fear in her eyes. Two Eagles did not like seeing it, for he knew she was afraid of his reaction to what she had done.

"How did this happen?" he asked thickly. "How is it that you are with my cousin who I thought was dead?"

"Your cousin?" Candy said, her eyes widening. "Spotted Bear is your cousin? And . . . and . . . you thought he was dead?"

"His mother and my father were sister and brother, though both are now in the Hereafter," Two Eagles said. "And, *ho*, I thought my cousin was dead. I knew he had been scalped. I went for his body to give him burial rites, but I could not find it. I thought that the enemy had taken it and desecrated it still further."

"He was afraid to come home because he saw himself as a Ghost, one of the living dead," Candy murmured, so glad to know that Two Eagles had not heartlessly turned his back on Spotted Bear.

"You have not yet explained why you are with him," Two Eagles said solemnly.

"The other day, when I went looking for Shadow, I got lost," she said. "Spotted Bear came to my rescue. He explained everything to me about his appearance and why he had not returned home because he was a Ghost. He also told me that if you knew of my association with him, I might be sent away, considered taboo to all Indians. That is why I didn't tell you. Please forgive me, for had I known that you would want your cousin home with you, even though he had been scalped, I would have gladly told you."

She hung her head, then raised it again and gazed into Two Eagles's eyes. "Shadow came for me today and led me to Spotted Bear's tepee, where he lay ill and terribly feverish," she said. "I had a kindness to repay to him. That is why I went to see if something was wrong. Thank goodness I did."

"You said you had a kindness to repay," Two Eagles said tightly. "At . . . any . . . cost?"

"I hated thinking that I might lose you over this, but I couldn't leave Spotted Bear alone again, possibly dying," Candy said, once again fearing that Two Eagles would not forgive her.

Why else would he look so stern?

Suddenly Two Eagles rose to his feet and went to Candy.

He swept her into his arms. "It is good that you showed my cousin such kindness," he said. "I would expect no less from you. You are a woman of good heart."

"Then . . . you . . . aren't going to turn me away?" Candy asked, searching his eyes. "I am not taboo to you?"

"You could never be taboo," Two Eagles said, then stepped away from her and knelt beside Spotted Bear. "Nor could you, cousin. I truly thought you were dead. Had I known you were alive, I never would have stopped searching for you until I found you. I would have taken you home and seen to your healing myself."

Out of the corner of his eye he saw that some of his warriors had shied away, moving back from Spotted Bear. Obviously they feared him because he had lived through a scalping.

Two Eagles ignored his men's ignorance and would speak to them later about it.

Right now all that was important was to get his cousin home so that he could be medicated.

"But . . . I . . . am a Ghost," Spotted Bear said, his voice fading with each word. He glanced over at the warriors. "They . . . see . . . me in that way. They . . . fear . . . me."

"Not for long," Two Eagles reassured him. "I shall speak to them. I will make them understand that it is wrong to fear those who have lived through a scalping. In my village, no one who has survived such a thing will ever be feared or called a Ghost."

"Thank you, cousin," Spotted Bear managed to say before falling again into an unconscious state.

"We must hurry," Two Eagles said, going to his horse and removing a blanket from his travel bag.

He went back to Spotted Bear and wrapped him in the blanket even though he already had many on him.

It seemed that no matter how many blankets were on him, Spotted Bear still shivered from his fever.

This gesture of Two Eagles was to make a point to his warriors. He wanted them to understand that they should, without reservation, share their blankets with this fallen man, a man who had hunted with them, who had enjoyed evenings around the large fire with them.

Just because he no longer had hair, he was not any less a Wichita warrior!

Two Eagles hurried to his warriors and explained to them how this had come about, and what Two Eagles was going to do. "Above all else, my warriors, you must look at this man, my blood cousin, with love and respect," he said firmly. "He has lived through what none of you, I hope, will have to do, and he is no less a warrior for it." He looked slowly from man to man. "Do you understand what I expect of you?"

They grunted and nodded in unison.

Two Eagles watched as each took a blanket from his bags and went to place it on Spotted Bear.

Candy was so touched by this show of affection, tears swam in her eyes.

Two Eagles smiled at his cousin, then spun around and hurried to his horse, where he swung into his saddle.

Candy was already in hers. She was ready, even eager, to ride again.

She knew the importance of getting Spotted Bear to his people's shaman so that he could have proper treatment for the fever. She just hoped it wasn't too late.

"You do forgive me, don't you, Two Eagles, for keeping the truth from you?" Candy asked, bringing his eyes to her.

"You know I do," Two Eagles said, smiling broadly at her. "You are my woman. How could I stop loving you for any reason? I have vowed my love to you, and it is forever. Do you hear? Forever."

He swallowed hard and looked over his shoulder at Spotted Bear, who lay in a deep sleep. Then he gazed into Candy's eyes again. "It is unbelievable that he lived through the scalping, for the horrible signs of what was done to him are so visible," he said, shuddering. "He is a man of much bravery to live through such a horrendous event, and then he had the courage to keep to himself because he did not want to bring trouble into my village. He saw himself as a Ghost. How can he have thought that I could ever see him in such a way?"

"I had no idea that he was your cousin," Candy said, glad that they were near the village.

She glanced down at Spotted Bear. He hadn't stirred again.

She looked then at Shadow, who had caught up with them. She smiled when she saw that her wolf stayed close by Spotted Bear's side.

She caught a glimpse of one of the wolves following them. It remained hidden in the dense forest at the left side of the trail.

She imagined that the wolves feared for their friend Spotted Bear's life and hated being separated from him!

"We are almost home," Two Eagles said, drawing Candy's attention back to him. "I shall ride ahead and prepare my people for Spotted Bear's arrival. I shall also prepare my shaman. It is all in his hands now, whether my cousin lives or dies."

Candy watched him ride away; his warriors continued on with her and Spotted Bear.

When they arrived at the village, everyone was standing outside, looking guardedly at the man on the travois.

Candy knew that there would be some who might never accept Spotted Bear's presence in their village.

But that mattered not.

What did matter was that finally Spotted Bear was home, truly home, and his chief had accepted him, and his shaman was awaiting him.

Candy rode onward and stopped before Crying Wolf's lodge, where Two Eagles stood, waiting.

Candy dismounted while Two Eagles gently unwrapped the blankets from around Spotted Bear, then lifted him into his arms and carried him inside the shaman's lodge.

Candy waited outside.

When Two Eagles came out again, she gazed into his eyes as he looked lovingly into hers.

"He is now under the care of our shaman," he said. "*Hiyu-wo*, come, my woman. Let us go

251

home. There we will await word about my cousin's condition."

Candy saw that their horses had been taken away and that the warriors had returned to their homes. She also noticed that everyone in the village had resumed their normal activities.

When Candy and Two Eagles were inside their tepee, where Shadow was already asleep on her pallet, Two Eagles placed his hands at Candy's waist and turned her to face him.

"Thank you for being the woman that you are . . . a woman whose heart is loving and giving," he said thickly. "Had you not gone when Shadow came for you, my cousin would have died."

"He might still," Candy murmured.

"He is in good hands, so I doubt that he will leave this earth just yet," Two Eagles said. He took her by the hand and led her down beside his lodge fire, which was now only glowing embers. "If he was strong and brave enough to have lived through the scalping, he will not allow an ordinary fever to take him away from the life that now awaits him. I will make it all up to him; he will soon forget that time he felt he no longer belonged among his own people."

Candy was relieved that he still loved her and wasn't angry that she'd gone to help Spotted Bear. She was thankful that he had found her that day of her own misfortune, when she was crawling away from the massacre. She now knew that nothing would ever stand between them and their devotion to one another.

"I'm so tired," Candy murmured, easing into Two Eagles's arms as he held them out for her.

"Sleep," he said, holding her close. "I shall hold you and watch you. I find it hard to take my eyes off you. You are everything precious on this earth."

Candy melted into his embrace.

She went to sleep with a contented smile on her face.

Chapter Twenty-eight

The soul unto itself
Is an imperial friend—
Or the most agonizing spy
An enemy could send.
—Emily Dickinson

Candy was awakened abruptly by a sound like hailstones pummeling the tepee, yet the glow of the rising sun through the buckskin proved it was not a stormy morning.

"What can it be?" Candy asked, hurrying into a dress as Two Eagles threw on his clothes.

The sound increased in volume, and Candy jumped in alarm when something strange began falling through the smoke hole, crackling and popping as the objects fell into the flames in the fire pit. It sounded to her like corn popping.

She gazed, wide-eyed, as she recognized the objects.

She said "grasshoppers" at the same time that Two Eagles said "locusts."

"Lord, I can't believe my eyes," Candy said as she stared at the insects falling into the flames, their bodies popping at contact.

"We're being invaded by a swarm of locusts!" Two Eagles said, hurrying to the entrance flap. He shoved it aside, flinching when more locusts flew inside the tepee.

He dropped the flap closed, but not before he had seen what was happening outside. The sky was black with the swarm of locusts. They were dropping onto everything in his village; all of the tepees were crawling with them. He could hear the whinnying of the horses in the corrals as their flesh was struck by the insects.

"How bad is it?" Candy asked.

"I have never seen this many at one time," Two Eagles said, watching as more insects continued to fall through the smoke hole.

"I remember one time long ago, when my father was stationed at Fort Jefferson Barracks in Missouri, grasshoppers came in such great numbers that everyone's crops that year were ruined by them," Candy said, shuddering.

She remembered the horrible insects getting caught in her hair that day. She would never forget how she'd fought in vain to remove them as she ran to her house. Her mother had finally managed to get them out, but not before some had burrowed in so deeply that those strands of hair had to be cut in order to remove the horrible insects.

"It is good that our crops are already harvested or we would have lost everything," Two Eagles said, less tense now that the thumps against his lodge covering were beginning to lessen.

"But there are surely those who have not had their harvest yet," Candy said, swatting at a locust that had landed on her arm. She shivered as she plucked the creature from the sleeve of her dress and tossed it outside.

"Perhaps you should stay inside while I go to see about the horses," Two Eagles said.

"I would rather go with you," Candy said. "I want to see what damage the grasshoppers have done."

"You call them grasshoppers while I call them locusts," Two Eagles repeated, sliding his feet into his moccasins as Candy did the same. "Why is that?"

"That is what we have always called them," Candy said. "Back when they were so bad in Missouri, they were said to be Rocky Mountain locusts, yet we called them grasshoppers because they looked like the insects we normally saw in the summer in Missouri."

She flinched when another locust fell down through the smoke hole and settled on the inside skin of the lodge, clinging upside down, its bulging eyes looking slowly around it.

"They came that summer day in sky-blackening swarms, devastating all vegetation in their path," she said as Two Eagles plucked the insect from the wall, studying it as he held it closer.

"A relief and aid society was organized, but only to help people whose skin was white," Candy said.

"The Indians that lived in that area, the peaceful Shawnee, lost everything that year, yet they received no assistance."

She watched Two Eagles hold the entrance flap aside and release the insect into the air rather than kill it, and she thought what a kind man he was.

"No public outcry was heard for the hungry Shawnee, but they would not allow themselves to beg," Candy said. Even then she had felt the plight of the red man, yet she was too small a child to offer them any help.

She had begged her father to help the Shawnee, but he had told her to mind her own business. He had told her never to offer redskins any kindness, for if she did, they would never stop asking things of her.

It was as though fate had determined that eventually her father would be shown no pity by red men, just as he had never shown pity to them. The Sioux had come and taken his life, as though they had known of the man's past transgressions against men and women of their skin color.

Even children.

Yes, she had heard about her father's raids on villages where no one was left living, man, woman, or child. But she had not wanted to believe such stories about her father. She had closed her eyes to the truth.

But when she had seen the head of the Wichita chief stored in that jar, she had to believe the very worst of her father.

Candy stepped outside with Two Eagles, gasping when she saw the thick layer of locusts on the ground, some dead, some alive and crawling above a heap of their own kind.

Slowly people emerged from their tepees, stunned speechless by the sight.

Candy winced when she stepped farther outside beside Two Eagles, each step crunching locusts beneath their moccasins.

One by one, people came together in the center of the village to discuss what had happened, as Two Eagles, Candy, and several warriors hurried to the corrals to check the condition of their horses.

Candy clung to Two Eagles's arm as she stepped up to the corral with him. The horses were now contentedly munching the locusts as though feed had fallen from the sky.

The horses were not harmed, their hides too thick to be hurt by the insects.

Two Eagles stroked his midnight-black stallion's sleek mane, then turned back to Candy. "My people have much to do now," he said decisively. "We must be sure to gather up all of the dead locusts and rid ourselves of them, or the stench will soon be all but deadly."

He went to the center of the village, where everyone still stood.

"We must work tirelessly until the insects are gone from our village," Two Eagles announced. He looked past the tepees to the river, then in another direction, where their crops had just been removed from the communal garden.

"We will take them to our empty garden, pile

them up, and burn them," he said. "Let us begin now. We should not stop until all are removed."

Everyone joined in the work, scraping up the locusts and placing them in baskets.

Candy worked as hard as anyone, laughing when Shadow romped and chased an occasional locust that had escaped the fire.

As the sun climbed high in the sky, Candy's back ached fiercely, but she still stayed with the others, glad to be able to see the ground again in the village; soon the hard work would be over.

She stopped for a moment when she saw Two Eagles gazing off in the direction of Proud Wind's village. She knew that he was wondering whether Proud Wind and his people had brought in their harvest before the locusts arrived.

Chapter Twenty-nine

Nymph of the downward smile
and sidelong glance,
In what diviner moments of the day
art thou most lovely?
—*John Keats*

Candy was exhausted from cleaning up the piles of dead locusts. She stood with the others as they watched the terrible things go up in smoke in the middle of what had not long ago been a garden filled with ripe corn.

Even the sentries had been drawn from their posts to help clean up the debris.

Candy gazed at Two Eagles as he stepped beside her. "I'm so glad that's over," she murmured, wiping a bead of perspiration from her brow. "But the stench. It's horrible."

"The wind is changing," Two Eagles said, wiping a smudge of black soot from her cheek. "The smell of death will soon go in the opposite direction."

Candy reached up and brushed some soot from his skin, then turned with him as they heard the sound of a horse and wagon approaching the village.

Worry filled Two Eagles. "It must be whites, for no Indians travel by wagon," he said tightly.

He waved at his warriors, bringing them quickly into a circle around him. He instructed them to take the women and children and stay inside their lodges. They were only to come out if they saw a threat. In that case, they were to come out in full force, carrying firearms.

He then rushed back to Candy. He led her quickly to their tepee, closing the flap behind them.

"Stay here," he said as he gently placed his hands on her shoulders. "Let none of the white people see you. You know the dangers."

"Yes, I know," Candy said, yet she felt strange hiding from her own people.

"I must go and see what brings the white eyes among my Wichita people," Two Eagles said, placing a hand on Candy's cheek. "I will send them away quickly," he said, only pausing long enough to brush a comforting kiss across her lips before he left.

Candy knew she must not be seen, but she longed to hear what had brought the strangers into the village. She stepped to the closed flap and leaned an ear close to it.

Two Eagles stood just outside the entrance flap, his arms folded across his bare chest, as the wagon drew closer and closer.

He stiffened when he saw a white man at the

reins, and several children, boys and girls of various ages, in the back of the wagon. He quickly counted nine children and noted that they were poorly dressed. Their cheeks were gaunt and pale, their eyes anxious as the wagon came close enough for Two Eagles to look into them.

What confused him was that there were so many children, but no woman with them.

Did they have no mother?

His eyes narrowed as the wagon stopped a few feet from him and the white man gave Two Eagles a look that he recognized too well. It was a look of superiority, as though this man saw himself as better than someone whose skin was of a different color.

The children aroused pity in Two Eagles's heart. But he felt deep hatred for this white man whose eyes spoke of his unfriendliness.

"What do you want of me and my people?" Two Eagles asked, his arms folded defiantly across his muscled chest.

"Food," the man said icily. "I have seen your corn crops. I know that this was a good year for you. I had a good crop, too, but it was not harvested before the grasshoppers came and ate it. My children are hungry. I have come to demand that you give me some of your corn, and other vegetables that you have harvested. I know you have enough to spare."

Two Eagles frowned. This man had no right to demand anything of a proud Wichita chief or his people.

Two Eagles glared at the man. Then his eyes went to the children again, and he knew that he could not deny them food just because their father was crude and unthinking.

Two Eagles started to respond, to tell the white man that he would give them some of his stored food, but before he had the chance to say it, the impatient white man drew his gun and aimed it at Two Eagles.

When Candy heard a pistol being cocked, she went cold inside. In a matter of moments she could lose the man she loved, for she knew it had to be the white man who had cocked the gun; Two Eagles was standing outside weaponless.

She looked over her shoulder at the cache of weapons in the teepee.

Her heart pounding, she rushed to it and grabbed up a rifle, saw that it was ready for firing, then went back to the entrance flap.

She had just started to step outside when she heard Two Eagles talking. He was still trying to handle this situation peacefully, and she felt it was not her place to interfere, not yet anyhow.

But if she was needed, she would step outside and show that rude man a thing or two!

Trembling, she leaned her ear close and listened again to what Two Eagles was saying, admiring his bravery and patience.

"White man, threatening a powerful Wichita chief with a firearm is not wise," Two Eagles said flatly. "Ask in a civilized manner for food and it will be given to you, but demand it at gunpoint and your request will be ignored. No one forces Chief Two Eagles to do anything he does not want to do."

"Must I remind you that I am the one with the gun?" the man snarled, still holding the pistol steadily aimed at Two Eagles's gut.

"Look behind you, *wasichu*," Two Eagles said, slowly smiling when he saw how those words made the man flinch. The white man looked behind him and saw the many warriors standing there, their arrows notched on their bowstrings.

"*Ho*, yes, you might succeed at killing Chief Two Eagles, but then *you* will die at the hands of my warriors," Two Eagles said, again slowly smiling when he saw the white man grow pale as he lowered his pistol.

"Lay the firearm aside," Two Eagles said, standing his ground.

The man nodded and placed the pistol on the seat beside him, then once again looked at the many arrows pointed at him.

"Now what?" he gulped out. "Are you going to allow me to leave? Or . . . are . . . you going to take me as a captive?" He looked over his shoulder at his children, then into Two Eagles's eyes. "And . . . what . . . of my children?"

"They are going to be given food enough to last for many sunrises," Two Eagles said. He nodded at two of his warriors. "Go. Take food from where it is stored for the winter. Bring enough for these children. Place it in the wagon with them."

Two Eagles gazed into the man's eyes again. "My people had an abundant harvest this year before the locusts arrived," he said. "There is enough to share with your children."

Two Eagles waited for the man to thank him, but was not surprised when he didn't. Instead the *wasichu* sat there grabbing the bags of corn, pumpkins, and beans as the warriors handed them to him.

Once the bags were in the wagon, the man still didn't thank Two Eagles, but instead looked past him at his tepee, as though he was thinking now of something more than food. Two Eagles wondered if the white man had seen Candy before he had led her inside his lodge.

Without another word, the white man grabbed his reins and slapped them against his team of horses. Again the man looked over his shoulder at the tepee, then gazed coldly into Two Eagles's eyes before heading out of the village.

Candy breathed a sigh of relief that the man had left without one shot being fired. She had never been prouder of Two Eagles than now. He had stood there with courage as the man had held him at gunpoint, and then had given the man's children food! Thanks to Two Eagles's kindness, the white children would have food for their tiny bellies.

Chapter Thirty

Let knowledge grow from more to more,
But more of reverence in us dwell.
—Alfred, Lord Tennyson

Hawk Woman huddled in her tepee, trembling. She had heard the voice of the man who had demanded food of Two Eagles. Even without seeing his face, she had known it was Albert Cohen. The man she had fled was there at the village where she had taken refuge.

He must be living nearby. How else could he have gotten to the Indian village so soon after the locust attack?

Now she knew that she would have to be more careful. She could never allow Albert to know she was there.

She also knew that desperate measures must be taken now to make Two Eagles love her instead of

Candy. She needed his love in order to keep her safe from the wicked man who had been banished from his own people, the Mormons.

If she were Two Eagles's wife, he would stop at nothing to keep her safe . . . and happy.

A slow smile quivered across her lips as she thought of a way to torment Candy so that she would want to flee back to the white world, where she truly belonged. Yes, the first time Two Eagles left Candy behind at the village, Hawk Woman would take action against her rival!

But thoughts of the child she'd left behind made Hawk Woman tremble at the knowledge that her daughter was so close. She longed to see Penelope, even though she knew she could never actually embrace her.

But . . . just . . . one look!

No, she thought angrily. She couldn't bear the pain of looking upon her daughter, even though she knew she could find Albert's home and sneak close enough without the evil, cruel man knowing it.

Yes, she was devious now in more ways than Albert would have imagined possible. But she was smart, too, and knew that she must forget Penelope, for Two Eagles was more important to her now. He was her future. She *would* be his wife!

Chapter Thirty-one

Oh, cease! Must hate and death return?
—*Percy Bysshe Shelley*

Candy watched Two Eagles and several of his warriors ride from the village; she understood why he didn't want her to go with him to Proud Wind's village, to see how his people had come through the locust attack. It was too soon after the white man's appearance in the village for Candy to go out where she might be seen.

Two Eagles had told Candy that the man had peered intently at his tepee as though he might have seen her hurry into it.

If so, Candy had to be careful, for if that man's wives were dead, would not he be on the lookout for another woman to raise his children?

Candy went back inside the tepee and noticed that Shadow was not there. She always worried when her wolf disappeared for any amount of time, for she knew that one day she might not see her again.

Sorely tired from all the work she'd done cleaning up the locusts, Candy sat down beside the fire for a while. Then, realizing how tired she was, she crawled over to her bed of blankets. She rolled one blanket down halfway, stretched out on the others, then gasped with horror when she found herself being attacked by ants.

She leapt from the bed, swatting at the ants, which were on her dress as well as her legs and arms. The sting of their bites burned her flesh.

After ridding herself of the nasty bugs, Candy knelt down beside her bed and rolled the top blanket down.

She felt the color drain from her face when she saw that someone had placed a bullhorn plant, with its many ants, in her bed. When she had disturbed the plant by crawling between the blankets, the ants had swarmed from it.

"Who would do this?" she whispered, aware now just how badly she had been bitten. The bites had turned into red welts on her flesh, burning as if someone had touched her skin with a hot poker.

Then it came to her who had to be responsible. There was only one person who hated her enough to want to cause her such discomfort.

Hawk Woman.

Surely while Candy was away from the tepee

bidding Two Eagles good-bye, the spiteful woman had placed the bullhorn plant, with its ants, in Candy's bed.

Trying not to focus on the terrible bites, Candy angrily tossed the bullhorn plant outside and then picked up the blanket where many of the ants were still crawling and went to Hawk Woman's lodge.

Candy didn't announce herself but instead went inside and dropped the blanket at Hawk Woman's feet. Some of the ants rushed from the safety of the blanket onto Hawk Woman.

As they crawled up her bare legs, Hawk Woman swatted at them, crying out when they bit her.

"Yes, the bites sting, don't they?" Candy said bitterly. She placed her fists on her hips. "Will you stop at nothing to make my stay here at the village uncomfortable? Don't you know that nothing you do can discourage me from staying? I will never leave Two Eagles. And why can't you realize that Two Eagles doesn't love you? He's going to marry me. Do you hear? Me!"

Hawk Woman brushed the blanket and ants aside and stood quickly. She leaned her face into Candy's. "Never," she hissed. "Do . . . you . . . hear me? Two Eagles is never going to marry you." She smiled wickedly. "I'll make certain of that. Someday, some way, you will see who the true winner is."

"You are a demented woman," Candy said as Hawk Woman's warning sent ice through her veins.

She slowly backed away from Hawk Woman, then made a quick turn and left.

She stopped, trembling now from the burning sting of the bites as well as from the fear that came with her enemy's threats.

Yes, Hawk Woman was an enemy, and something had to be done about her once and for all!

But for now, all Candy could think about was how badly the welts hurt her.

She rushed to Crying Wolf's lodge and spoke his name outside. She was relieved when he drew aside the entrance flap right away.

"Come inside," he said in his kind, soft voice. "Sit by the fire. Tell me, how did you get those bites?"

Candy stepped past him, then sat down on a thick cushion of pelts beside his lodge fire. She held her arms out for him to examine.

"Ant bites," he said, then questioned her with his old, pale brown eyes. "How did you get them? These are from ants that live in bullhorn plants. Did you accidentally rub up against one?"

Candy didn't want to whine, to complain about Hawk Woman to the shaman.

"Yes, that's what I did," Candy murmured, not actually telling a lie, for she had rubbed against the bullhorn that had been "planted" in her bed!

"You now know how painful these ants are, so you must be more careful around them," Crying Wolf said kindly. "Many of my people, especially children, have come to me with such bites. I know how to medicate them. By nightfall much of the swelling and sting will be gone."

"Thank you," Candy said.

She sat there quietly as he ministered to her while her mind kept seeing the spiteful look in Hawk Woman's eyes. She tried not to shudder when she recalled her evil laughter. She had never met anyone like Hawk Woman before, which gave her enemy an advantage over her.

But she would not let such a woman get the best of her.

"There you go," Crying Wolf said, drawing Candy's attention back to him. "You should already be feeling better."

Candy was aware that the white cream he had spread over her bites had taken a lot of the sting from them already. She smiled as he put his medicinal vials back inside his huge bag.

"Thank you so much," she said. "You seem to know how to work miracles."

"That is why I am my people's shaman," Crying Wolf said, smiling broadly. "It pleases me to know that I have been able to help you."

Candy rose to her feet. "I feel strangely sleepy," she said, yawning.

"In the ointment that I placed on your burns is an herb that makes one relax," Crying Wolf said, standing and taking her gently by the arm. "Do you need assistance to your lodge?"

Candy yawned again as she fought off the urge to sleep. "No, I'll be fine," she murmured, giving him a hug before stepping from his tepee.

As the sun hit her eyes, Candy saw Hawk Woman through the golden haze. A sudden uneasiness swept through Candy, for if she was in a drugged stupor, Hawk Woman might try to take advantage of her.

Trying to look as though she wasn't drugged, Candy managed to get inside her tepee.

But as soon as she did, she fell in a half faint on her bed. Remembering the ants that had been there, she managed to crawl away, then got to her feet long enough to take the blankets outside and shake them.

Again she felt Hawk Woman's eyes on her.

Candy ignored her and hurried back inside the tepee, turning quickly when she heard movement behind her.

She had expected to see Hawk Woman there, but instead it was Shadow.

Candy dropped to her knees and welcomed Shadow in her arms. "Where have you been?" she asked. "Don't you know how much it worries me when you leave?"

Shadow snuggled closer.

"Yes, you know, don't you?" Candy said softly.

Having enough strength left to rearrange her blankets, Candy stretched out on the bed with Shadow next to her, snuggled as close as she could get.

"What must I do about that terrible woman, Shadow?" Candy whispered, her eyes slowly closing.

Candy just wasn't certain yet whether she would tell Two Eagles about Hawk Woman's latest act of hate. She would decide by the time he returned.

But for now, sleep was all that mattered to her.

As her eyes drifted closed, she was glad that Shadow was there to keep her safe while she slept. Hawk Woman wouldn't dare try anything while Shadow was near.

Chapter Thirty-two

Ah! Who shall lift that wand of magic power,
And the lost clue regain?
—Henry Wadsworth Longfellow

Candy was awakened from a sound sleep by the distant howling of wolves. She leaned quickly up on an elbow, already aware that Shadow was no longer cuddling against her, as she had been when Candy had fallen asleep.

Instead she found Two Eagles sitting beside her bed, gazing lovingly at her. "You are home," Candy murmured, starting to sit up, then stopping when she saw what he held in his hand. It looked like the bullhorn plant she had thrown outside.

Sitting up slowly, she looked at Two Eagles again as he held the plant out toward her.

"Why would I find this outside the entranceway?" he asked, glancing at the red welts on her arms. Even with the creamy white medicine covering them, he could see how inflamed the bites were.

Then he searched her eyes with his.

Feeling uneasy, Candy was at a loss for words. She wasn't yet ready to tell him what Hawk Woman had done. She realized she wanted to solve this problem with Hawk Woman herself. She needed to be the one to finally put her in her place!

He tossed the plant into the lodge fire, then reached behind him and brought a bag out for Candy to see. "Crying Wolf stopped me after I arrived home and told me of your problem with the ants," he said. "He said he was not sure how you got bitten by them, but thought I might want to bring more of his special medicine for you to use before we retire for the night."

"He is so kind," Candy murmured, hoping that Two Eagles would not insist on knowing how she happened to have been bitten, or pursue the question of how the plant had wound up beside his lodge entranceway.

She felt careless now for having left it there. She should have burned all traces of the plant.

"Let me put the cream on now," Two Eagles said. He opened a vial and dipped his fingers into the white liquid; when it dried, it looked like chalk on the skin.

Candy held one arm out and then the other as he gently applied the medicine to her bites. Then she lifted her skirt so that he could medicate those on her legs.

"You now know the dangers of being anywhere

near those ants, or the plant in which they live," Two Eagles said, looking quickly into her eyes. "But something tells me I did not need to tell you that. I feel that someone else is responsible for this. Why do you not share the name with me? Or need I ask? It was Hawk Woman, was it not? She placed the plant in the tepee. You did not see it until it was too late and the ants were attacking you."

Candy swallowed hard, lowered her eyes, then gazed into his again as he finished treating the last bite on her legs.

"I have no real proof who did it," she said.

"No proof is needed," Two Eagles responded. "You and I both know without proof, for I have seen Hawk Woman's behavior toward you. Her jealousy is making her behavior even uglier."

"Did you ever see her behave any better?" Candy blurted out, then wished she had held her tongue. She did not want to become vindictive like Hawk Woman.

She would not lower herself by such behavior. From now on, she would watch her words more carefully when she spoke of Hawk Woman to Two Eagles.

"I will warn her against her continued spiteful behavior toward you," Two Eagles said, replacing the vial in the bag, to return it tomorrow to Crying Wolf.

Candy reached a quick hand to his arm. "No, please don't," she murmured. "It has become a 'woman thing.' Let we women work it out between us."

"I could stop it now with only a few words," Two Eagles said, reaching out and gently touching her on the cheek. He was glad the ants had not ventured to her face.

"No, please," Candy said. "Now that I know how much she resents me, I can be more careful."

Then she reached for his hand and held it lovingly on her lap. "And how did you find things at Proud Wind's village?" she asked softly. "Did they come through the locust attack as well as we?"

"No, they were not as fortunate," Two Eagles said, sliding his hand free. He turned toward the fire and gazed into its dancing flames. "They had not yet harvested their crops. Most were destroyed."

"How horrible," Candy gasped. "What are they going to do?"

"There is always the hunt," Two Eagles said, turning toward her again. "I plan to go on a hunt with my friend Proud Wind and help bring home much meat for his people. The women will prepare it so that it will last them the whole winter."

"But they need more than meat for their survival," Candy maintained.

"*Ho*, and they will have what they need," Two Eagles said, turning toward the fire again and lifting a log into its flames. "Our harvest this year was one of the best we have ever had." He turned slow eyes to her again. "We will give them half of what we have put into storage."

Candy's eyes widened. "But you already gave the white man so much," she said softly. "Can your people truly chance losing any more? What if it is a much worse winter than usual? What would you do then?"

"I will estimate what we can risk giving away and what we must keep in case we do have a bad winter. Again meat will help fill my people's stomachs, for my warriors are good hunters. I am not all that concerned about sharing food with my friend and his people," Two Eagles said, confidence in his voice.

"When will you take food to Proud Wind and his people?" Candy asked, hating for him to leave again so soon.

She was uneasy that Hawk Woman had gotten the best of her today. What else might the woman decide to do to Candy?

Yes, she was afraid. But she wouldn't let Hawk Woman know it, or Two Eagles.

She didn't want him to feel that he must be with her every moment in order to keep her safe. She wanted to prove that she was not the meek and helpless woman her appearance made her seem. She might be petite, but she was strong enough to take care of herself.

"Many of my warriors are already on their way to Proud Wind's village with food," Two Eagles said.

"So you can stay with me tonight?" Candy said, glad she would not have to spend an entire night without him so soon after what Hawk Woman had done.

"For tonight, *ho*, I am here to stay," Two Eagles replied. He wanted to make love with her, yet knew that as long as the welts were so painful on her skin, he would not touch her in that way.

He eyed the blankets, and then Candy. "I have already bathed," he said softly. "I am ready to sleep if you are."

"Yes, that sounds good to me," Candy murmured, then gazed at the closed entrance flap. "I just wish Shadow hadn't left again."

"How long has she been gone this time?" Two Eagles asked.

"I'm not certain," Candy said, sighing as she stretched out on the blankets with Two Eagles soon beside her. "She was here when I fell asleep. And now she is gone."

"I heard the wolves howling in the distance as I arrived back at the village," Two Eagles said. "They were probably calling to Shadow even then."

"I heard them, too, upon awakening," Candy said. "Shadow couldn't have been gone for very long. Surely she will come back soon."

She wanted to snuggle up to Two Eagles, but the sores on her arms and legs were too uncomfortable for her to lie beside him.

Slowly her eyes closed and she felt the peacefulness that came when sound sleep was near.

"I will be leaving early tomorrow," Two Eagles said, drawing Candy's eyes open again.

"Where will you go?" she asked.

"On the hunt with Proud Wind," Two Eagles said. He noticed the worried look in her eyes. "It is best that we hunt now in order for his people to prepare the meat before the sharp winds of winter come."

"Of course I know I can't go with you, so I won't ask," Candy murmured. She winced when she turned and a blanket brushed against her bites.

"Anyway, I'm not feeling well enough to go very far on a horse."

"I'm certain you can find something to occupy yourself with while I am gone," Two Eagles said. He leaned close to her and brushed a soft kiss across her lips. "But make certain Hawk Woman is nowhere near you."

"Once we are married—" Candy began, but he interrupted her.

"Once we are married, Hawk Woman will finally know that she has to look elsewhere for a husband," Two Eagles said firmly. "And it will have to be someone outside my village. There is not one man among my unmarried warriors who would want her in his bed."

Chapter Thirty-three

I regret little,
I would chance still less.
—Robert Browning

Restless with Two Eagles off on the hunt, Candy had decided to do something constructive with her time. She could not bear to sit in the tepee and wait for Two Eagles to come back home. She was walking in the woods to gather herbs to season their supper. She wanted to prove to him that she had learned which herbs were edible.

She knew now that although the Wichita's basic foods were meat, corn, squash, and beans, there were many other plants, such as edible roots and greens, available near the village in the forest, along the riverbanks, and in the open fields.

She already knew that searching for food was a constant project, particularly among the women.

Her welts no longer burned, and she was not so afraid of Albert Cohen right now. The true threat to her well-being was back at the village.

Hawk Woman.

She was now constantly on Candy's mind, for Candy knew that she had to be alert at all times in case that spiteful woman tried something else to harm her.

She sighed, for she felt safer away from the village while Two Eagles was gone than in it. She was finding this walk through the trees wonderfully relaxing.

"I will certainly surprise Two Eagles when he comes home tonight and finds a pot of greens cooking over the fire," she whispered, proud that she now knew how to make a tasty meal.

But she had so much more to learn, and she would. After she was married, she wanted her chieftain husband to be fed well enough so he could perform his duties to his people.

She smiled almost wickedly when she thought about how he must have his strength for other things which included only his wife!

The sun was just barely making its way through the thickness of the trees overhead, looking like golden threads as it slanted downward. Candy walked on, occasionally looking over her shoulder to make certain she would not get lost, as she had that other time she had left the village alone.

She did not have Shadow to keep her company, for the wolf was still gone.

Candy wished there were a way to encourage her

pet to stay with her, but in the forest was a pure white wolf that had chosen Shadow as its mate. Now there was a bond between them that no one could break.

She wondered where the wolves were staying now that Spotted Bear was no longer living in his tepee. Surely they missed his company. When she had visited him this morning to see how he was doing, he'd told her that he missed the wolves.

But he was happy to be home among his people and would never leave again, not now that they, for the most part, accepted him among them.

She was glad that he had recovered from the illness that had caused his terrible fever. She would never forget the heat of his flesh against her hand that night.

His fever was gone now, and each day he was stronger.

She smiled as she thought about the food she would prepare over the fire for Two Eagles. She would take some to Spotted Bear as well. His people had worked together to erect a tepee for him. The women were kind to him, taking him food both morning and night, as well as water from the river.

Some warriors had taken Spotted Bear their buckskin clothes, so that he would not have to return to his home in the woods for his own.

That gesture of kindness proved just how glad the warriors were that one of their men had returned home, even though he had been scalped and left for dead.

He was no longer seen as a Ghost. He was Spotted Bear again.

Suddenly hearing Two Eagles's warnings about leaving the village alone, Candy stopped when she found a thick bunch of delicious-looking greens.

She set her basket down and fell to her knees to begin gathering handfuls of the greens. When she felt she had enough of those, she began plucking herbs and placing them in the basket with the greens.

The aroma of flowers wafted to her, drawing her eyes to some wild roses climbing up the trunk of a huge oak tree. They were pink, tiny, and beautiful. She would have flowers awaiting her beloved's return, as well as a good pot of food.

After gathering enough herbs, she went to the rose vine. It seemed a miracle that this part of the forest had been spared the terrible scourge of the locusts. It must have been the thick foliage on the trees that had saved the roses from the ravages of the insects.

She did see a dead locust here and there, and even an occasional one alive on a low tree limb, its round, beady eyes seeming to look through Candy.

She ignored the insects and was now contentedly plucking stems of roses, wincing when she pricked her fingers now and then with the thorns.

A movement nearby, the sound of a snapping twig, made Candy stop what she was doing. Had she grown too confident, maybe even careless?

Her heart thumping inside her chest, she slowly turned toward the sound.

Her heart seemed to fall to her feet when she saw the shadow of someone hiding behind a tree not far from where she stood frozen on the forest floor.

Searching inside herself for a measure of strength, she turned, and then began running.

Chapter Thirty-four

O breathe a word or two of fire.
Smile as if those words should burn me.
—John Keats

She knew she wouldn't get far, but she couldn't just stand there making it easy for whoever had come upon her in the forest. She could already hear the pounding of feet behind her on the hard earth and knew that the man was gaining on her.

Her insides froze when she felt strong arms grabbing her around her waist. In the next moment she was shoved painfully to the ground.

She was yanked around so that she now lay on her back with a full view of the one accosting her.

She didn't recognize the man, but the moment he spoke, the voice gave him away. It was the man who had come and demanded corn and other vegetables after the locust attack.

She started to scream, but he was quicker. He clasped one hand over her mouth, while his other held her wrists together above her head, his knees straddling her.

She felt sickened by the leer on his face because she knew that this man intended to rape her.

"I got a glimpse of you just before you hurried into the tepee when I came for food at the savages' village," he said, laughing throatily, his piercing green eyes seeming to bore holes through her.

He wore a thick red beard, and his hair was stringy and greasy as it fell down past his thin shoulders.

He had a bulbous nose, with wide nostrils that flared each time he breathed.

His teeth were uneven and yellow. His lips were a strange purplish color. "When I glimpsed the golden hair, I thought I'd finally found the lady that escaped me sometime ago," he said.

He gazed at her hair, then looked into her eyes again. "Yep, she had the same golden hair, but she wore hers long." He laughed once more. "What happened to yours? Did the savages try to scalp you?"

His words seemed to swirl around inside Candy's head as her fear built. He seemed wicked through and through.

And what had he said about a woman who had escaped him? Could that be Hawk Woman, who would be Sara Thaxton to him?

But if this man was Albert Cohen, where were his wives, for Hawk Woman had said he had many?

Of course, she thought quickly to herself, he

wouldn't have brought his wives with him when he came for food with the children, realizing their presence would bring undue attention to him. It just wasn't natural to have so many wives, and he surely kept his polygamous marriages to himself whenever possible.

"Got you wondering about me, don't I?" the man said, laughing boisterously. "Well, let me tell you something, pretty lady. You ain't who I thought you were, but you'll do just fine anyhow. You'll be a sweet, lovely lady to add to my family of wives and children. You're even prettier than the one who got away. And tiny. I like 'em tiny. They make the prettiest kids."

Sickened by his bragging about his vile deeds, Candy felt she might vomit.

She swallowed hard to keep the bile down. But it was difficult.

She knew that if Two Eagles didn't find her soon, she could be many miles away and out of reach by the time he came after her.

"Yep, I'm taking you to join my other wives," he said, letting go of her wrists so that he could get a handkerchief from his rear pants pocket.

He laughed when Candy began clawing at his face, her fingers unable to make contact with his flesh because of the thick beard.

Soon he had gagged her with the red handkerchief, its stiffness making Candy realize that he had used this thing to blow his nose.

He yanked her up from the ground and thrust his face into hers. "If you try anything like that again, trying to claw my face with those long fingernails of yours, you'll regret it," he growled out. "Now just accept your new lot in life. You are going to join my other wives. You are going to bear me many children."

He gripped her by an arm and began half dragging her away from where her basket and digging knife lay beneath the tree. The plucked roses looked up like small smiling faces as they lay amid the bright green of the herbs.

"Why were you with the savages, dressed like a squaw?" he asked, knowing that she couldn't answer him with the handkerchief tied around her mouth. "You must've cooperated with them, or else why would you be allowed to leave the village and go alone into the forest?"

He snickered into her face. "You've bedded up with one of 'em, ain't you?" he said. Then his eyes widened. "It must've been the chief, for it was the chief's tepee that you hurried into to hide from me."

Candy glared at him. He looked proud as punch over his discovery.

She felt sick to her stomach to know that if Two Eagles didn't return home soon, she might be sharing a bed tonight with this filthy man.

They walked onward now in silence. Candy was yanked forward time and again when she tried to hesitate.

And then she saw a wagon up ahead and a team of two horses. No one else was there.

"It won't be long now," the man said as he pushed Candy toward the wagon, then lifted her and threw her into it as though she were no more than a sack of potatoes.

He climbed in after her and tied both her wrists and ankles.

"There, that ought to hold you," he said, then shoved her down flat onto the floor of the wagon. "But I've got to keep you hidden." He yanked up a couple of blankets and covered her with both of them. "That oughta do it."

Candy shivered with fear even though she was hot beneath the blankets. Her captor sat down, snapped the reins against the horses' backs, and took off.

She realized that he had not gone far before he stopped, yet it was far enough that no one from the village would easily find her.

She felt as though her life had come to an end, for there was no way that Two Eagles would know where she was, unless the wagon had left good tracks along the ground.

Yet Two Eagles would not know where to begin looking for her. He had no idea she was going to go into the forest today.

She stiffened and listened when she heard many voices, mainly of women. They were asking the man what was beneath the blankets.

Candy hoped they would feel sorry for her when they saw that she had been abducted and would find a way to free her.

But that didn't seem logical, for if that was possible, wouldn't they have fled this evil man, themselves, at their first opportunity?

She flinched when he suddenly threw the blanket aside, revealing Candy to his many wives and children. They stood all around the wagon, their eyes widening when they saw her lying there, gagged and tied.

He jumped into the wagon and forced Candy to her feet. He removed the gag from her mouth, and then the ropes at her ankles and wrists.

"This is my new wife," he announced, chuckling. "And she'll be giving you children a brother or sister."

Again Candy felt as though she might vomit.

Instead she stood stiffly as everyone looked her over carefully. Her breath was stolen away when he lifted her into his arms and half threw her over the side of the wagon, where she fell clumsily to the ground at the feet of the other wives.

She didn't look up at them, just waited for what would happen next.

"Get up!" the man shouted. "We've a piece to travel today to get you far from those Injuns. I haven't found my Sara, but you'll do instead."

Yes, Candy thought, this was the very man Hawk Woman had fled from. The banished Mormon.

Candy moved slowly to her feet, and as she did, she noticed one woman standing back from the others, a scarf over her head and partially over her face.

When the man went to the woman and yanked her roughly toward one of the wagons, cursing her as he ordered her onto it, the woman's scarf fell from her face.

Candy almost fainted when she saw who it was.

Her very own mother!

Candy saw a soft pleading in Agnes Creighton's eyes, and she understood. Her mother didn't want Candy to let the man know they were related.

She wasn't sure why, but she did as her mother wanted.

Candy watched angrily as he slapped her mother. "You'll learn to be more obedient," he growled. "Get on that wagon!"

Candy watched as the other women, except for one, who by her superior attitude seemed to be this man's partner, climbed frantically on board. The children scampered to get on the other wagon.

"Now it's your turn," the man said, placing a rough hand at Candy's wrist and shoving her. "Get in that wagon with the women, damn you."

Candy hurried aboard and sat down beside her mother.

As the man took the reins of the wagon filled with the women, his female partner took the reins of the wagon full of children.

Candy dared to slide a hand over to her mother's and gripped it reassuringly.

The man looked over his shoulder at Candy. "By the way, my name's Albert," he said, winking at her. "Albert Cohen. What's yours?"

Candy was certain about who she was with now and truly dreaded the days that stretched out before her.

"Your name?" Albert insisted, frowning at Candy.

She remembered proudly the Indian name that Two Eagles had given to her. She smiled smugly at

Albert. "Painted Wings," she said, seeing his look of disgust and not noticing how her mother had gasped at hearing it.

Candy laughed to herself, realizing that her decision to use her Indian name was the best thing she could have done under the circumstances.

She hated causing her mother to look at her in dismay, but she loved Albert's reaction to the knowledge that she saw herself as more Indian now than white.

He turned away from her and snapped the reins against the horses' backs, then looked at Candy again. "I'm going to work the Injun outta you," he snarled. "In many ways!"

Candy no longer felt as smug.

Suddenly she was terribly, terribly afraid, both for herself . . . and her mother.

Chapter Thirty-five

Shadow of annoyance
Never came near thee;
Thou lovest—but ne'er knew
Love's sad satiety.
—Percy Bysshe Shelley

Hawk Woman was stunned at what she had just witnessed. She had followed Candy into the forest and stood behind a tree, awaiting the moment she could slam her knife into Candy's back, when she had seen Albert Cohen step out of hiding.

What had happened then was still unbelievable to Hawk Woman.

Albert Cohen, the very man she had escaped from, had abducted Candy.

Had he just happened along and seen Candy alone and vulnerable, another woman he could add to his collection of wives?

Or had he glimpsed Candy when he had come to the village with his children to demand food? Had he known where the sentries were posted today and eluded them long enough to take Candy away?

Either way, Candy had played right into his hands by going into the forest alone to gather greens and herbs.

If he had waited another moment, it would have been Hawk Woman who surprised Candy. Hawk Woman had just yanked her knife from its sheath when Albert came into view.

A slow smile fluttered across Hawk Woman's lips and a look of victory entered her eyes. She was finally free of Candy, and she hadn't had to lift a finger to do it.

Even now she heard the wagon lumbering away, in it the woman who was planning to be "first lady" of the Eagle band of the Wichita.

Now if she could just play her cards right, that first lady would be none other than Hawk Woman.

She was going to try to portray herself as someone more gentle and caring than she had in the past. She now saw that gentleness was what attracted Two Eagles to a woman, not strength.

Yes, she would finally achieve her main goal in life. She would be the wife of a powerful Wichita chief—Two Eagles!

Sliding her knife back in its sheath, she gazed at the overturned basket of herbs, greens, and flowers. She laughed throatily when she interpreted these as the last remains of Candy, for no one, not even Two Eagles, would ever know who had taken her, or how to find her. Hawk Woman knew Albert Cohen well enough to know that he would leave the area quickly.

Feeling gay and lighthearted now that again she again had a chance to be the chief's wife, Hawk Woman almost skipped back in the direction of the village.

Yes, she knew she should report what she had witnessed, but hadn't she planned to kill Candy today, herself? This was even better. Albert Cohen had done the dirty deed for her.

She would not have the guilt of murder on her mind for the rest of her life. The burden of keeping quiet about Candy's abduction was not as heavy as the one she'd been prepared to shoulder.

Smiling broadly, she continued on her way back to the village. Suddenly, however, she found herself in the company of Shadow. The wolf fell into step beside her and gazed into Hawk Woman's eyes in a steady stare.

A coldness crept into Hawk Woman's veins as Shadow's eyes would not leave hers. It was as though the wolf sensed that Hawk Woman was guilty of not helping Candy in her time of trouble.

Hawk Woman wondered why the wolf had appeared now; she could not help thinking that it had to do with Candy's disappearance.

Hawk Woman gazed back into Shadow's eyes, wondering if the wolf could be that intuitive.

Unnerved, Hawk Woman tried to shoo Shadow away, but nothing would make the wolf budge.

Shadow stayed beside Hawk Woman as she broke into a run, panting, until she finally reached the village.

"Go away," Hawk Woman said, flapping her

CASSIE EDWARDS

hands at Shadow. But the wolf held her ground, her eyes still looking hard into Hawk Woman's.

Then Hawk Woman's blood seemed to turn cold as she heard the sound of horses arriving at the far end of the village.

She stiffened when she saw Two Eagles returning home, his many warriors already disbanding and going to their lodges, where their wives stepped out to greet them.

But Two Eagles had farther to go to his tepee.

Hawk Woman realized that she was standing right in front of his lodge.

She tried to hurry away from it, but Shadow blocked her path and stood there, gazing almost unblinkingly into her eyes.

Hawk Woman again tried to shoo Shadow away, but the wolf still didn't move. Instead she emitted a low growl from the depths of her throat.

Suddenly Hawk Woman was afraid of Shadow.

Hawk Woman had been taught by the Wichita that wolves were mystical in many ways. She had heard many myths about what they were capable of. She had always thought that the stories about wolves were just superstition.

But now?

Hawk Woman felt the strangeness of what was happening and truly feared Shadow, knowing that she had joined a pack of wolves that lived nearby. She feared that they might join Shadow at any moment now.

Two Eagles rode up and dismounted.

He gave Hawk Woman a quizzical stare, and then

302

noticed the strange behavior of Candy's wolf, which was staring almost without blinking up at the woman. He saw that Hawk Woman seemed almost terrified of Shadow, a wolf known for her gentleness.

Two Eagles knelt in front of Shadow and stroked her brown fur. "It is good to have you home again," he said, but realized that the wolf was paying no attention to him.

Shadow still stared straight up into Hawk Woman's eyes.

Feeling that something very strange was going on, Two Eagles rose to his feet and turned to Hawk Woman.

He was surprised to see strange fear in the woman's eyes. She was standing stiffly as she gazed, mesmerized, into the wolf's eyes.

Two Eagles was suddenly aware of something else.

He turned and stared at his tepee. He only now realized that Candy hadn't came from his lodge, as she would have upon hearing his voice. Candy always greeted Two Eagles with a welcoming embrace when he had been gone for any length of time.

He hurried inside his lodge, his heart filled with panic when he saw that Candy was not there.

He rushed back outside, but just before he could question Hawk Woman as to whether she had seen Candy, the pack of wolves appeared at the edge of the village, White Wolf emitting a low growl as he, too, focused on Hawk Woman.

His jaw tight, his eyes narrowed, Two Eagles went and stood before Hawk Woman, who still had not budged from her fearful stance. "Why is Shadow

303

acting so strangely, and what has drawn the pack of wolves to my village when they rarely come close enough for anyone to see them?" he asked, his eyes glaring into Hawk Woman's as she now met his gaze.

"Hawk Woman, what have you done? Where . . . is . . . Candy? Or should I ask, what you have done with her?"

Her heart pounding, feeling trapped, Hawk Woman slowly stepped away from Two Eagles. Just as she turned to run, Shadow lunged for her and stopped her by sinking her teeth into the skirt of the woman's buckskin dress.

Now knowing that something was very wrong here, Two Eagles went to the woman and gripped her by her shoulders. "Where is Candy?" he asked forcefully. "Where is my future wife?"

Hearing him call Candy his future wife seemed to snap something inside Hawk Woman. "I hope Candy is dead by now!" she screamed. "For I expect Candy will try to fight off the man as soon as he removes her bonds, giving him no choice but to kill her. He wants tame women . . . not hellcats."

"The . . . man?" Two Eagles said tightly. "What man?"

"Albert Cohen," Hawk Woman said. "He was the one who came and demanded food from you. I hid from him. He now has your Candy."

Rage filled Two Eagles's being. His fingers dug into Hawk Woman's shoulders. "Tell me what happened," he demanded. "Did you stand by and allow that white man to abduct my woman? Were . . .

you . . . laughing as you watched? Did you truly believe that if Candy was gone, I would allow you to take her place?"

Hawk Woman's words were frozen inside her, as her heart seemed to be frozen. She felt as if her world had just been broken in half.

She hung her head in defeat, then raised her eyes back up and looked defiantly at Two Eagles. "I will tell you nothing else," she spat out. "Do you hear? Nothing!"

Two Eagles fought off the urge to hit her. He had never hit a woman before.

But this creature standing before him was not a woman!

A fire entered his eyes that made Hawk Woman suddenly afraid of Two Eagles for the first time in her life.

Chapter Thirty-six

Love laughed again, and said, smiling,
"Be not afraid."
—*John Bowyer Buchanan Nichols*

Hawk Woman had never seen such fire in Two Eagles's eyes.

She was very aware that his shouts had brought the people from their homes. Even now they were gathering around Two Eagles and Hawk Woman.

Following White Wolf's lead, the wolves were moving closer, something no one had ever seen before.

Hawk Woman flinched when Two Eagles's grip grew tighter on her shoulders. Her knees were trembling so violently she could hardly stand.

"Tell me everything you know about what has happened to my woman," Two Eagles said in a low hiss as he leaned his face closer to Hawk Woman's.

When she still didn't answer him, he shook her so hard her teeth clacked together.

Truly afraid for her life now, Hawk Woman knew she must give him the truth or possibly die right there, with Two Eagles's people as witnesses.

"Please stop!" she cried, tears streaming from her eyes. "I'll tell you everything."

But only she knew that she would not actually tell him everything. She would never tell him of her intention to kill Candy before she was abducted by Albert Cohen.

"I am waiting," Two Eagles growled, still holding her tightly by her shoulders. "Tell me now, or I will take you to the white man you escaped from as I go and save my woman from him."

"No, oh, please don't make me leave the safety of your village," Hawk Woman pleaded, her heart racing at the thought of ever having to be with Albert Cohen again.

She loathed the man. He was a beast!

"I will allow you to stay, but only if you give me the answers I seek," Two Eagles said, slowly dropping his hands from her shoulders.

He placed his fists on his hips. His jaw tightened.

"I am waiting," he said flatly.

"Alright, I'll tell you," Hawk Woman said, glad that his fingers were no longer digging into her flesh. She knew she would have bruises there, for her skin throbbed from the punishment of his grip. "I went into the forest to gather greens for my evening meal."

She swallowed hard beneath his steady stare. It

felt as though he were looking right into her soul and might know a lie when he heard it.

But she had to try to convince him that what she was telling him was what had really happened.

"But I didn't get the chance to gather anything," she said. "I . . . I . . . came upon a dreadful scene of abduction just as Albert Cohen grabbed Candy and dragged her away. Candy had a basket and was gathering her own greens, and had just plucked roses from a vine when he took her."

Two Eagles grew cold inside as he imagined his woman being forced away by the evil white man.

And there had a been a witness to the crime!

Again he placed his hands on Hawk Woman's shoulders, his fingers squeezing into her flesh. "When you saw my woman in trouble, why did you not hurry back to the village to seek help?" he said heatedly. "Had you done this, my men might have gotten there before the white man traveled far with Candy."

But before Hawk Woman could reply, a thought came to Two Eagles that made a flood of hot rage fill his veins.

He dropped his hands away from her as he leaned into her face. "You are not telling the truth," he said, his teeth clenched; his hands were doubled into tight fists at his sides. "You never leave the village alone for any reason. You know the danger, especially after you saw the man you escaped from come into my village. You have stayed within the perimeters of the village ever since your arrival here, so that no white man or woman could see you. You always feared that word might spread that a golden-haired woman was living among the Wichita."

He paused, inhaled a shaky breath, then spoke again. "You have never left my village except for baths, and even then you were safe because of the sentries who protected my people's women as they bathed. Yet you left today?" he demanded hoarsely. "Tell me the truth. Why were you in the forest while Candy was there? You followed her, didn't you? Why?"

He suddenly yanked Hawk Woman's knife from its sheath and held it up to her face. "Is this the true reason you were there?" he asked in a low growl. "Was it your plan to make certain only one golden-haired woman lived in my village? Had you planned to kill Candy and blame the evil deed on someone else?"

Hawk Woman's eyes wavered; then she bolted and ran, but she didn't get far. The pack of wolves went and encircled her, White Wolf inching closer.

"Two Eagles!" she screamed, trembling. "Please do something. Don't let the wolves kill me."

The wolves parted to make way for Two Eagles as he strode up to Hawk Woman and grabbed her wrists.

"Take me where you saw my woman last," he demanded. "Then I will punish you for the evil in your heart later."

White Wolf suddenly made a quick turn and loped back into the dark shadows of the forest, with the other wolves following him.

But Shadow stayed with Two Eagles as Hawk

Woman led him into the forest to the scene of the abduction.

Two Eagles seemed to die a slow death when he saw Candy's basket and the spilled greens and herbs that she had gathered before her abduction.

He bent to a knee and picked up a lone pink rose. He caressed its petals. He had always compared his woman's skin to the softness of a rose petal.

He was keenly aware of Hawk Woman turning and running away from him. He allowed it, for he could assume that she wouldn't get far. The wolves were near and had surely seen her flight.

He paused when he heard her scream and then beg for mercy. He knew that the wolves had stopped her.

Several warriors had followed Two Eagles into the forest. Now they came up to him solemnly as they saw Candy's basket and were touched by her attempt to gather greens for their chief's dinner.

Hawk Woman screamed again.

Two Eagles felt no mercy for the woman, but he had no choice except to send his warriors to take her back to the village. Deep in his heart he would have preferred to leave her at the mercy of the wolves, who knew the evil of this woman's heart.

"*Looah*, go," he said as he nodded at two of his warriors. "Get Hawk Woman. Take her to the tepee that my woman used upon her first arrival at our village. Guard her. Do not let her leave, no matter how hard she begs."

The warriors nodded and ran in the direction of Hawk Woman's continuing screams.

Two Eagles fell to his knees and studied the tracks

that had been made by Candy and her abductor. He saw which direction they went.

Suddenly Shadow barked and nudged Two Eagles in the side with her nose.

Two Eagles looked down at Shadow and knew by her behavior that she wanted him to follow her. Could she know where Candy was?

He smiled at the thoughtful devotion of his warriors as he saw some of them ride up, leading Two Eagles's stallion. They had stayed behind at the village only because they knew he would want his horse.

Two Eagles mounted his stallion, and soon they were riding through the trees, Shadow leading the way.

Chapter Thirty-seven

Today or this noon
She dwelt so close,
I almost touched her.
—*Emily Dickinson*

Low in spirits, and aching all over from Albert
Cohen's rough handling, but so glad to have found
her mother, Candy sat beside her in the wagon.

They both made sure that Albert didn't realize
they were related. They had no idea what his reaction would be, but they were afraid he was capable
of anything.

When they had stopped several times to drink at
various streams, Candy had mingled among the
women, trying to look nonchalant as she asked them
to band with her, to get the best of Albert. But none
of the women had the courage. There was fear in
their eyes as they told Candy to leave them alone
and not bother them anymore.

As the wagon wheels rumbled onward along the packed earth, with the forest at their left side, Candy felt her buttocks ache as she sat on the floor of the wagon, each bump in the road causing a sensation like sharp pins sticking into her flesh.

She gazed over her shoulder into the distance, in the direction of Two Eagles's village. She was devastated to know that she would never see him again, or be held in his loving arms.

She would cherish those times with him, especially the nights, when he had taught her the true meaning of love. If she closed her eyes, she knew she would be able to hear his voice, smell his flesh, and feel the wonders that come with those moments when they had came together in the final throes of passion.

But she feared that love was hopeless, for she didn't see how Two Eagles could possibly know where to look for her. The abduction had been so swift, it was all like a blur to her now.

She turned her eyes forward again, finding it too painful to think about Two Eagles and what they had meant to one another, and what they could have been.

They had talked of children. Oh, to have a child in Two Eagles's image would be something she would have treasured.

But that was never to be, unless she found a way to escape the clutches of this madman. Fortunately, he had not yet approached her sexually. He knew the importance of placing many miles between himself and the Wichita village, for the farther he traveled, the less chance there was of the Wichita finding him and the women and children who were his family.

Through tears, Candy eyed the rifle that Albert always kept beside him on the seat of the wagon. He had made it clear he would use it if anyone tried to escape, or if anyone happened along and questioned him about why he had so many women and children with him.

Candy knew he would not let anyone interfere in his life. He would shoot anyone who tried.

She knew that it would not be long before he felt it was safe enough to stop for a full night. She suspected that every time he stopped for a night of rest, he chose a different woman to spend that night with him.

Chills rode Candy's spine to think about him choosing her. Surely he would want to see if she had been worth all the effort it had taken to abduct her.

"I was foolish to go into the forest alone," she whispered to her mother, who for the most part sat silently beside her, her face pale, her eyes empty and hopeless. "But I will not give up hope. I must believe that somehow Two Eagles is even now following the tracks which will bring him and his warriors to me." Candy had told her mother about Two Eagles and the way he had found her after the massacre at Fort Hope.

"Shh," her mother whispered back to her. "If Albert hears you talking to me, he might stop and give us both a lashing with his whip."

Candy's eyes widened. "He does that?" she whispered, seeing how her mother was cowering against the side of the wagon, so afraid she looked like a tiny woman, not the strong-willed person Candy had always known.

Her mother nodded, confirming that he did use a whip to make his wives obedient to his every whim.

Agnes then turned her eyes away from Candy so that even if Candy did whisper to her, she would not hear.

Agnes already had scars on her back from the day she had told Albert she wouldn't tolerate his touching her ever again. Furious, he had yanked the whip from the wagon, and as everyone watched, he lashed her, over and over again, until she had crumpled to the ground, begging for mercy.

That night he had asked her forgiveness as he applied ointment to her back where the whip had cut into her flesh. He had told her she would be his favorite woman now and he would give her many things he did not give the others.

She had bravely, brazenly spat in his face.

She could even now feel the sting of his hand as he slapped her and then shoved her to the ground and took her sexually as the other women, even the children, watched.

She had been taught a lesson that evening, one that she would never forget. She gave in to him now every time he ordered her to his bed.

Worse, she was afraid that she was with child. It was terrible to consider, not only because it would be this madman's child, but because of her age. She knew she was too old to have babies.

In all her life she had only been able to carry one child to full term. The other times she had lost the baby in the early stages of her pregnancy.

She hoped that if she was pregnant now, she would lose this child, too.

Confused as to why her mother was ignoring her, Candy wiped tears from her eyes. She tried to focus on finding a way to escape the lunacy of this man. If she did, she would bring help back for the other women and their children.

She would be so proud if she could find a way to help these people, especially the children. There was much sadness in their eyes, for they knew their future was bleak.

There would be no schooling, no freedom, no love. They were there only to satisfy this madman's need to have as many children and wives as possible.

With determination tightening her jaw, Candy looked around her, and then up at the angle of the sun in the sky. She was trying to figure out how long she had been traveling since her abduction, and how far she was from Two Eagles's village. The two wagons were so loaded down with belongings and people, Albert could not travel quickly. Candy knew Two Eagles could catch up to her if only he discovered the wagon tracks.

Candy started when she felt her mother nudging her in the side with an elbow, drawing Candy's eyes quickly to her.

When her mother nodded to the left, where the trees grew thick along the side of the road, her eyes widened. She caught sight of several wolves racing by in the shadows of the forest, keeping up with the wagon. Among them was not only White Wolf, but also her beloved Shadow!

They had somehow known that she was in danger and how to find her. They had come to rescue her. But how could they achieve it? Albert would start shooting the wolves as soon as he saw them.

She prayed that they would stay hidden until later when camp was made. After Albert was asleep, it might be possible to escape. Albert had only one woman on his side: Gretchen, who knew how to shoot a firearm as accurately as a man and would not hesitate to kill not only wolves, but any woman who attempted to escape while Albert slept.

But Candy knew that the wolves were stealthy and could move incredibly fast.

She smiled, for she believed she would not be a captive for much longer.

Chapter Thirty-eight

My heart is quivering like a flame,
As morning dew, that in the sunbeam dies,
I am dissolving in these consuming ecstasies.
—Percy Bysshe Shelley

Candy's heart thumped wildly as she caught a glimpse of Two Eagles riding hidden amid the trees alongside the road.

Then she saw movement behind him and recognized several of Two Eagles's warriors.

Her pulse raced as she watched White Wolf edging closer to a clearing beside the beaten path of the road.

Then suddenly White Wolf leapt out and onto the seat of the wagon, catching Albert so off guard he didn't have time to grab his rifle.

In a flash, White Wolf knocked Albert off the seat. The rifle was knocked off as well and landed at Candy's feet.

She grabbed it and held it on Albert while White Wolf kept his teeth clamped on Albert's right arm. At the same time Two Eagles and his warriors came out into the open and surrounded the two wagons.

Out of the corner of her eye, Candy saw the woman she detested grabbing for her rifle.

Two Eagles noticed, too, and took aim with his rifle. He shot Gretchen's firearm out of her hand just as she pointed it at him.

Through all of this, Albert was screaming, begging Two Eagles to call off the wolf.

Two Eagles rode up and patted White Wolf, and the animal released Albert's arm. He then leapt from the wagon to rejoin his pack.

The moment White Wolf let go, Albert eyed Candy and his rifle. He made a lunge for the firearm, but Two Eagles was faster. He grabbed Albert by the throat.

When Albert tried to wrestle free, his own struggling caused his neck to crack, killing him instantly.

Two Eagles laid the dead man aside. Then he reached down and pulled Candy into his arms.

Sobbing, she twined her arms around his neck and clung to him.

After she had collected herself, and realized that all was well again with her world, she leaned away from Two Eagles. She smiled at her mother, who was still sitting in the wagon, seemingly awestruck by all that had happened.

"Two Eagles, this is my mother, Agnes," Candy said, gesturing toward her with her free hand. "After she left Fort Hope, she ran into Albert Cohen.

She thought he was a kind man offering her assistance, but soon realized how wrong she was. She became his prisoner."

Two Eagles eyed Agnes strangely, then asked, "How could you name your child Candy?"

This broke the strain of the moment. Everyone except Gretchen laughed in unison.

Two Eagles carried Candy from the wagon and gently placed her on his steed, then mounted behind her.

He looked at the women and children. "You are now free to go wherever you want to go," he told them. "You are no longer captives of this white man who lost sight of decency long ago."

Candy gazed at her mother, then turned her eyes up to Two Eagles. "Can my mother come home with us?" she asked softly.

Agnes stood up and climbed from the wagon.

She came up beside Two Eagles's horse and took Candy's hand in her own. "Honey, I'd rather not," she murmured. "I would rather continue my journey now that Albert isn't here to stop me. I'm anxious to go where I can perform on the stage again. Dancing is in my blood."

She laughed softly. "Yes, I know I'm probably too old for anyone to want to see me dance, but I must give it a try," she said. She would not trouble her daughter with the possibility that she might be pregnant with the madman's child.

It was not necessary.

She knew almost without a doubt that before long she would lose the child, as she had in the past. Then she would finally have her life back again, one that she could live on her own terms.

Agnes turned and gazed at the other women and children. "Do you want to go with me to find civilization again, to truly know the meaning of freedom?" she asked, smiling at the women she had grown close to, and then the children she adored.

They all said "yes," as though in one voice.

Candy slid from the horse and went to her mother. Trying hard to understand a woman who would choose to live far away from her only daughter, she embraced her mother. "Mama, is this what you truly want?" she asked, leaning away from her so that they could gaze into each other's eyes. "If so, we might never see one another again."

Agnes looked past Candy and smiled at Two Eagles, then held Candy's hands. "I think I'm leaving you in good hands," she said. "And I believe we will see one another again. It's just that I need something different than you do. Please understand."

"Mama, I hope you find that something and will be happy," Candy murmured. "You deserve it. I know how unhappy you were for so long with Father."

"He only thought of himself, no one else," Agnes said thickly. "The day I left was the first time in years that I knew freedom."

"And then it was stifled again by that terrible man," Candy said, glancing at Albert's body and shuddering at what his intentions had been for her.

"Yes, that terrible man," Agnes said, stiffening at the memory of those long nights with him, and especially those times when he had beaten her almost to death.

Agnes stepped away from Candy and climbed aboard the wagon. She shoved Albert's body off the seat to the back of the wagon, then covered him with a blanket.

She then took her seat and grabbed the reins as the other women and children took their places in the wagons.

"I'll hand his body over to the authorities at the next town or fort, whichever we arrive at first," Agnes said, her back straight, her long, russet-colored hair blowing in the gentle breeze. "I love you, daughter, forever and ever."

"I love you, too," Candy said, blinking tears from her eyes.

Two Eagles dismounted and stood at Candy's side as the wagons rolled away. The people in them had looks of hope and faith now, such as they had not known while Albert Cohen was alive.

Candy's mother's wagon didn't get far before Agnes turned and smiled at her over her shoulder, then said, "I love you . . . Painted Wings."

Candy was touched deeply by her mother use of her Indian name. She realized now that her mother had truly accepted her daughter's new life.

Candy nodded as her mother's eyes turned away from her and Agnes Creighton continued on her journey.

"Painted Wings?" Two Eagles asked, drawing Candy's eyes to him.

"Yes, I told Mother the beautiful name that you gave me and . . . and . . . she approved," she said.

Her insides turned warm with love for this wonderful Wichita chief when he embraced and kissed her.

And then he held her away from him and gazed into her eyes. "Are you ready to go *wissgutts*, home?" he asked, searching her eyes.

"Yes, ah, home," Candy murmured. "For a while I didn't know if I would ever see it, or you, again."

She flung herself into his arms. "Thank you for rescuing me," she whispered, then felt something leaning against her leg.

She turned and gazed down and found Shadow there, gazing up at her. She knew that if wolves could smile, her wolf would be smiling now. She knelt down and embraced her pet. "Thank you, too," she said.

Shadow leaned against Candy for a moment, then ran off to where White Wolf and the other wolves awaited her arrival.

Tears came to Candy's eyes when White Wolf and Shadow touched noses, then turned and disappeared with the others in the shadows of the forest.

"I hope we see her again," Candy said, wiping tears from her eyes.

"With such affection that is between you and the wolf, I can promise you will see Shadow again," Two Eagles said, taking Candy's hand and leading her back to the horse. "*Hiyu-wo*, come, my woman. We have things awaiting us."

"Things?" she said as he lifted her on the horse.

"*Ho*, things," Two Eagles said, chuckling as he mounted behind her. He held her with his left arm and lifted the reins with his right hand.

Soon they were on their way home, with so many beautiful promises of tomorrow awaiting them.

Chapter Thirty-nine

I wonder, by my troth, what thou and I
Did, till we loved?
Were we not wean'd till then?
—John Donne

Filled with resentment at the knowledge that everything she had done to get Two Eagles to care for her had been in vain, Hawk Woman sat and glared into the glowing embers of the fire. She was being held prisoner in the same tepee that had been Candy's jail until . . .

"Until Two Eagles took her into his lodge," Hawk Woman whispered to herself, her jaw tightening. "That woman has gained everything since her abduction, while I have lost all that was important to me."

Yes, she had lost her freedom; she didn't even know what her final fate would be when Two Eagles returned home to deal with her.

Yes, she had lost him, and all hopes of ever having him.

"And all because of that prissy, tiny thing that came into my life at the wrong time," Hawk Woman said as she continued to talk out loud to herself.

Yes, she had to find a way to get back at Candy once and for all. Somehow she would find a way to make her pay for interfering in her life.

Suddenly a shriek of pain pierced the air outside the tepee. Hawk Woman heard someone cry the name of the warrior who had been assigned to stand guard outside the tepee.

She hurried to the entrance flap and drew it aside just enough to see what was happening.

Her eyes widened when she saw Bold Bear's wife run to him, tears pouring down her cheeks as she told him that their daughter, Evening Star, had fallen and it looked as though she might have broken an arm.

Hawk Woman's heart raced and a cunning smile quivered across her lips when she saw Bold Bear leave his post in panic. Obviously, he had forgotten his duty of guarding Hawk Woman the moment he heard about his daughter's misfortune.

She watched him go with his wife into the shaman's lodge, leaving Hawk Woman alone, with no one guarding her.

Her heart thumped wildly when she saw everyone rushing to stand outside the shaman's tepee, concerned about the little girl's injuries.

Realizing just how easy it would be to leave, Hawk Woman didn't waste another minute.

Although she knew she would be forced to leave the safety of the village without a weapon, this was a chance she had to take. Hawk Woman opened the flap more widely and took another quick look around her.

She still saw no one anywhere except outside the shaman's lodge.

Cackling beneath her breath, she sneaked from the tepee, stepping lightly, then ran around the side until she was safely at the back where no one would see her.

She stood there for a moment, panting, her eyes on the corral. She knew that if she was to get far away before Two Eagles returned home, she had to use one of his horses.

She smiled cunningly again, for although she had not ridden a horse since she had came to Two Eagles's village, she knew her skills would not desert her. Her father had taught her how to ride a horse almost the minute she could walk.

Realizing that the people's interest in the injured child could last for only a short while, Hawk Woman ran to the corral and chose one of the fastest steeds.

She took the roan from the corral and planned to walk the horse until she was far enough from the village that the sound of his hooves hitting the earth would not be heard. Once she did mount the steed, she would waste no time. She would ride hard and long until she found someone who would provide protection as she traveled toward civilization.

But she would be careful this time whom she approached. The last time she had asked for help, it had gained her nothing but a life of drudgery with Albert Cohen.

"And a daughter who never knew me," she said stiffly.

She glanced down at her attire. Anyone who saw her would question the way she was dressed. She would say that she had been held captive by Indians and had succeeded in escaping their clutches.

Smiling, she knew that part of her story would be true, for she had had no choice but to escape the Wichita.

When she was far enough from the village, Hawk Woman mounted the horse bareback and sank her heels into its flanks, sending it into a thunderous gallop across open land.

Feeling free with her golden hair flying in the wind, as it had when she was a child riding her father's horses, Hawk Woman closed her eyes. She thought of yesteryears and times precious to her.

She couldn't believe how she had changed into someone vile and mean . . . someone who had even planned to do murder. As a child, she had been a good clean person.

She had even learned many verses in the Bible and attended Sunday school every Sunday with her parents.

She opened her eyes, her jaw tightening when she recalled who had changed her.

Albert Cohen.

He had made her into someone vile and mean, but deep inside herself she still held a portion of that child her parents had adored.

Tears filled her eyes. How she wanted those times back again. But she knew it was impossible to go back. Both her parents had perished and she had been forced to find a way to live on her own.

That need had brought her to the point where she had been taken in by Albert Cohen and his syrupy words.

She shook her head to clear it of these thoughts. Now all she should be concerning herself with was getting as far away from the Wichita village as possible. Therein lay her true danger, for once the Wichita discovered that she had escaped, warriors would be searching for her high and low.

She rode hard until the moon climbed high in the dark heavens, and even then she continued. She was afraid to stop for the night. She must find the strength to ride until she found someone who would take her in.

"There has to be something out there for me," she whispered to herself.

That thought, which gave her a measure of hope, made her continue onward. Then she caught sight of a flickering ahead that caused her to draw a rein and stop. She saw a campfire through a break in the trees. Her heart leapt with gladness, for surely fortune had smiled on her. Here was a fire, where she might camp for the night and perhaps even find food.

But she had to be wary. She must get close enough to take a good look, and then decide whether to show herself.

She dismounted and grabbed the reins, then walked stealthily into the shadow of the trees with the horse. She stopped abruptly when she saw two wagons that she recognized.

"Albert's," she whispered to herself, everything within her going cold.

She peered intently ahead, trying to see who sat around the fire.

When she saw only women and children, she felt even more nervous. Albert must be up to his usual nightly game of choosing one of the women and taking her to his blankets in the back of one of the wagons. The others would sit by the fire, trying not to think of what he was doing to the chosen one.

Someone else came to mind. "Penelope," she said, peering harder to see if she could see a girl her daughter's age among the children.

But it was too dark and everyone was sitting too close together to see clearly. The aroma of baked rabbit wafted toward Hawk Woman, making her stomach ache with a hunger she had felt only one other time in her life . . . when she had fled Albert Cohen and had gone days without food before Two Eagles had found her.

Then someone else came to mind. Candy! Apparently, Two Eagles hadn't found the wagons in which his woman was being transported.

She smiled wickedly as she thought of Candy being the one in the wagon with Albert.

"Little Miss Prissy, how do you feel now that you are no longer in the arms of your Indian lover?" she hissed.

But again she thought of Two Eagles. He was surely somewhere close, searching for Candy, and

Hawk Woman didn't want to be the one he found instead.

She gave the children one last look, again thinking of her daughter, then shrugged. She wasn't born to be a mother anyhow. Albert had actually done her a favor by cutting her ties with her daughter.

And now she had also cut her ties with the Wichita people.

"It was never meant to be," she said, her eyes narrowing. "I'll find a new life somewhere, where I'll be appreciated."

The most important thing now was to get farther away from this area.

She walked her horse away from the campsite, then swung herself onto it again. She cackled into the wind as she pushed the steed into a hard gallop.

Chapter Forty

You kissed me! My heart, my breath, and my will
In delirious joy for a moment stood still.
—Leigh Hunt

The moon had replaced the sun in the sky. Night sounds were all around Candy as she rode with Two Eagles on his steed. Exhausted from her long ordeal, she cuddled against him, safe within his arms.

She closed her eyes and tried to blank out the worst of her abduction. She was thankful that Albert Cohen hadn't had a chance to rape her.

Thank heavens she was back with her beloved one, safe and untouched.

Yes, she was the lucky one to have gotten away from that fiendish man before he ruined her life, as he had ruined so many.

The children. She would never forget the haunted, empty looks in their eyes. When they grew old enough to have families of their own, they would find it hard to explain how they had been conceived and raised.

But, fortunately, thanks to Two Eagles, those children had been given a second chance. Although they had lived a degrading life up till now, they did have a chance now of bettering themselves.

"We are almost home," Two Eagles said, interrupting Candy's train of thought.

She sighed and gazed up at him. "I'm so glad. I don't think I've ever been this tired," she said. "I hope I will have no more ordeals like this. All I want is to marry you and bear your children. I want to be at your side as you lead your people. I hope nothing else will stand in the way of our happiness."

"We will marry *nahosah*, tomorrow, after you have a good night's rest," Two Eagles said, smiling at her. "My woman, soon you will be my wife."

"I feel as though I already am," Candy murmured, smiling.

"And I already see myself as your husband," Two Eagles said thickly.

"When I was a small girl I envisioned myself having a big wedding and walking down the aisle of a church dressed in white," Candy said softly. "But I no longer have such fantasies. I am living real life with the man I adore. And I *will* be dressed in white on my wedding day . . . the whitest of doeskin."

"No one could be as lovely as you, no matter what you wear," Two Eagles said, leaning forward to brush soft kisses across her brow. "You are my Painted Wings."

336

"Yes, Painted Wings," Candy said, sighing. She smiled up at Two Eagles. "I shall never forget my mother's reaction to the name. She actually accepted that I had a new name. I imagine she understood, once and for all, just how much I resented having been given a name that embarrassed me."

Candy snuggled closer to Two Eagles and rested her cheek against his powerful chest once again. "It was so good to see my mother again," she said. "After she fled into the night, to escape not only my father but military life in general, I did not want to think about what sort of trouble she might find out there on the trail all alone. Of course it is horrible that she was forced to endure life with Albert Cohen, even if for a short while, but at least she was still alive."

"And now she will finally find the sort of life that she hungered for," Two Eagles said. "You must always think that she will be happy in her new life, especially now that she is free of Albert Cohen."

"But there are many more like him out there who prey on women," Candy said, shuddering. "Still, I do believe Mama will be alright. She is perhaps the strongest-willed person I have ever known. I still can't believe she stayed with my father as long as she did."

The low sound of thumping drums came to Candy in the soft night breeze, causing her to lift her head from Two Eagle's chest.

She gazed ahead, where she could now make out the shine of the river in the distance; the moon lent the water a white, magical sheen.

She could smell the smoke of the outdoor fire that was always burning, morning and night, in the center of the village.

She also caught the scent of venison cooking over someone's cook fire.

A serenity she had never known before swept through Candy. She was finally home again.

Yes, home.

This was her home now, and would be until she was placed among the Wichita in their burial grounds.

She hoped that she would take that path to the hereafter before Two Eagles, for she wasn't certain she could bear wrapping him in his finest furs and lowering him into the ground, never to see his smiling face again.

She shivered at the thought and shook herself out of her morbid reverie.

This was a time for rejoicing. She was home again, safe and sound, and her man had said that he would be taking her as his wife tomorrow.

"Tomorrow," she whispered.

"Did you say something?" Two Eagles said, bringing her eyes to his.

"Yes, I said 'tomorrow,' " she said, smiling sweetly into his eyes. "I have waited all my life for tomorrow, for it was destiny that led me to you. That I am finally seeing my destiny fulfilled causes a sweetness inside me I can't describe. I am so happy, Two Eagles. So very, very happy."

"That day, when I saw you crawling along the ground after the Sioux massacre, even then I knew that destiny had brought us together. But I would not allow myself to think further about it, for at that moment I had other plans for you," he admitted. "I saw you as the opportunity to avenge what your father had done to my uncle, even though I did not know you were that man's daughter. That I had found someone alive from the massacre, who was somehow aligned with that murderous fiend, was enough for me."

"I am so glad that it was not you or your warriors who attacked the fort that day," Candy said, closing her eyes to shut out the images of Malvina and her father with arrows in their bodies.

For a moment Two Eagles's insides tightened. If the Sioux had not arrived that day ahead of the Wichita, it would have been Two Eagles and his warriors firing those deadly arrows from their bowstrings.

He did not like thinking about keeping anything from his woman, but he could not chance losing her, or her respect, were he to tell her the truth about that day.

No, he would never tell her. It would be a secret that would go to the grave with him.

He was glad that events had turned out as they had. If he and his warriors had arrived earlier than the Sioux, who was to say whether his Painted Wings would have lived through the ordeal? If not, both his and Candy's destinies would have been denied!

"I don't believe I've ever seen stars shine as brightly as tonight," Candy said as she gazed at the star-speckled sky. "There is a star in the northern sky that seems much brighter than usual."

"That star in the north is known as the 'Ghost Bear,'" Two Eagles said. "It is said that a man who was traveling in the far north came upon another man who said, 'This is my burial place. I live in the far north. If you accept whatever I offer you, I will give you power. You shall have power over the herbs to cure people, for I am a medicine man. If an accident should happen, or if sickness should arrive, I will give you a way to heal. In your doctoring you should look to the sun, for my powers are derived from him. Before you begin doctoring, offer me smoke.' The man was then informed that it was the Ghost Bear who was talking to him, and upon looking again, he saw that it *was* a Ghost Bear. The man looked back and the Ghost Bear had become a star. That star is the one you see tonight that is the brightest of them all."

"I shall always remember that when I gaze upon that North Star," Candy said. "I want to share something with you that I had once thought about that brightest star in the heavens."

"And that is?" Two Eagles asked, smiling down at her.

"When I lost my beloved grandfather and was missing him so much, one night as I lay in my bed looking out my bedroom window, something caught my attention in the sky. It was a star that I had never seen before. It was so bright! Suddenly I thought of my grandfather and felt it was he looking down at me. To me he was that star."

"And so you have the same feelings we Wichita have about that star. It is not always superstition that brings such tales from our hearts, but something very real," Two Eagles said softly. "That star brought your grandfather back to you that night. He is there now, as well, smiling down at you from the heavens."

"That is so beautiful," Candy murmured. "I love everything you tell me, whether it is myth or real. I long to be able to sit with the other women as we sew and bake and be as knowledgeable about such things as they."

"There is so much to tell you," Two Eagles said. "To feed a man or woman, to pray for him, to teach him—these are the greatest things anyone can do in the eyes of *Tirawahut*, our people's Great Spirit. In doing so, those who give willingly to others receive a blessing in some form, themselves."

They both went silent as Two Eagles rode into the village, his warriors disbanding on either side as they rode to their tepees and families.

His tepee was at the far side of the village, so it took him longer to reach his home, but he was always glad of its position. This way, he was able to see how everyone had fared while he was gone. It seemed that all was well tonight, which made him smile.

He rode onward, then just as he started to go to his corral, he saw something that disturbed him.

Bold Bear, the warrior he had left to guard Hawk Woman, was gone, and no one was there to take his place.

Nor was any smoke spiraling from the smoke hole

341

of the lodge where Hawk Woman had been held captive.

Then he saw Bold Bear running toward him. Many other people stepped from their lodges at the same time, their eyes directed toward Two Eagles.

All the while the drumming continued somewhere in the village.

"My chief!" Bold Bear cried, waving down Two Eagles.

"I wonder what's wrong," Candy said, hearing a strange desperation in Bold Bear's voice.

"I am not certain," Two Eagles said. He gazed into her eyes as he slid away from her and dismounted, then lifted his arms up for her.

She slid from the horse into his arms just as Bold Bear came up and stood stiffly before them, his eyes gazing uneasily at Two Eagles.

"My chief, she is gone," Bold Bear said, lowering his gaze.

"Who . . . is . . . gone?" Two Eagles demanded, even though he already knew. He turned slow eyes to the dark tepee, then looked again at his warrior.

"Where is she?" he asked.

"My daughter, Evening Star, was injured," Bold Bear said. He swallowed hard. "I was summoned. I went to her. I completely forgot about Hawk Woman and my assignment to guard her until you returned."

"Are you saying that she escaped?" Two Eagles asked, doubling his hands into tight fists at his sides. "You let that woman escape?"

Bold Bear nodded. "She has been gone now for some time, and she fled on one of your favorite steeds," he said. "I apologize. What can I do to correct my mistake? When you are a father, you will understand and see how a daughter comes first over everything else, especially if that daughter has been injured."

Seeing his warrior's despair, Two Eagles realized that he had not yet inquired about Bold Bear's daughter's welfare. "And Evening Star?" he said, unfolding his hands and lifting them to Bold Bear's bare shoulders. "How is she?"

"She is resting in her own bed in my tepee," Bold Bear said. "Crying Wolf cared for her and prayed over her. Even now the drums are playing to *Tirawahut*, so that my daughter will be stronger on the morrow."

"I am glad that her injury will mend," Two Eagles said, nodding. "And do not fret so much over our loss of Hawk Woman. Her escape takes the burden from my shoulders as to how she must pay for her sins against my woman."

"Several warriors left and searched for Hawk Woman but could not find her," Bold Bear said. "She seems to have disappeared into thin air."

"Wherever she is, I am glad she is not here any longer to wreak havoc on our village," Two Eagles said thickly. "But I do regret the loss of my prized steed."

"I have already replaced it with one of my own," Bold Bear said. "That is the least I can do after leaving Hawk Woman unguarded."

"That is not necessary," Two Eagles said, dropping his hands from his warrior's shoulder. "You take that horse and give it to your daughter so that she will have a horse of her own. Tell her it is a gift from both her father and her chief."

"You will do this for me . . . for my daughter, after I did not do as I was supposed to do?" Bold Bear said, marveling over his chief's kindness.

"The horse now belongs to Evening Star," Two Eagles said, smiling. He gazed over at Candy. "I have other things on my mind. Tomorrow is the day your chief will take himself a wife."

Bold Bear smiled broadly. "I will spread the word," he said. "Tomorrow will be a special day, not only for our chief but for all of our people. It is always a good day when a chief takes a wife, especially a chief as beloved as you."

Candy blushed as Bold Bear gazed into her eyes, smiled, then turned and ran around the village, shouting the news for everyone to hear.

Two Eagles took Candy by the hand and led his steed to his corral. Then he went to their lodge, led her inside, and tied the entrance flap closed.

Candy turned to Two Eagles as he placed his arms at her waist. "I am so happy," she sighed when he pulled her closer and gave her a meltingly hot kiss.

But Two Eagles realized how tired Candy was and did not venture farther than the kiss.

He lifted her into his arms and carried her to their bed, then gently laid her down on it.

He went and placed more wood on the fire, then stretched out beside Candy.

He smiled when he heard more drums now, and singing, for everyone was celebrating his wedding day. It would not be long before the moon would disappear and the sun would replace it in all its glory.

"Tomorrow I become a bride" were Candy's last words before falling into a deep, sweet sleep, with Two Eagles nestled close.

"Yes, *nahosah*, tomorrow," he said, drifting off to sleep himself with one arm draped across his woman.

Chapter Forty-one

I love your arms when the warm, white flesh
Touches mine in a fond embrace.
—Ella Wheeler Wilcox

Many years later
January, the moon of Difficulty

It was a crisp, clear night. A group of wolves stood among soft shadows thrown by the three-quarter moon of this brand-new year.

Sitting by the warm fire in the tepee, Candy smiled at the sound of the wolves. She knew that Shadow was among them, a part of the pack now, as were the offspring she'd borne over the years.

Ho, yes, it was a new year, and Candy was thrown back in time to the New Year celebrations of her past at forts where her father had been stationed.

Last night, at the Wichita village, there had been

347

no celebration as December turned into January, bringing with it the new year.

But she needed nothing else to celebrate when she had everything she had ever wanted. She had a wonderful marriage of eight years, and two beautiful children.

Both of their children had their father's skin color, and their seven-year-old son, Leaping Deer, even had Two Eagles's midnight-black eyes and hair.

But their daughter, Gentle Rose, had Candy's blue eyes, which were beautifully set off by the copper of her skin and the darkness of her hair which she wore in two long braids.

Candy's hair was long again, and like her daughter, she wore it in two long braids down her back.

Spotted Bear was a big part of the Wichita's lives; no one even noticed his disfigurement any longer. His happiness made Candy so proud because she had helped make it possible.

Her thoughts drifted to something else. She could not help smiling as she thought about the tattoo on her right breast. Although she had the same three concentric circles around one nipple that were required of all Wichita women, she had one more tattoo.

To pay homage to the name Painted Wings, which everyone now called her, she had requested a tattoo in the shape of a butterfly on one of her ankles. It was very tiny and beautiful, one she proudly displayed as her chieftain husband's wife.

And then there was Shadow. Candy did not get to see her wolf as often as she would like, but enough to keep track of her and her various litters; she had now given birth to twelve pups. One of these, a male, was as white as the whitest snows of winter, with its father's mysterious blue eyes.

It was that wolf, who was the oldest of them all, having been born several minutes before the others of the same litter, that seemed to be in charge of the rest. Like his father, he seemed born to lead.

At this moment, both of Candy's children were out in the snow, sometimes sledding, sometimes skating on the frozen ice in the nearby lake, or having snowball fights.

All of those things kept them coming and going from the tepee to change into dry clothes.

She didn't mind their changing clothes so often. She was an expert seamstress now and enjoyed making clothes, especially dresses for herself and her daughter. She had learned the art of beading, and all of the family's clothing was beautifully decorated with beadwork.

She was sitting beside a cozy fire, stringing beads on a length of thread.

She loved the dizzying array of colors, which would grace the matching dresses she had planned for her daughter and herself.

When she dropped a bead and it rolled toward the fire, Two Eagles came into the tepee just in time to rescue it.

Candy smiled up at him, seeing how his copper cheeks had a rosy tint to them from the cold. "Thank you," she said, taking the bead as he gave it to her.

She gazed at his moccasins, which had snow

caked on them. He quickly removed them and set them close to the fire, replacing them with dry ones.

"How are the children?" she asked, maneuvering the lost bead onto her string. "Do you think they have been out there long enough? The wind has picked up. Hear how it is howling around the lodge?"

"I imagine they will come in soon, for the wind is colder now," Two Eagles said as he removed his fringed jacket and laid it close to the fire to dry.

After lifting a large log onto the flames, he sat down beside Candy. "And how is the child in your belly faring?" he asked, reaching over and placing the palm of his hand on the round swell of her stomach.

"When spring comes, making everything beautiful, our child will be another flower to add to the wonders of nature," Candy murmured. "It will be another daughter. I feel it in the way it kicks just like our first daughter did." She laughed softly. "Sometimes it feels as though it is trying to kick a rib out of place."

"I would say we are having a strong son instead of a daughter," Two Eagles said, smiling proudly.

"*Ho*, perhaps," Candy said. She set her beading aside and scooted closer to Two Eagles, nestling in his arms as he reached out and embraced her. "I am so happy. Things are wonderful, Two Eagles. I feel so blessed."

"Life is good to us all," Two Eagles agreed. "Not only our family, but all of our village. We continue to have abundant harvests, and the hunts are always good, even though the buffalo are fading from this area. As the white settlers encroach more and more on what was once only the land of the Wichita, I see few buffalo."

"They kill buffalo when they don't need to," Candy said tightly. "I believe they do this only to keep the buffalo from our people. It is disgraceful. I wish I could do something to stop such waste, but I would not dare appear before the President in Washington dressed in doeskin. I would be seen as a traitor to my country and perhaps locked up forever."

"Do not worry about such things as the dissappearence of the buffalo, or anything else that has to do with matters in Washington," Two Eagles said. "Being a wife and mother is the best thing a woman can be."

"*Ho*, I know, and as I said before, I am so very, very happy with my life," she said. She turned her eyes up to look into his. "My husband, it is a new year. It will be as good to us as all years past. I feel it in my bones."

"*Ho*, or even better," he said, chuckling.

"I must admit that I miss one thing," Candy said in a teasing fashion, for she did not miss what she was about to tell him at all. It just seemed strange not to be a part of a New Year's celebration as she had celebrated each new year when she was growing up.

"And that is?" he asked. "Tell me, and I shall see that you have it."

Candy leaned away from him.

She moved to sit in front of him, feeling the fire

warm on her back. "I doubt you can," she said, looking mischievously into his eyes.

"I will try if you will only tell me what you are talking about," Two Eagles said, taking her hands in his.

"I miss the fireworks that my father and the soldiers at the forts always shot off on New Year's Eve," she said, in her mind's eye recalling how beautiful the fireworks looked against the dark heavens.

"Fireworks?" Two Eagles said, lifting an eyebrow. Then he smiled. "Ah, *ho*, fireworks," he repeated before she had the chance to say anything else. "I am familiar with such things. Let me tell you about my first experience with fireworks. Do you wish to hear it?"

"*Ho*, please tell me," Candy said, truly loving his tales of his past experiences. She could listen to him talk way into the night, once he got started.

"Long ago, on a cold night of the new year, in the middle of the night I heard the firing of guns," Two Eagles said. "My father shouted the word 'enemy,' which meant that he felt that our village was being attacked by our enemies. My father grabbed his firearm and thrust one into my hand although I had not had much practice yet with rifles, while my mother sat trembling and afraid that we would soon be dead."

"And then what?" Candy asked, her eyes anxious. "Were you attacked?"

"There was no attack at all," Two Eagles said, smiling as he remembered that night so well, and how stunned he and his father were when they saw beautiful colors spraying across the sky.

"My father and I both knew that firearms could not make such designs in the sky as we saw," he said. "I went with my father. We stealthily moved through the night until we came upon those who were making the noises. It was French Canadian half-breeds camping downriver from our village. They were firing off what I now know are called fireworks. We watched until there were no more; then we returned home."

"Was that the only time you ever saw fireworks?" Candy asked.

"No, after that we saw them often on the night of the new year, but they were being sent into the sky from behind the walls of the forts," he said.

"When we first came to Fort Hope, we had fireworks displays," Candy said, then frowned. "But my father stopped them after the Sioux came near to watch one year. That unnerved my father enough that we never had fireworks again."

"I learned ways to make my own fireworks," Two Eagles said proudly. "Put on your coat and come outside. I shall show our children, and those playing with them, as well."

Anxious to see what he was going to do, Candy pulled on her warm coat, then went outside with Two Eagles after he had put on a dry buckskin jacket.

She waited for him by the entranceway as he chose four arrows from his quiver. Then she saw him pick a cartridge from his cache of weapons and slide it into his front jacket pocket.

They left the tepee and went to stand beside the large outdoor fire.

The children soon gathered around and watched Two Eagles as he prepared things for his display of fireworks.

He cleared the snow from a small patch of land and broke the cartridge, spilling the gunpowder on the ground.

He then went beneath the trees close to his tepee and found some dried grass that was not covered by the snow.

He took this grass back to where everyone stood, curiously watching and waiting.

He tied these tufts of dried grass around the points of the four arrows and dipped them into the gunpowder. Then he held the point of one arrow into the flames of the huge fire. Immediately he shot the arrow straight up into the sky.

Rushing through the air, the arrow flared, making a bright red glow in the sky. As the arrow paused at the apex of its flight, flames shot outward, spectacular in the night, before it fell back to earth.

The children squealed.

Candy stared, amazed that the gunpowder hadn't ignited the moment it was set into the flames but seemed to wait until just the right moment to send its lovely sprays of color into the dark heavens.

"It was so beautiful," she murmured, watching as Two Eagles prepared another arrow for the same spectacular flight.

When all four arrows were fired, and the smell of gunpowder was heavy in the air, the children all moved in close around Two Eagles, asking questions so quickly he could only laugh.

"On another, warmer night, when your toes aren't freezing in your moccasins, I shall show you the fireworks again," Two Eagles said, gathering up his arrows and walking with Candy back toward their tepee.

"It was so beautiful," Candy said as they stepped into the warmth of the tepee. "It's so amazing how you did that."

"My father taught me, as did his father teach him," Two Eagles said. "You see, they had fireworks long before the white people."

Shivering from the cold, Candy stepped closer to the fire. She placed her back to it as Two Eagles removed his jacket, then came and removed hers.

"My woman, my Painted Wings, do you truly know how much I love you?" he said, sweeping his arms around her and drawing her close as the children came in, shivering, their eyes bright.

"I believe so," she said, laughing softly as she watched the children shake off their coats. "You show me in so many ways."

She placed her hands on his cold cheeks. "Do you know how much I love you?" she asked, searching his eyes.

"*Ho*," he said, taking her hands and leading her down beside their lodge fire. He leaned closer to her so that only she would hear what he said. "I wish I

355

could take you to bed. That would be our own private way of celebrating the new year."

"Later tonight," Candy said, knowing that would be the soonest they could make love.

"*Ho*, later," he said, but he did not wait to lower his lips to hers, to give her a fiery passionate kiss.

"My Painted Wings," he whispered against her lips. "My beautiful Painted Wings."

She sighed with happiness, having found everything she had ever wanted in the arms of this wonderful, kind, and handsome Wichita chief . . . her savage beloved!

As he held her now, he sang a rejoicing song of his people to her and their children, one Candy knew already because she had heard it often through the years of her marriage to Two Eagles.

She joined in and sang with him as their children sat, listening. . . .

"*Nawq, Atuis,*
Now, O father,
Irir ta-titska,
Our thanks be unto thee,
Ir-rur-ahe!
Our thanks!"

LETTER TO THE READER

Dear Reader,

I hope you enjoyed *Savage Beloved*. The next book in my *Savage* series, which I am writing exclusively for Leisure Books, is *Savage Tempest*, about the Pawnee tribe of Nebraska. The book is filled with much passion, intrigue and adventure.

Those of you who are collecting my Indian romance novels and want to hear more about the series and my entire backlist of books can send for my latest newsletter, bookmark, and fan club information, by writing to:

Cassic Edwards
6709 North Country Club Road
Mattoon, IL 61938

For an assured response, please include a stamped, self-addressed, legal-sized envelope with your letter. And you can visit my Web site at www.cassieedwards.com.

Thank you for supporting my Indian series. I love researching and writing about our beloved first Americans.

Always,
Cassic Edwards

ATTENTION
BOOK LOVERS!

Can't get enough of your favorite **ROMANCE**?

Call **1-800-481-9191** to:

* ✳ order books,

* ✳ receive a **FREE** catalog,

* ✳ join our book clubs to **SAVE 30%**!

Open Mon.-Fri. 10 AM-9 PM EST

Visit **www.dorchesterpub.com**
for special offers and inside
information on the authors you love.